BREAKAWAY

DUSK BAY DEMONS
BOOK 2

MAGGIE ALABASTER

TRIGGER WARNINGS

Hey lovely reader. Your mental health matters, so read with care. This book contains violence, stalking, kidnapping and mild somnophilia. In depth somnophilia is contained to the bonus scene, which is an optional download.

CHAPTER 1

SINCLAIR

"Yeah, absolutely, when we know *anything*, I'll be sure to loop you in. Thank you *so* much for reaching out. Have a great day."

I pressed end on the call and dropped the phone beside the half full mug of cold coffee. Elbows on the desktop, I rubbed my jaw with my fingertips. My face hurt from smiling into the bloody phone for the last week.

The response I was allowed to give to each call was the same, official script.

'The police are still investigating the alleged incident here at Demons Arena. I'm sorry, I don't know any more than that right now.'

Don't call me, I'll call you.

Of course they kept calling. Most days, the phone rang again almost as soon as I hung up. They knew as well as I did, I couldn't tell them anything but they tried anyway, pushing and poking, hoping I'd slip up.

Working in the PR department for the Dusk Bay Demons ice hockey team, I couldn't *afford* to slip up.

That might get me killed. Or worse, fired.

Yeah, priorities.

"I have to give you credit for not telling them to fuck off." Elenna Christakos leaned her hip against the side of my desk. The assistant equipment manager was one of my best friends. She also wrote romance books that would wear out any girl's vibrator.

"I was extremely tempted," I admitted. "I have to put together a press release that'll shut them up." That would be easier said than done.

I raised my hands to my temples and massaged them. After work, I had a date with a long bath, glass of wine and a good book.

"If anyone can do it, you can." She tucked a strand of dark hair behind her ear. "You're the best at what you do, that's why the Demons hired you."

"You're slightly biased," I told her. She was sweet, but her faith in me might be a little misplaced.

"Not at all," she said. "If anyone can explain why the door to the arena was blown in and people died, it's you."

"Gas leak?" I joked weakly.

This was Dusk Bay. Attacks like the one on the arena weren't common, but it was difficult to sell them as an accident.

Families like the Brantleys, the Bells and, to a lesser extent, the Fiorellis, held a lot of power in the city. And by that I mean they basically ran the place. And competed with each other.

No one would buy the gas leak explanation.

"Zombie invasion?" Elenna joked. "Exploding Zamboni?"

"Both of those are more plausible than a gas leak." I bit back a smile. "The GM was *not* impressed with the mess they made. Apparently he doesn't mind the players leaving blood on the ice during a game, but using the rink for a shootout?"

I lowered my hands to my lap and sat back in my chair. "Let's just say he was ticked off."

"None of that was our doing," Elenna reminded me. "Aidan's plan was to get to Geneva Mancini before she came after any of us." The Demons' head coach was one of her partners. The equipment manager, Finley Howard, was another.

"Tell that to the GM," I said wearily. "On the other hand, don't. I don't think he wants to know."

Horatio Jones was all about denial when it came to who was really in charge in Dusk Bay. He knew as well as the rest of us, but pretended not to. Sometimes I wished I could do the same.

"That zombie invasion idea is sounding more and more plausible," she joked. "What better place to come for fresh brains?"

I grimaced. "Is that going to end up in a book some-day? Hockey playing zombies?"

"It wasn't going to, but now you mention it..." She smiled and pressed her finger to the side of her cheek, as though contemplating it. "I could model one on Coast Riggs."

Her dark eyes appraised me carefully, watching for my response with undisguised amusement. She was sweet, but she could stir shit with the best of them. Especially when it came to my unrequited crush on the Demons' centre.

I managed not to blush. "How about you model one on Orion instead?" The defensive player was the third of her partners. Defensive in both meanings of the word. He gave off more 'touch her and die' vibes than anyone I've ever met.

"I could do both." She was lost in thought now, already working out characters in her brain. "Coast, the cocky centre zombie, and Orion, the quiet but intense defence zombie."

I laughed and shook my head at her. "You know if you write it, I'll read it, but don't you think Coast has a big enough ego?"

The guy was smoking hot, all muscles and charm, and he knew it. The puck bunnies adored him. Hell, women who didn't care for hockey panted after him.

He barely knew I existed. Why would he when he could get any woman he wanted? Except for Elenna. He flirted with her once in a while, and somehow lived to tell the tale. I guessed he liked to live dangerously.

Although, Aidan might not kill the Demons' best centre until his career was over.

Maybe.

Aidan wasn't known for keeping his temper contained.

"He does, now you mention it," Elenna said. "He probably thinks we're talking about him right now." She glanced behind her, like he might be right there, listening.

"We are," I pointed out. "But we're definitely *not* talking about his six pack or speculating on the size of his cock."

Thinking about both, yes, but not *talking* about them.

"I'm not." Elenna gave me a sly smile.

I needed to be less obvious.

"Of course not, you have three gorgeous guys at home who all adore you. You probably have more orgasms than you know what to do with."

No, I wasn't jealous at all. I mean, I had a drawer full of vibrators.

"Maybe you should forget about Coast and find someone else," Elenna suggested. "There's tons of single, hot guys in Dusk Bay. Hell, there's tons of them that work here at the arena. A girl can barely turn around without tripping over one of them."

I sighed. "I know, you're right. I need to forget about

him. He's just a guy." A hot guy I was attracted to, but that was all it would ever be. A crush. The sooner I got over it, the better.

"Exactly," Elenna agreed. "Maybe you should go on that dating app, Kinkyr, and see what happens."

"Knowing my luck, I'd be paired up with an *actual* zombie," I said dryly. "Maybe one that works in the accounting department."

Elenna laughed. "Come out with us after tomorrow night's game then. If nothing else, you'll have fun. Or you might hook up with someone new. Wren is coming."

Wren Valentine was our other best friend. The petite redhead always made nights out more fun. She was one of those people who left their filter at home, if she ever had one. It was one of the things we loved the most about her.

"I'm always up for a night out." I was definitely up for a hookup. If not with Coast, then maybe another guy from the team. Or someone not related to the Demons.

Whatever, as long as they were generous with their orgasms. I couldn't remember the last time I had one that I didn't give to myself.

"Great. I think we could all use some relaxation after the attack, and the scrutiny from the police and journalists. Aidan has been inundated with questions he's not allowed to answer. Finley is about to fend them off with hockey sticks. I think Orion is ready to shoot the next person that asks us anything related to the other night." She looked frustrated and tired. As over it as I was.

"I'll do my best to write something that puts all of this to bed," I said. "At least where the press is concerned. Any word on the Fiorellis?"

"Aidan says they've been suspiciously quiet," Elenna said slowly. "By now, they're aware Geneva and Jamison are dead. It's only a matter of time before Nicholas and Celine decide to get revenge." She wrinkled her nose.

"Against Coast," I said softly. He was the one who killed both of them. Jamison under Aidan's orders, and Geneva to protect Elenna. Even if Nicholas and Celine were pleased about the death of their stepmother, they'd be furious their brother was dead.

One way or another, they were bound to come after Coast at some point. The idea gave me shivers up and down my spine.

That, right there, was a good reason to stay away from him. Of course, it made him more attractive, not less. I'm wired that way, whether I liked it or not. Drawn to danger.

I grew up in Dusk Bay. Violence was nothing new to me. I'd killed people out of necessity. I wasn't scared to do it again.

"Against Aidan too, potentially," Elenna said softly. "He was supposed to be working with them against Geneva. He thinks they may have told her his plan, so she acted first. He's not sure how she knew otherwise. It's possible someone betrayed us."

She frowned and looked over at me. "You know he'll do whatever he can to keep Coast's name out of it. None of Geneva's people survived. The only way they'd know is if—"

"Whoever betrayed us to Geneva does the same to Coast," I concluded.

"Right," she said. "My guys are working as quickly as they can to figure out who it was. If they can get to them first, they will."

"I hate the thought it might have been one of the players on the team who betrayed us," I said.

"So do I," she agreed. "But it could have been anyone. There's plenty of staff in the arena. One of them might have been planted to work against the Brantleys."

Caleb Brantley, the second oldest of the seven brothers, owned the team. Someone would be sent to keep an eye on the Demons for that reason alone. Not knowing who I could trust, apart from Elenna and her guys, sucked.

Presumably I could trust Coast, unless he was trying to throw everyone off his trail. Killing Geneva and Jamison would be the perfect way to do that. No one would suspect him then.

Of course, now I was suspecting him. Sort of. I didn't want to, but it was difficult to dispute my own, hopefully flawed, logic.

"We'll find out who it is," Elenna assured me. "I don't

need to tell you to keep your eyes open. The smallest thing could lead us to whoever it is."

I nodded. "I'll keep an eye out for anyone who does anything strange, like eating pizza with a knife and fork."

She snorted. "That's weird, but I don't think it's particularly suspicious."

"It's *extremely* suspicious," I joked. "Almost as suspicious as people who drink decaf."

She sniffed. "There's nothing wrong with decaf. It's better for Aidan. He gets wound up enough as it is." Her brown eyes widened slightly, as though she was thinking about something specific.

The polite thing to do would be not to agree with her too vigorously. Aidan put the 'wound' in 'wound up.' In both pronunciations of the word wound.

She correctly interpreted the reason for my silence. "I know, I know. It's who he is. He doesn't hold back in sharing what he thinks and feels. Especially when he's angry."

Which was most of the time. I'd never met anyone with as explosive a temper as Aidan Draeger. On any given day, he could be heard growling, yelling or snarling at someone, usually one of the players.

I doubted the words 'holding back' were in his vocabulary. I didn't know how Elenna put up with him, but she loved him. He loved her. As far as I could tell, she was the only person on the face of the planet he was ever truly soft with. As soft as a man like he could be.

"I suppose that's better than guessing what someone is thinking and feeling," I said.

"Are we talking about Coast again?" She seemed happy to change the subject.

I was about to say we were, but instead I said, "Coast Riggs who? I'm going out tomorrow night to meet someone new and forget all about him." I nodded firmly.

And I was going to get laid if it was the last thing I did.

CHAPTER 2

SINCLAIR

"Commiserations." I raised my drink in the direction of Aidan and Orion. I downed a gulp before I slipped into a chair beside Wren.

The Demons lost by two points, in a hard-fought game. The side of Orion's face was bruised, where he got an elbow from the opposition's enforcer. Right before he slammed him into the boards and ended up in the sin bin.

No one was holding back tonight.

"We'll kick their asses next time," Finley said. The red-haired equipment manager was always smiling, relaxed, especially in comparison to Aidan and Orion. He was like the sun peeking out from between two thunderclouds. Still with a faint Irish lilt, after living in Australia for the last ten or fifteen years. The more he had to drink, the more pronounced it became.

"We should have beaten them *this* time," Orion

growled. "If he hadn't pulled me off right in the end—" His resentful gaze swivelled toward Aidan.

Elenna put a hand on his arm. "It is what it is. Next time, you'll clobber them."

Orion turned to look at her, his expression softened a fraction. He clearly loved her. If anyone tried to mess with her, he'd smash their heads in without a second thought.

Why couldn't I attract a guy like that?

I exchanged glances with Wren, who was clearly thinking the same. She had a bit of a thing going on with Tiberius 'Tiger' Pennington, the Demons' first string left defence, but who knew if that was going anywhere anytime soon? Tiger was almost as volatile as Aidan. He and Coast constantly gave each other shit. I wasn't sure if they hated each other or just liked to stir each other up. Maybe both.

"We better win next time," Aidan said. "If we don't, we can kiss our chance at the Goodall Cup goodbye." He glanced at Orion like it was all his fault.

Orion glared back.

If I didn't know better, I'd think the two guys didn't like each other either. I suspected they just liked to out glare at each other.

Men.

While the rest of them chatted, I let my gaze wander around the pub.

Hazards was the favourite hangout of the Dusk Bay Smashers, the local rugby team, but the Demons frequented the place from time to time. The atmosphere was always good, and the hamburgers cooked in the restaurant at the back were the best in the city. Possibly in Australia.

I picked up my glass and found it empty. "I'm going to get a refill, does anyone want anything?" I stood and took my glass back to the bar.

"Hey, can I buy you a drink?" Javey Montanez, the Demons' left wing, stepped up to me and offered a tentative smile.

I'd only exchanged a handful of words with him in the past. He was one of the quieter players, often over-shadowed by guys like Coast and Tiger. I'd never really looked at him before, but I looked now.

His dark hair was cut short on the sides, but long enough to curl at the back of his neck. His eyes were deep, chocolate brown. The kind a girl like me could lose herself in.

His body was all toned, lean muscle trying to escape from black jeans and a dark blue shirt under a black leather jacket. A tattoo trailed down the side of his neck, over skin a bunch of shades darker than mine, before disappearing under his collar.

What was it a tattoo of? All I could make out right now was a reptilian tail.

A piercing in his tragus winked in the light.

I smiled up at him. He had to be at least six foot three or four. Taller than my five foot ten.

"Sure," I said casually. I didn't want to look

desperate or anything. I certainly didn't want to look like his proximity made my panties wet.

He smelled like some kind of spice. Cinnamon or nutmeg, or something that reminded me of baked goods.

Would it be too forward of me to offer to nibble on his loaf?

He smiled as though he had no clue I was mentally undressing him. "What would you like?"

Your tongue on my clit.

"Vodka and orange, please," I said instead.

He nodded and leaned over the bar to give our order to the bar attendant. He tapped his card and handed me my drink.

I smiled my thanks and sipped through the straw before stepping away from the bar.

"Commiserations on tonight's game. You played really well though." He had, hadn't he? Probably. If not, it seemed like the thing to say. Male ego and all that.

He followed me over to a quieter corner of the pub and shrugged. "Thanks. It was a tough one. I think… Most of us keep remembering the other night." The side of his mouth dipped down.

"Right." I'd forgotten about that. "You were held at gunpoint, weren't you?"

That would have been an ordeal for anyone. Badass or otherwise.

I quickly added, "I mean, you don't have to talk about it if you don't want to."

"It's okay," he said. "They reckon the best way to recover from something is to talk about it. We're banned from saying anything to the press or anyone outside the Demons, and most of the guys won't open up. I don't mind, if you want to listen."

"Of course." I gestured for him to continue. Being a good listener made me good at my job. Problems were easier to solve if I fully understood them.

He glanced down into his beer, then back up again. "Sitting on the ice in jeans is cold as fuck." His lips curved back up.

"Is that what you got from the experience?" I asked, teasing lightly. "Nothing about guns, just how cold the ice was."

People dealt with trauma in different ways. He may use humour to deal with his. Not to mention hiding behind a mask of shyness. What would it take for him to open up to me? Why did I want him to? I wanted to get to know him better. Was that answer enough?

He chuckled. "It's the thing that stands out the most. That and, you know, wanting to get out alive. Coach had our backs, like he always does." His gaze flicked over to Aidan, then back again. "I wasn't too worried."

I didn't buy that, but I wouldn't call him out on it. He was one of the ones who wrestled armed men to the ground when Aidan and the others stormed in. He could have very easily ended up dead. Thank fuck he hadn't.

"I'm sure you would have dealt with it if Aidan hadn't," I said. "You guys aren't beaten that easily."

"Not by people with guns." He sipped his drink. "If they were armed with hockey sticks, we would have been screwed." Lines around his eyes crinkled with amusement.

He was adorable.

"Right." I drew the word out. "You would have been totally pucked. Unless you had sticks too. You could have challenged them to a game."

He grinned. "They would have been beaten either way." He had a look in his eye, like he would have smashed the crap out of all of the attackers, single-handedly, if necessary.

I shouldn't be surprised to see violence bubbling beneath the surface. He was a Dusk Bay Demon, after all.

"That's hot," I said without thinking. Shit, did I say that out loud?

Whatever, I didn't want to take it back, it *was* hot.

Was he actually blushing? He ducked his face for a few moments.

"Can I tell you something?" he asked.

"Do you eat pizza with a knife and fork?" I asked.

He looked back up, confused. "No."

"Then you can tell me something," I concluded. He wasn't *that* kind of strange or suspicious, that was reassuring. "If you still want to, because that was a strange question."

"It's not the strangest thing I've ever been asked," he said. "I wanted to say that I've been trying to work up the courage to talk to you. You're usually surrounded by other people, especially other guys on the team who are, I dunno, more interesting than me."

"Who says you're not interesting?" I raised my chin and my eyebrows and looked at him questioningly.

"I do," he said. "When I'm not on the ice, I'm the guy in a corner reading a book. I'm not outgoing or funny. I'm just…me." He shrugged.

"I think you're very interesting," I said firmly. "I also like to read."

I hardly knew him, but I wanted to see what was underneath his shy exterior. And what was underneath his clothes. I was almost certain he was picking up that vibe too.

This could be the perfect start to moving on from my crush on Coast. We might even go somewhere, who knew?

I was usually drawn to outgoing guys and that hadn't ended well yet. It wouldn't hurt to look outside the box.

"What do you read?" he asked.

"Palms," I replied immediately. "Want me to read yours?"

"Um, sure." He held out his left hand.

I trailed the tip of my finger down his lifeline, from the heel of his hand to between his thumb and pointed a finger. My fingernail lightly slid over his skin.

His Adam's apple bobbed. "What do you see?"

"You're going to live a long life," I told him. "You'll eventually die in bed with a woman younger than you."

"That's very specific," he said.

"Isn't it?" I glanced up at him and grinned. I was almost certain he was twenty-five. A year older than me. I looked back down and turned his hand around. "You've never been married."

"Never," he agreed. "You can see that on there?"

"You don't have a tan line on your ring finger," I said.

He laughed. "That's observant. I'm starting to wonder if you can read palms at all."

"Because my reading is so dubious?" I cocked an eyebrow at him.

He grinned. "Well, a little bit, but your powers of observation are on point. What else can you tell about me just by looking?"

I made a show of regarding him carefully. "You like beer. Or you're very good at *pretending* you like beer."

He laughed again. "That's incredible. I don't know how you do it." He sipped his beer.

"A magician never reveals their secrets," I said, tapping the side of my nose. "I can also tell you don't get into trouble, or you're very good at covering it. But I know that because I've never had to help repair your reputation."

He eyed me over the rim of his glass, his lips barely touching the side. "Yet."

"Let me update my assessment then," I said slowly. "You're planning some trouble of some kind. You might even be hoping to get caught. How many older siblings do you have?"

He looked surprised. "Three. Two brothers and a sister. Why?"

"You have that air about you. If you tried to do something bad, people either didn't notice, or they let you get away with it because your older siblings had done it all before you. Am I right?"

He lowered his drink. "Nail, meet head." He looked like he was going to continue, but then said, "Do you want to get out of here?" He jerked his head towards the door, before downing the rest of his beer.

"Yes, I do, very much." I finished my own drink, took his hand and let him lead me out the door.

CHAPTER 3

JAVEY

The only place I've ever had confidence was on the ice. From the moment I laced up my first pair of skates and picked up a hockey stick, it was the one thing I wanted to do. One of the few things I was good at. I left it all out on the rink every time. Held nothing back.

Off the ice, I was the complete opposite. Awkward, introverted. When the press gathered around, I left the talking to the other guys.

I didn't mind any of that, it was what it was. Until now.

Now, I wanted Sinclair to see me. Really see me. To understand me and not run away.

I half-expected someone like Coast or Phoenix to follow us out and ask why the hell she was leaving with me.

I asked myself the same question, but shoved it away faster than my stick on the puck.

Her hand was warm in mine. *My* hand, not one of the other guys. No one followed us out. No one confronted me or questioned her choice. She didn't change her mind once she stepped out into the cold night air.

If anything, she seemed more certain. Curious about me, wanting to know more.

I wanted to know more about her. I needed to know everything. Everything I didn't already know.

I'd been watching her for quite some time without her realising. Without her seeing me. Almost as good as I was at hockey, I was good at hiding. Either in plain sight, or in the shadows. I wore black to blend into the night. My presence concealed while I stood outside her house, seeing her moving around inside. Watching through cracks in the curtains while she stripped off naked. While I wrapped my hand around my cock, and…

Now, it was just us. We walked for a block or two, enjoying the relative quiet. Traffic hummed past, but the sound of throbbing music grew more and more faint.

"You were going to tell me about your family," she said.

I glanced over to her. Why was a woman as gorgeous as Sinclair Rooney giving me the time of day, much less walking with me through the streets of Dusk Bay late at night?

"I was?" I asked.

"You don't have to." She glanced back at me, her

chin tilted up. I liked that she was tall, but still had to look up to look at me.

She said so much with her blue-eyed gaze. She truly wanted to understand me. Not Javier Montenez, the winger and hockey demigod—I didn't consider myself quite at god status—but as Javey. Fuck, I wanted to hear my name on her lips. Needed to hear her scream it.

"There's not much to tell apart from what you already figured out," I said. "I'm five years younger than my next oldest sibling. By the time I was born, there was no toy they hadn't broken, no wall they hadn't scribbled on, few bones they hadn't broken." I shrugged. I was long past feeling sorry for myself.

"So you had to work extra hard to get noticed?" she asked.

"Mostly I didn't bother," I said. "If I was sitting in the corner reading a book, I wasn't causing any trouble." I was okay with them leaving me alone. I liked my own company.

"That sounds lonely," she said.

"I guess so. Like you said, when I wanted to do something I shouldn't, I didn't get noticed." I smiled.

"What did past Javey get up to?" Her tone was teasing, but the sound of my name on her lips was music. Hah-vey.

"Mostly making friends with people my parents wouldn't have approved of," I said. "A few who worked for the Brantley family or people like them. When you've learned to blend into the background, it gets you all sorts of places."

The skin on the back of my neck prickled. Were we being watched?

I didn't look back. I kept my focus on her. Outwardly at least.

Inwardly, I was on alert for anything. Even before the attack on the arena, I was always watching out, always ready. Since the attack, the sensation of being followed, or something coming had increased tenfold.

The fact I was there that night made me a target. I was starting to regret asking Sinclair to leave with me. If anything happened to her because of her proximity to me…

"I'm sure it does," she was saying. "No one suspects the shy hockey god."

"Exactly," I agreed.

"So how does a guy who grew up not being noticed end up playing professional hockey?" she asked.

"We used to ice skate at the local rink on the weekends, and I was good at it," I said simply. "I was asked to join the team. I almost said no, but then I figured it would give me more time on the ice. Turns out, I was good at hockey too."

I wasn't bragging, just stating a fact. Hockey came as naturally to me as breathing. Chasing the puck, blocking shots, making goals, checking opponents into the boards, it was in my blood.

"My brothers used to say it's because I spent so

much time by myself, playing with my stick." Assholes. They were more interested in kicking a ball around. I left that to them, I couldn't kick for nuts. Never bothered to try very hard. If I did, I'd be compared to them the entire time. Fuck that.

Sinclair laughed. "And now you're laughing all the way to the net. And the bank too, I guess." She worked for the Demons, she'd have a fair idea how much I earned.

"I'm doing okay," I said. Between the money I made playing hockey, and the bonuses from doing the occasional job for Caleb or Reuben Brantley, I could comfortably retire.

What would I do if I did? I didn't know what I'd do with myself without a hockey stick in my hand.

Her smile froze and her hand tensed in mine. A moment later, she forced herself to relax and spoke as though nothing was going on.

"Where are they?" She didn't look around either. She kept her eyes on me or the footpath in front of us. She grew up in Dusk Bay, she was well aware of its shady side. Her instincts were almost as finely honed as mine.

I wanted to tell her I didn't know what she was referring to. To reassure her there was no one around but us.

We'd both know I was lying. I didn't want our relationship to start with lies. Not even when the truth could kill us both.

"I'm not sure." I spoke in the same tone I'd used for

the last handful of minutes. Casual, friendly, if slightly reserved. "My place isn't far from here."

"Good," she said. "Because I don't think I can keep my hands off you for much longer." Her voice was husky, hotter than hell. She might be the fucking end of me.

I was one hundred percent here for it.

My heart raced, my cock hardened. If it wasn't for whoever was watching us, I'd find a place to pin her to the wall and get my hand under her jeans. I might have anyway, but it was the middle of winter. I wanted to get her off, not freeze her clit off.

"Me either." If this was a dream, I didn't want to wake up until I'd come inside her.

A small part of me, in the very back of my mind, expected one of my teammates to come running up and try to whisk her away. I'd punch them in the face and keep walking.

As far as I was concerned, she was mine. I planned to find a way to make this permanent. The moment I saw her, I'd decided that. One way, or another, she belonged to me.

I stopped in the shadow of a building, tangled my fingers in her hair and dragged my lips over hers. Just once, just lightly, but long enough to let sparks fly between us like crackles of electricity.

Heat surged through me. My cock was hard.

She groaned against my mouth, her tongue sliding over my lips, tasting me.

Before I changed my mind about fucking her out in the cold, I tore myself away from her and tugged her to keep walking. Our steps were faster now.

The sensation that we were being watched increased as we approached my apartment building. My body tingled, caught between aching for her, and extreme caution.

"In the black car on the corner," she said like she was talking about the weather.

"I see them," I said.

Two of them, not making any attempt to hide their presence. To the casual passerby, they'd appear as nothing more than a couple of people hanging out, maybe making out.

To me, to Sinclair as well, there was nothing casual about their presence. I was starting to wish I had a gun in my pocket. Or a hockey stick in my hand. Hell, a nice hard puck right between the eyes would do.

"I think they've seen us," she said.

The car doors started to open.

"Keep walking," I said, half my attention on the car, the rest on her and the distance to the front door of my building. "We're just people walking down the street."

"Right." A hint of nerves snuck into her tone.

They immediately put me on edge. I had to keep her safe, whatever the cost to me.

"Montanez." Sawyer Mancini stepped out of the car, followed by a man I didn't recognise. One of his minions or associates, I presumed.

"Mancini," I replied, neither friendly nor unfriendly. Merely acknowledging his greeting. I slowed my steps, but didn't stop.

"I think you know why we're here."

To cock block? His timing couldn't have been worse. Or mine couldn't. If I hadn't approached her in Hazards in the first place…

Sawyer's gaze slid up and down Sinclair appraisingly. Appreciatively.

Fucker. I wanted to knock his teeth out for looking at her that way.

I came to a stop now, pulling Sinclair behind me. "Enjoying the fresh air?"

Sawyer chuckled. "Such a fucking comedian. You should give up hockey and take up stand-up. You'd kill your audience every night." His eyes narrowed, his words deliberately chosen.

"I'll leave the killing to you," I said. I made to step away when he raised a hand to stop me.

"I buy that you leave the killing to other people," he said slowly. "I want to talk about who you leave it to."

"I have no idea what you're talking about," I said.

"My mother's attack on Dusk Bay Arena." Apparently he was done skirting around the subject. "Her death and that of Jamison Fiorelli. You were there." He wasn't asking.

"I remember being held at gunpoint by Geneva's people," I said. I wasn't beating around the bush either.

"You can confirm who killed her." Also not a question.

"I can confirm it wasn't me," I said. "Everything else happened so quickly. One minute she was about to shoot an unarmed woman, the next minute she was dead." Good riddance as far as I was concerned.

"Shot by Coast Riggs," Sawyer said. "So was Jamison."

"If you're so sure, why are you asking me?" I asked.

"You're not denying it." Sawyer's eyes narrowed. "But I'm not asking you. I know exactly what happened. I'm here to make you an offer." He tilted his head so his gaze skirted around me, to Sinclair.

If it wasn't for her hand in mine, I might have rammed his teeth all the way down his throat. Choking on them would be worse than me just knocking them out.

"What offer?" I didn't try to keep the growl out of my voice.

He straightened up. "Information. That's all. You won't have to kill anyone for me." He laughed like he said something hilarious.

"What information?" It was Sinclair who asked. "We've already covered for your family. We made the attack out to be much less than it was. Otherwise you'd have a swarm of police at your door."

Which they probably deserved.

"We appreciate that," Sawyer said smoothly. "But there's always more that can be done. That's where my old friend Javey comes into this." He looked back at me. "You owe me a couple of favours anyway. I'll be claiming those."

I wanted to tell him to fuck off, but Sinclair looked at me sharply. If she was done with me after this, Sawyer might be losing a testicle or two.

I exhaled, my breath making mist in the cold air.

"What do you want?"

CHAPTER 4

SINCLAIR

"So you worked for the Fiorelli family?" I held the coffee cup in both hands and inhaled, the smell tickling my senses.

I'd kept myself at a comfortable distance from Javey while I processed what Sawyer said.

"Once or twice." Javey sat on the arm of the couch, his own coffee in his hands. The frown hadn't left his face since Sawyer and his associate drove away, leaving us alone on the footpath.

"They paid well, and at the time I needed the money. I was playing hockey as an amateur and doing whatever jobs I could to get by. I was sure I could go pro, but I needed to eat. It was that or work for my uncle Pedro in his butcher shop."

"Squeamish?" I asked.

"No," he replied. "I never aspired to be a full-time butcher. Neither kind."

I couldn't picture him slicing meat for human consumption, or slicing humans for torture, fun or profit. On the other hand, it was often the quiet ones who preferred that way of life.

Deciding it was cool enough, I took a sip of my coffee. "Can I ask you something?"

"Of course." His expression was guarded. He was clearly uncertain what conclusion I'd come to.

Honestly, I hadn't come to one yet. I liked him, but if he was working with the enemy…

"Someone inside the Demons is working with them," I said slowly. "Someone who knew what Aidan had planned. They told Geneva and she acted before he could."

"I don't know who would have done that." Javey took a sip of his own coffee. Some of the tension left his body. "It wasn't me. I'm sure you noticed how cagey Sawyer was about knowing what happened to his mother and stepbrother."

I had noticed that. I didn't know Sawyer well, but from what I'd seen, cagey as fuck was what he did.

"Now he wants you to report on the Demons' movements," I said. "No prizes for guessing why."

"He's going after Coast." The sides of Javey's mouth drew back. "Potentially Aidan as well."

"What are you going to do?" I asked. "Are you going to tell him anything?"

"I don't know," he admitted. "I saw the way he was

looking at you. If I don't do what he wants, he might do something to you."

I felt my face pale. The milky coffee threatened to curdle in my stomach.

The possibility Sawyer might use me to get to Javey, or anyone else, hadn't crossed my mind. Now it had, I didn't relish the idea. I wasn't blind, I saw Sawyer's interest, but it wasn't returned in the slightest. He was an attractive enough guy in his own way, if you're into slippery eels. Or the kind of animals that eat their young if they get in the way.

Honestly, I was surprised he was interested in any kind of revenge for his mother's death. He should be ecstatic he could step into her shoes.

Javey caught the expression on my face. He set aside his coffee and walked the handful of steps to me. He took my mug from my fingers. He set that aside too, and curled his hands around mine.

"I won't let anything happen to you." His voice was deep, resonant in the otherwise quiet of his apartment.

The sound sent shockwaves of need right to my pussy.

"I'll do whatever I have to do to keep you safe."

"You hardly know me," I argued weakly. My heart was racing hard enough to fly right out of my chest.

He leaned in until his breath brushed my cheek. "I know you better than you think. I've been watching you for a long time. Hoping for a chance to talk to you and to get to know you."

I shivered. "You have?" I said lightly, in spite of the catch in my voice.

"I have. I know you live in a cute brick cottage on Battersby Street," he said. "You go to bed late and always rush to get ready for work in the morning."

I swallowed. "Lots of people do that."

He could have been guessing.

I knew he wasn't.

"You wear black, lacy underwear." He leaned in closer.

"You drove past and saw it on the washing line." Holy shit, was he saying what I thought he was saying?

"You have a tattoo on your left ass cheek that says 'bite me.'" He lightly bit my right earlobe.

I startled slightly, but my panties were drenched. I should get out right now, run and never look back. I really should, but I didn't want to. I mentioned I was drawn to danger.

"You've been stalking me?" I whispered. It really *was* always the quiet ones.

"Not stalking, just...learning," he said slowly. As if somehow there was a difference.

When he lowered his mouth to mine I didn't pull away. I kissed him back.

He let my hands go and gripped my waist.

I wrapped my arms around his neck and pulled him closer.

He pressed his leg between my thighs and rubbed it against the gusset of my jeans, right past my pussy.

I groaned and rubbed myself against him, setting my clit on fire between layers of fabric.

"Javey…" I breathed softly.

"Sin," he said, equally breathless. He cupped my ass and pulled me forward until he could pick me up and wrap my legs around his hips. Without breaking our kiss, he carried me to his bedroom and laid me down on his king-sized bed.

I unwound my legs and let him unbutton my jeans and tug them down my hips. I lifted them up off the bed to help him, while pulling off my coat, jumper and shirt.

He unzipped my boots and pulled them off so he could get my jeans off my feet. He tossed them aside. I lay on his bed in my panties, bra and bright pink socks. He looked down at them and grinned.

"Cute."

I wriggled my toes. "I thought so."

Apparently he didn't agree, because he grabbed both socks by the spare fabric around my toes and pulled them both off before throwing them over his shoulders.

"Cuter, but still overdressed."

"Yes, you are," I told him. "It seems like you've seen a lot of me, but I haven't seen enough of you." I propped myself up on my elbows and cocked my head expectantly.

If I was going to let him get away with stalking me,

it was the least he could do in return. That, and a *bunch* of orgasms.

He smiled at me, then proceeded to strip off slowly. Layer by layer ended up on the floor, revealing more of his taut muscles, chiselled abs and a slightly protruding belly button.

"And you call my socks cute." His outie navel was a hundred times cuter.

He glanced down at it and shrugged before pushing down his boxers and letting his thick erection spring free. He wrapped a fist around his length. "Is this cute too?"

"That's not the word that comes to mind." I rolled over onto my knees and crawled over to the end of the bed.

"What do you think you're doing?" He raised an eyebrow at me.

I looked up at him. "I was thinking your cock looked so tasty, I might try it out."

"Oh, really?" he said in a tone that made my heart race harder.

"Really." I stopped with my face a couple of centimetres from the tip of his cock. Close enough to see moisture leaking from the end.

I grabbed his ass with one hand and pulled him towards me so I could slide my lips around his head. I swirled my tongue around his tip, licking over that bead of pre--cum. I hummed in appreciation of the taste of him before taking more of him into my mouth.

I always enjoyed giving blowjobs. It made me feel powerful and in control. After that conversation with Sawyer and Javey's admission that he'd followed me, it was exactly what I needed.

Later, we'd discuss the extent of his—learning—and set some boundaries, but for now I wanted him at my mercy.

He twined some of my hair around his fingers, holding me close as he slowly rolled his hips and thrust. At the same time, he groaned, his breath coming quicker and quicker.

"Sin, your mouth feels incredible. I'm going to…" He grunted. "I'm going to come."

I cupped his balls and massaged them, pushing him closer and closer to the edge.

I looked up at him, watching his face. His eyes were almost closed, eyelids fluttering, long lashes brushing his cheeks. His lips were slightly apart, one side of his face pulled back in a grimace of concentration.

I watched him come. Felt his balls tighten and release. Heard him grunt and groan before he squirted a mouthful of warm, sweet and salty cum into my mouth. I sucked harder while he came, milking him for every drop.

Finally, he sagged and I slid my mouth off him. I looked him right in the eyes while I swallowed down every drop. I was right about him being tasty. His cock and his cum were both delicious.

"Holy shit, that was incredible." He blinked a few times, still coming back down from the rush.

I smiled. "Yes it was." Watching him come turned me on more than ever.

"I want to return the favour." He placed his hands on my shoulders and pushed me back down to the bed. He hooked his fingers through the top of my panties and tugged them down and off. He bent my knees and placed my feet on the very edge of the bed before kneeling in front of me.

"You have a beautiful pussy." He looked at me admiringly. More than admiring, he seemed proud, like he was looking at something that very much belonged to him. Or at least, that he *wanted* to belong to him. He'd have to prove himself with that tongue of his.

He lowered his face to my pussy and started a long, slow exploration of every millimetre of my pussy and clit. He teased and tasted every little bit, missing nowhere, like a man determined to thoroughly learn every tiny part of me and what I like.

By the time he slipped a finger inside me, I was on the edge of coming, so close he'd be able to taste it.

He slipped in another finger and turned his hand around to massage me inside and out.

"Javey." That was part appreciation, part pleading with him. For what, I don't know. He was giving me everything I wanted and more.

"Come for me," he said, his voice muffled by my pussy. "I want to hear you."

I moaned and slipped over the edge into the most wonderful abyss. An almost bottomless pit of fireworks, exploding volcanoes and possibly a couple of flashes of lightning.

My whole body exploded along with it. My nerve ends tingling and singing, celebrating the joy of the amazing sensation passing through my whole body.

I didn't know if I screamed or shouted his name, maybe both, but I wasn't quiet. The whole building probably heard me come. I didn't give a shit. Let them know how good he made me feel. Let them be jealous they weren't the ones he was touching, caressing, coaxing to come for the longest, longest time.

After at least a minute or two, I drifted back down to earth, breathing heavily and trying to catch my breath. I flipped back against the mattress while his fingers were still inside me. His tongue still lapped my sensitive clit until my orgasm faded away.

Only then did he pull away from me, rise and encourage me to climb under the covers with him.

CHAPTER 5

Chair feet scraped across the floor. They stopped right in front of my desk before someone plopped down on it and sat with his arms crossed on the top of my desk, body angled forward.

I recognised the tattoos on Coast's forearms, but continued to tap away at my laptop for another minute or two.

Finally, I closed my laptop and looked up at him.

"Did you want something?" Did he have to be so fucking good looking? Dirty blonde hair, blue green eyes, chiselled chin. When he smiled, dimples popped out in both cheeks.

He should be illegal. Instead, he was making my panties wet without saying a word.

"You and Javey can't happen," he said, unflinching.

I sat back in my chair. "Says who?" I couldn't decide

if I was pissed off or not. That might depend on what he said in the next thirty seconds.

He cocked his head. "Says me. And the fact you hardly know the guy."

"I hardly know you either," I pointed out. "Why should what you say matter?"

He grinned. Yeah, there were those fucking dimples.

"First of all, I'm me," he said, as though that was self-evident. "Second of all, I wouldn't rule out the possibility of him being connected to some unsavoury types. Thirdly, the way he looks at you is borderline obsessive."

"No offence, but you being you doesn't inform my decisions," I said slowly. "Secondly, that's obvious because he associates with you and the other Demons."

He grinned broader. "Ouch."

I flashed him a quick smile. "Thirdly, maybe a girl wants a guy who's obsessed with her. At least with a guy like that, I know where I stand." Was that healthy? Probably not. Did I give a shit? Maybe a little. It was still better than mooning over someone who fucked a different puck bunny every night.

"That's an interesting take on it," he said. "The Demons weren't the unsavoury types I was referring to. Although, I conceded your point about them being dubious, especially me. If we weren't, they'd call us the Angels instead."

I laughed. "That would definitely be a misnomer."

"He told you, didn't he?" Coast frowned. "About his

occasional affiliation with the Fiorelli family. You know they want me dead, right?"

"Yes. Yes. And to be fair, they'd probably be happy if we were all dead," I said. "But they do want some of us dead more than others." Before he could say anything to that, I added, "Javey isn't working with them against us."

"Are you sure about that?" I couldn't remember him looking serious before, but he did now. "Someone is."

"I know they are, and we'll find out who, but like you said, he's borderline obsessive. Would he do anything that would hurt me?"

"Depends what side of the border he ends up on." Coast shrugged. "I want you to be careful, okay? I like the guy, but I don't want you to get hurt."

"Why do you care?" I asked, more blunt than intended.

I probably imagined the tips of his ears turning pink. His bravado didn't slip for a moment.

"I wouldn't want to see any pretty girl get hurt." He leaned back and laced his fingers behind his head. "That would be a waste."

"Wouldn't want to damage a perfectly good pussy." How cynical did I sound? Cynical enough. "Or mouth."

"I'm starting to think you only perceive me as some kind of man whore," he said dryly.

I shrugged. "If the helmet fits."

He grunted softly. "That sounds like a challenge. Have dinner with me."

I blinked. I must have misheard.

"What did you say?"

"I said, have dinner with me," he repeated. "I'll prove to you there's more to me than just a dumbass, horny hockey player."

"I never said you were a dumbass," I pointed out.

He chuckled. "No, just the rest of it. Give me a chance to prove you wrong."

"Why?" I asked.

He leaned forward. "Because it'll be fun. What have you got to lose?"

Nothing, I supposed. Javey and I were nothing more than friends who spent the night together. I didn't belong to him. Someday, maybe, but not now.

"Fine, one dinner," I said. "We'll see if you prove me wrong or not."

"Great, I'll pick you up at six." He handed me his phone so I could enter my address and phone number.

Should I be pleased he didn't know my address already, or not? Did he know Javey did? That Javey had been to my place and watched me? Was that what this conversation was about?

I concluded it was more likely he didn't know. His warning wasn't that specific. Or maybe he didn't want to freak me out. Given what some of these guys got up to, stalking was probably a minor offence. Especially since Javey seemed to have no intention of harming me in any way.

I handed his phone back.

Coast tapped on the screen. A moment later, mine rang on my desk.

He smiled. "Just checking you gave me your real number."

"Does that happen often?" I asked. "Women give you a fake number?"

"More often than I'd like to admit," he said. "Most don't want more than a casual hook up. Sometimes being me is a real beach."

I rolled my eyes playfully at his pun. "I'm sure it is."

"At least they all get wet," he continued. "Right before they…*wave* goodbye."

I snorted. I wouldn't make fun of his name, but it was cute that he did. He didn't take himself too seriously.

"I should warn you though." He rested his arms on my desk again. "One date with me and you might be caught in a rip. My current can get very strong."

"I'm a good swimmer," I said. "I used to surf. I can still take on a six foot swell."

He grinned and glanced down at his groin. "I don't need to brag, I have you to do it for me."

I laughed. "I was talking about your height, but if you want to think I was suggesting your cock is six feet long, go ahead. You'd be dragging it around the ice if it was."

"What if I told you it's not always my hockey stick I'm using to hit the puck?" His eyes twinkled with amusement.

"I'd suggest you're cheating and kicking it along with your skate," I replied. "But I know you wouldn't cheat. You're not that kind of guy."

"Aren't I?" He cocked his head at me. "What kind of guy am I? Apart from a horny hockey player."

"You said it yourself, you like a challenge," I said. "Where's the challenge if you're not fighting to win? Isn't it better to know you earned every goal? Every win? Besides, if you cheated, you'd get kicked off the team."

Or end up in a shallow grave.

"Accurate on every point," he said. "I love a good, hard victory. Working up a sweat and pounding your opponent." His eyes were locked on mine.

His innuendos were making it hot in here. I was trying very hard not to picture him on his back, while I rode him relentlessly. Even if he didn't have six feet in his pants, I was sure what he had was substantial. He didn't seem like the type of guy to overcompensate.

"I see you're feeling what I'm feeling," he said. Yeah, he was smug when he said it.

Coast Riggs would never not be cocky as fuck. Unfortunately for me and women everywhere, it was part of his charm.

"In need of more coffee?" I suggested. "That's more or less a permanent state of mind for me and most of the people here."

I gestured with one hand around the office. PR and marketing shared one big office. The Demons' logo adorned the largest wall, and the door leading out into the arena.

Desks were separated by partitions, most covered in information like the season schedule, the Secret Santa sign up information from two years ago and a collection of random puppy photos.

Every so often, the office manager came through and pulled down old information, but until then it gathered, layer over layer.

"Maybe you should try decaf?" he suggested.

"Maybe you should wash your mouth out with soap," I teased. "We don't tolerate profanity like that in here."

He laughed. "What do you tolerate?" He slid around closer and spoke in my ear. "If I sat you down on your desk and ate you for lunch, would they tolerate that?"

Holy fuck.

I swallowed. "They might want you to feast on them too."

"I only want to feast on you," he said.

Before I could respond to that, he was on his feet and pushing the chair back where he found it.

"I'll see you at six." He winked before strolling out of the office like he hadn't left me in a virtual puddle on my chair.

"I don't know if this is a good idea," I admitted.

"Of course it is." Wren finished fixing my hair and stood back for a good look. "You like him, he likes you."

"I like him, he wants to get into my panties," I said.

"I still don't see the problem," she said with a laugh. "You've been wanting that for how long?"

"The way you say that makes me sound like I've been pining for him for years." I leaned back and also inspected her work. "It hasn't been that long. At least as long as you've been pining for Tiger."

"I have not been pining." She stepped forward and smoothed down some hair at the back. "Lusting, yes. Pining, no."

"What's the difference?" I much preferred talking about her and her love life than mine. Such as it was.

I'd told her about Javey and the night we spent together. Predictably, she was concerned about him hiding outside my house and peering through windows. She knew I could handle myself, and I would. If he lurked around outside, I'd invite him in.

"One means I want to fuck him and the other means I can't live without him," she said.

"What's it called when it's both?" I teased.

"Love." She wrinkled her nose. "I like him, but I'm not ready for that. Besides which, I'm thinking of embracing Elenna's model for relationships."

"You're collecting men for a harem?" I asked.

She sat down on the end of my bed. "Why not? Tiger is cute, but he's not the only guy around. And he may not be enough to fulfil all of my needs. It works for Elenna, why not us?"

I swivelled around in my chair. "I hadn't given it much thought, but you're right. Why not us? Do you think Coast and Javey can share me?"

"I think if they can, you'll have an amazing time." She smiled.

"And if they can't, they might actually kill each other." If Coast lived long enough for that. I wasn't worried about the Fiorellis going after him while we were out having dinner, because, like I said, I can look after myself. I also got the impression they were biding their time. Waiting until Coast and Aidan were in the same place together. Not surrounded by other people who could fight back. I'd say they wanted to avoid harming innocent people, but this was Dusk Bay. Innocent people were thin on the ground at best. Along with the Forellis' morals. They wouldn't care who died, as long as they won.

"Maybe Coast and Javey could work it out in a more civilised way," she said with a sly smile. "I suggest naked mud wrestling."

"Whatever the problem, you always suggest it can be solved with naked mud wrestling." I gave her the side eye.

"Traffic congestion?" I suggested.

"That can totally be solved with mud wrestling, try again." She gave me a 'give it to me' gesture with her fingers.

"The plight of the rainforests?" I suggested. "The debate over which is better, *Star Wars* or *Star Trek*? The existence of pink marshmallows?"

"I think you've proven my point, but what's wrong with pink marshmallows?" She frowned.

"Nothing, I just think marshmallows should be any other colour than pink." I didn't really care about the colour of marshmallows as much as I did getting a response from her. Knowing Wren, she'd take up the pink marshmallow cause, just because she could.

"I think they're perfect in pink, but how did we get to this subject? We were talking about your love life."

"Actually, we were talking about yours," I reminded her. "You were telling me how you were going to have fifteen boyfriends. Two for each day of the week, one for the morning and one for the night. And then a spare."

She laughed. "That's way too much testosterone for me. I'd settle for three or four. Although, seven doesn't sound bad."

Seven sounded like too much testosterone to me, but I just shook my head at her and laughed.

"If you're happy with seven boyfriends, then I'm happy for you," I said. "You could have your own hockey team. Six on the ice and one on you."

"I don't hate the sound of that," she said with a smile. "But you keep changing the subject. You want to go out with Coast, right?"

"Yes, I do, I just don't want to give him the wrong impression," I said slowly.

"What is the wrong impression, exactly?" She fixed me with a firm look. "Don't tell me you wouldn't fuck him, given half a chance, because I know you would. You'd like to get to know him better, wouldn't you? What wrong impression would having dinner with him give?"

"I don't know," I admitted. "I guess you're right."

"Of course I'm right," she said. "I might have sucked at school, but I'm smart in other ways. Including knowing that you and him would be as adorable together as you and Javey would. And if it doesn't work out, at least you get to have some great sex."

"Yeah." I had my doubts about a lot of things, but not that Coast would be anything other than amazing in bed. He certainly had enough practice at it. Practice I hoped to benefit from.

I wasn't afraid of my sexuality and I wasn't going to shame anyone else for theirs. Especially if it led to me getting lots of orgasms.

"It would also be nice to have someone else to live vicariously through," she said. "Elenna doesn't share too much anymore. She's probably too busy getting laid."

She pouted, but she was as happy for our friend as I was. Who wouldn't want their best friend to have three adoring partners? She was a lucky woman.

"You really do need that harem," I remarked. "Or another few vibrators. Have you and Tiger not…"

"I don't know what's going on with him," she said. "There's an attraction there, but we seem to keep skirting around each other. Just as I think something is getting going, something comes up."

I snickered.

She rolled her eyes. "Something other than his cock. His phone rings and he has to leave immediately. He never says why, he just goes. At this rate, my pussy is going to close up."

I moved over to sit beside her and put an arm around her. "Poor thing. There's nothing worse than a neglected pussy."

"Exactly," she said. "That's why I need a harem. If he's too busy to fuck, I can go to another one of the guys."

"That sounds like as good a reason for it as any," I said. "As long as you, you know, care about them too."

"Of course," she said. "That goes without saying.

Relationships are hard work, but if we all wanted it enough, we could make it happen."

"Do you have any idea *where* Tiger is going?" I asked.

"Nope," she said lightly. "He won't say a word. I mean, I don't want to push him. We don't know each other well enough for me to pressure him into giving me any answers. It's just that one minute we're making out and the next he's out the door. When I see him again, he pretends like nothing happened. No explanation, no apology."

"I'm sure whatever it is must be important," I said. "Otherwise, he's crazy to walk away from you." We both knew it was probably something related to Brantley family business, I saw that on her face. If that was the case, she'd never get an answer. Unless she got deeper involved. Which was by no means out of the question.

"That's what I keep telling myself," she said. "Maybe nothing is meant to happen. I should go and chase one of those other fish that apparently live in the metaphorical sea."

"Or better yet, don't chase guys at all," I said. "There's no reason why you can't have half a dozen chasing you."

"See, this is one of the reasons I love you so much," she said. "You're so good for my ego. Not in a bad way though. You're right, they should be chasing me. Or at least, putting in the effort. I don't need chocolates and roses."

"Just naked mud wrestling." I grinned.

She laughed. "Yes, just that. Lots of that."

"To clarify, would you be participating or only watching?" I regarded her as though I was completely serious about the question.

She looked back at me in the same way. "I'm not sure. I might start by watching and then participate if the mood strikes me. I don't want to commit too much."

"That's fair enough." I said with a nod. "I wouldn't want to commit myself to something that would end up with mud up my ass either."

We both laughed.

Mine tapered off with a sobering thought. "You don't think there's any chance that Tiger is the one telling the Fiorellis about Aidan's plans, do you? I mean, he would know and if he's disappearing suddenly..."

She winced. "I'd like to say absolutely not, but the truth is I don't know for sure. Like I said, I don't know him that well and he's not likely to tell me something like that. He knows I'd tell Elenna and she'd tell Aidan. He'd be signing his own death warrant. If Aidan didn't kill him himself, he'd make sure someone did."

"Right." That made me wary of talking to Elenna about Javey. If I mentioned anything about his ties to the Fiorellis, that may be *his* death warrant. If Aidan didn't kill him, he might send Coast to do it for him.

That would make our potential relationships very awkward. To say the least.

"What is it?" Wren asked. "You really think Tiger is the spy?"

"I hope not." I hesitated, then told her what Javey told me. "It's in the past and he didn't have that much to do with them," I said quickly.

"But you're not so sure," she guessed.

"I want to believe it, but for all I know, it could be Coast telling them everything. He was very willing to kill Jamison and Geneva. That might have been to cover his tracks."

"You believe that?" she asked.

I shook my head. "No. I don't want to believe any of the Demons are working against us. I really don't. But someone is, and until we know who, we need to be on our guard."

"That sounds like you're planning to stand Coast up," she said.

"I'm not," I said. "I'm going to be extra careful, that's all." I had every faith that Aidan and Finley would find out who betrayed them, and deal with them. Then we could all breathe a little easier. Right up until the time we had to deal with the rest of the Fiorellis and Mancinis.

Preferably before they made a move on Coast.

CHAPTER 7

COAST

"I said I've got this." I adjusted the phone against my ear while pulling my keys out of my pocket and pushing one into the lock. "I can handle myself."

Aidan's dry tone came down the line. "I'm sure you can. All I'm saying is watch your back. And be careful with Sinclair Rooney. If anything happens to her, I'll have to have you killed at Elenna's insistence."

I laughed, but he probably wasn't joking. Elenna looked sweet, but she was very protective of her best friends. Only an idiot messed around with people like that.

They say a lot about me, but no one ever calls Coast Riggs an idiot. Not to my face anyway. Not unless they want to choke on their own tongue. After I rip it out.

"Don't worry about Sinclair, she's in good hands." I unlocked the door and pushed it open.

Something was off. I glanced around, but nothing

looked out of place. Boxes were still stacked every-where, waiting to be unpacked. After fire fucked up my last home, I'd barely moved in here. Something held me back from making it comfortable. Possibly the fact people wanted me dead. Unpacking wasn't top of my list of priorities.

"She better be," Aidan said. "Just remember you can still play hockey without a cock."

"That's debatable," I said distractedly. "I need all my body parts intact."

"What is it?" He clearly picked up on my unease.

"Nothing to worry about, Mum," I said as lightly as I could. "I'd never forget your birthday."

"Do you need help?" He sounded worried now. That was a quick change from threatening me to giving a shit. Then again, the threats were lighthearted, sort of, and the worry wasn't necessarily misplaced.

I laughed. "I don't know, Mum. I'm sure I'll sort something out. You know me, I'm a last-minute kind of guy." I stepped inside my apartment, all my senses turned on high.

"I'm sending someone over," Aidan said.

"All right, Mum, I'll talk to you later. Bye." I ended the call and shoved my phone into my pocket.

A couple of men stepped out of my bedroom. I didn't recognise either of them, but it didn't take a genius to guess who they were and why they were here.

One of them clicked his tongue. "Don't you know you're supposed to tell your mother you love her before you end the call? You never know when it might be the last time she hears your voice."

I shrugged like I wasn't concerned about the guns in their hands. "My mother knows how I feel about her. I don't need to tell her every time. Did you want something? You know breaking and entering is illegal, right?"

"So is murder," he said.

"Great." I swung my bag off my shoulder and lowered it to the floor. "That means you're not here to kill me."

"There's a fine line between murder and justifiable homicide," he said. "My boss sees this as the latter."

Fucking awesome.

"Before you kill me, you want to loop me in as to who your boss is? If I had to guess, there's a few I could go for. Narrow it down for me." I held my hands out, palms, raised. "Nicholas, Celine or Sawyer? There's a couple more, but those are off the top of my head."

"You seem to have made a habit of pissing people off," he remarked.

I grinned. "You have no idea. Every time my team wins, the list gets longer." Hockey team and Brantley family, they were one and the same to me. Caleb Brantley was my boss in legal and illegal activities.

He huffed. "I have some idea. You're a popular guy. So popular we almost drew straws to decide who was going to come here and take care of you."

I pressed a hand to my chest just over my heart. "That's so sweet of you. I guess you lost."

I lunged at the one who hadn't spoken yet, throwing myself at his torso in a tackle my rugby coach would have been proud of. He let out a grunt of air before he slammed back into the wall.

The impact sent a jolt through me, but I gritted my teeth and made a grab for his gun. While I wrestled him for it, I turned us both around, using him as a shield.

He elbowed me in the stomach. I grunted, but didn't let go of the gun or his wrist.

In a classic badass move I learned from my sister, I raised my foot and stomped down hard on his toes.

He let out a short cry of pain and loosened his grip on the gun enough for me to point it down and squeeze the trigger. The recoil jolted us both, but the bullet slammed it straight into his other foot.

This time his cry was longer and more pained.

"Son of a bitch!" He shoved back harder, trying desperately to cling on to the firearm.

I had to give him credit, because getting shot in the foot looked painful as fuck.

He tried to elbow me away again, but I forced the gun up and pulled the trigger again. I was trying for the left side of the other man's chest, but I'd take the shot in the right.

Sharing a gun like this was difficult at the best of times.

The bullet tore through the man's chest and out the back before embedding in the wall behind him.

"Fuck, I just had that painted." Trying my sister's tactic again, I stomped down, this time on the foot with the bullet in it.

The scream of pain was almost deafening, but he lost his grip on the gun and I grabbed it before it fell.

I turned and shot him point-blank in the centre of his forehead.

I ducked out of the way before he fell. He landed heavily, blood seeping, pooling around him. Shit, he'd leave a bloodstain on my hardwood floors. Brand-new floors, but exactly the reason I got rid of the carpet.

No, shit like this doesn't happen all the time, but often enough that I took precautions.

I clicked my tongue at the remaining guy, who was slumped against the wall. "You're making a mess."

"Fuck you." He raised his gun, but he was clearly in pain. His aim would be off.

I easily ducked aside from a bullet that would have ended up in my skull. Instead, it hit the window and lodged inside it.

Yeah, my windows have bullet-proof glass. Like I said, no one calls Coast Riggs stupid.

"It's not too late to walk out of here alive," I said. "Maybe you could take a message back to your boss to tell them to fuck off. I'm not that easy to kill." I frowned. "I guess if you took that message back to them, they'd kill you, right? You might want to think about working for someone else."

I meant what I said, he could leave if he wanted to. I could kill him, but in the scheme of things, he was nothing. Barely a blip on my radar. He was only here to kill me because he'd been told to, not because he gave a shit.

"I feel like you have three choices here," I said slowly. "You can leave now and go to hospital, you can die slowly, or you can give me an excuse to kill you quickly. If I were you, I'd take the first option."

Surprise, surprise, the fucker took the fourth option. He raised his gun and managed to get off a shot that hit the gun in my hand. It flew out of my hand and smashed into the wall.

He grunted and aimed again. Apparently he was good at working through the pain.

"Right, that's how you want to play it," I muttered. Shaking my hand out, I threw myself down on the floor and rolled. I dipped my hand into my hockey bag near the door and grabbed up the first thing my fingers closed around. My right skate.

I rolled again, dodging another bullet that splintered my new flooring.

Fucking hell. I was going to have to get that fixed too.

I jumped to my feet and threw myself at my attacker. Skate in both hands, blade out.

I jammed the blade into his throat and shoved back

as hard as I could. I pinned him to the wall while he gurgled, arms flailing, trying to dislodge me. I had at least three inches of height on him and a fuck ton more muscle. Not to mention a whole lot of pissed off energy for what they'd done to my apartment.

I pushed the blade in harder. Teeth gritted.

He gradually went limp, eyes bulging, face red. The gun slipped from his fingers and clattered onto the floor. Only when I was sure he was dead, did I let go and step back.

He slid down the wall all the way to the floor where he landed with a satisfying thud.

"They don't call them knife shoes for nothing," I told him. I wiped the sweat off my brow with the back of my hand and tossed the skate back into my bag.

"Looks like you have everything under control," Phoenix DiMarco drawled from the doorway.

I glanced over to see the goalie standing with his arms crossed over his chest, surveying the mess.

"You just missed the fun," I said dryly.

He stepped inside. "Actually, I got here just in time to see you kill a man with an ice skate. My only regret is that I didn't video it on my phone. That was fucking epic."

I grinned. "It was, wasn't it? The asshole had it coming." Should it have been that satisfying? Maybe not, but it was. I gave him the chance to walk away and he chose not to take it. His bad.

"I figured he wasn't a friend of yours." Phoenix

stepped in further and looked over both of the dead men. "You're a dick, but you don't usually go around killing your friends. Not that I know of anyway." He glanced over at me. "By the way, Mum sent me."

I grunted a laugh and closed the door behind him, in case any of the neighbours walked past and peered in. The sound of gunshots usually didn't go unnoticed. Even in a place like this.

"I figured he had. I guess I should say thanks for showing up." I could just as easily have *not* managed the situation. The shot that knocked the gun out of my fingers could have hit my hand.

That would have hurt like a bitch and potentially ended my hockey career. I enjoyed working for Caleb, but I loved playing hockey more. The fact I had a backup plan wasn't as reassuring as anyone might think. I didn't want to fall back on it, not anytime soon. Or at all. When I finished playing, I wanted to coach. Coach Coast had a ring to it. Coach Riggs sounded even better.

"Any time." Phoenix shrugged. "What else are bros for?"

Phoenix and I both grew up in Dusk Bay, we both worked for the Brantley family, but we both had bigger aspirations. We wanted to play hockey for as long as we could and then work behind the scenes on the legal side of things. Dabbling in the illegal once in a while. You could take the man out of Dusk Bay, but you couldn't take Dusk Bay out of the man. The money was too hard to resist.

"No idea, bro." I gave him one of those awkward, side-on hugs before stepping back and glancing at my watch. "Any chance you want to help me clean this mess up? I'm going to be late for a date with Sinclair."

"The cute blonde in PR?" He didn't hesitate to scoop up the dropped gun and the shattered one and put them aside to help me move the bodies over closer to the door.

"That's her," I said. "Is this where you ask for an introduction so you can muscle your way in?"

He grabbed one of the dead men by the ankles and grinned up at me. "Maybe, bro. Maybe."

CHAPTER 8

SINCLAIR

I didn't expect Coast to turn up on time. I certainly didn't expect him to have Phoenix with him.

Both players' hair was damp, like they'd recently showered. Both wore dark trousers, Phoenix with a dark grey henley, Coast with a blue button-down.

"I hope you don't mind Phoenix tagging along for the ride to the restaurant," Coast said. "He helped me to clean up a bit of a mess."

They exchanged glances before Coast explained what happened.

I listened with horror, but not surprise. Sooner or later, someone would have come after Coast.

"I agree with Phoenix," I said. "I wish he'd caught that on his phone so I could watch."

What? Just because I'm a woman, doesn't mean I wouldn't appreciate seeing Coast use his skate like that. Frankly, it was kinda hot.

Yeah, because I needed to find him hotter than I already did. If I wasn't careful, I was going to be in big trouble. As it was, my ovaries were following his every movement.

"I suggested to Coast we recreate it, but he declined." Phoenix followed us out to Coast's dark red SUV.

"I declined on the grounds you refused to be the victim." Coast grinned as he walked around to the passenger side and opened the door for me.

"I can't film it and be the victim at the same time." Phoenix slid into the back seat. "I suggested someone other than me. I can think of a few people off the top of my head who deserve to end up on the sharp end of an ice skate."

"Like who?" I clicked my seat belt and looked back at him.

"Anyone named Fiorelli or Bell, for a start," he said. "That kid at school who said I'd never amount to anything. My junior league coach, who said I'd never make pro. That dickhead centre for the Emus who thinks he's the absolute shit."

Coast jumped into the driver's seat and started the engine. "Yeah, he deserved to be smashed against the boards a few more times. Him and that smug prick from the Opal Springs Ghouls, the left-winger."

"If smug prick was a prerequisite for getting killed with an ice skate, the list would be very long," I remarked pointedly.

Coast glanced over at me and grinned. "Phoenix, I think she's implying we're smug pricks."

"We *are* smug pricks," Phoenix said without any hint of apology or modesty. "But with good reason, because we're fucking awesome."

"Hell yeah we are," Coast agreed. "So is Sinclair. Right, Sunflower?"

I looked over at him. Sunflower?

"I'm not that awesome," I said. "I'm just me. Sinclair Rooney from PR."

"There's nothing *just* about you, Sinclair Rooney from PR," Coast told me. "I'm sure PR stands for perfect… Something starting with R."

Phoenix snorted with laughter. "You're such a dumbass."

"I'm thinking we drop Phoenix off by the side of the road," Coast said. "Maybe outside Nicholas Fiorelli's house."

"You wouldn't do that," Phoenix said. "First of all, you love me too much. Second, you need me to keep the puck out of the goal when it gets past you."

"I concede the second point," Coast said. "But if the team had two of me, they wouldn't need you."

"If the team had two of you, no one else would fit into the arena. Your ego would take up all the space," Phoenix scoffed.

I laughed at their banter. "Are you two always like this?"

Coast grinned. "No, sometimes we're mean to each other."

He glanced back at Phoenix before turning his attention back to the road. "Seriously, we've known each other since we were kids. We give each other shit, but when push comes to shove, he helps me bury the bodies and I help him do the same. Or in the case of today, leave them where the people that sent them can find them. Disappearing doesn't send a strong enough message as clearly saying we can deal with whatever shit they throw at us."

"Even if they mess up Coast's new paintwork and floorboards," Phoenix said.

Coast winced. "Yes, someone is going to pay for that."

"Your insurer," Phoenix said. "I'd love to be there when you explain how the damage happened this time."

"Fuck that, I'll just get it fixed myself," Coast said.

"Is it safe to go back there?" I asked. "Maybe you should stay somewhere they can't find you. Or at least, somewhere unexpected."

We all knew there was nowhere the Fiorellis couldn't find someone if they wanted to.

"That's a good idea," Phoenix said.

"I'll think about it." Coast drew up outside Gianna's restaurant, one of the most exclusive restaurants in the city, with a view over Dusk Bay.

"I was lucky to get us a table at short notice, but I

pulled a few strings." Coast killed the engine and walked around to open my door.

I scowled at him, because I was capable of opening a car door, but I stepped out anyway. "Will Phoenix be joining us?"

"Phoenix would love to," Phoenix said before Coast could say no.

Coast gave him a look with a raised eyebrow, but then shrugged. "I guess it wouldn't hurt. It's only dinner." He levelled a finger at Phoenix's face. "But you pay for your own food. And if three becomes a crowd, you fuck off."

He wasn't backwards in coming forward.

"Noted," Phoenix said easily.

I always had the impression he was difficult to get along with, but maybe he just didn't like crowds. With just the three of us here, he seemed a lot more relaxed. Less likely to be a PR nightmare that would end up on my desk on Monday morning.

In theory.

Coast grunted and placed a hand on my lower back to guide me in through the wide glass doors.

My first impression of Gianna's was of candlelit opulence. The walls were all painted black. Gold sconces were set in the wall every metre or so.

Tables were spaced to give some measure of privacy. Black tablecloths draped over their surface and grazed the dark wood floor.

One wall was entirely taken up with windows, overlooking the sparkling lights of the bay. In summer, those windows would be open, letting in the breeze and the scent of sea air. Right now, they were closed tight, to keep out the cold.

Coast nodded to Kennedy Knight and her three boyfriends, Mannix, Ares and Ice, as we filed past.

Ice responded with a nod and a smile, but the other guys looked at Coast and Phoenix like they'd strangle them with their bare hands if they got too close to Kennedy.

In a place like Dusk Bay, that was exactly what would happen. Guys around here were known for being possessive.

I smiled at Kennedy as I followed the guys to our table. I didn't know her well, but she seemed nice enough.

She smiled back before returning to the conversation with her boyfriends.

"This is nice." I slipped into my chair.

We had a table in the corner, me in the middle, the guys on either side, all facing the room. Now I realised why Coast was so agreeable to having Phoenix along. He got attacked in his own home. This was him being cautious with himself and with me. Possibly with Phoenix as well. He must be more rattled than he was letting on.

"I asked for a table in the corner," Coast said, confirming my suspicions. "We can never be too careful. Not even in here."

"I hear Gianna keeps a shotgun right beside the kitchen door," I said.

"If anyone is going to do that, it would be Gianna," Coast said. "She doesn't like anyone interrupting her diners."

"Has she ever used it?" I asked.

"Not that anyone knows of." It was Phoenix who answered. "It might not be true, but it's a good deterrent. That and no one wants to be banned from coming here. I recommend the ravioli."

"It's not as good as the carbonara," Coast said.

While the guys argued over the merit of the pasta, I let my eyes wander around the room. Everyone seemed deep in conversation. I recognised a few faces.

One of the players from the Dusk Bay Smashers rugby team sat with his girlfriend on the other side of the room. A couple of people high up with the Brantleys sat on the other.

I recognised a couple of local celebrities and a rock star or two. Some out with people other than those they were married to, clearly intimately acquainted. Not that that was any of my business. If they decided to cheat, that was up to them. They wouldn't get any sympathy from me when everything came crashing down around their ears later.

"Sunflower?" Coast apparently asked me something and I totally missed it.

I turned to him. "Sorry, what did you say?"

"I just asked if you wanted some wine," he said.

"Right, sure." I smiled.

"If this is too much, we can go somewhere else," he suggested. "If you'd prefer burgers —"

"No, this is fine," I said quickly. "I love pasta." I loved burgers too, but I wasn't going to pass up the chance to eat here. I may never get another opportunity. Gianna's was usually booked out over a year in advance.

He nodded and gave our order to the server when they stopped at our table. They quickly wrote it down on a small pad before sliding away. Servers in places like this were trained to blend in with the furniture as much as possible. Not to intrude on diners' experiences or personal space.

I wondered if I could learn to be as unobtrusive as that. Probably not, or I'd have had a career as an assassin or something. I should probably stick to PR.

"Are you all right?" I asked Coast. "It's not every day you get attacked in your own home. At least, I hope it's not."

He grinned with all his usual cocky swagger. "Of course I'm all right. It takes more than a couple of attackers to rattle me."

"What is the number exactly?" Phoenix filled a glass with water from the jug and took a sip. "Four? Six? Just out of curiosity, not future reference."

Coast eyed him doubtfully. "Sure, bro. I don't get rattled. Some day they might throw enough at me to kill me, but until then I'm going to keep on keeping on."

"It's okay to not be okay," I said. "I've been rattled every time I had to kill anyone. I can say the same for everyone else I know." Especially Elenna. She didn't say as much, but I had the impression she felt like she had blood on her hands after she shot someone in the head. She was always wringing her hands like she couldn't wash it away, even when her hands were so clean the skin was almost raw.

"I know," Coast said. "It's also okay to be okay. Okay?"

I held up my hands in surrender. "All right. But if you ever need to talk, you know where to find me."

"Me too," Phoenix said. "I'm sure there's some bro code thing about supporting each other when we kill someone with a perfectly good ice skate. I don't really know the protocol for things like that. I'm just guessing here." He shrugged one shoulder and downed the rest of his water.

"That sounds accurate to me," I said. "Whether it's an ice skate or a bullet or strangulation by rubber chicken."

They both laughed and looked at me like maybe I was out of my mind.

I spread my hands. "Sometimes a girl has to do what a girl has to do. For the record, it was the kind that squeaks."

They laughed again.

"I knew you were my kind of girl," Coast said.

"Funny, I was going to say the same thing," Phoenix said.

They exchanged glances and something passed between them. I wasn't entirely sure what, but I had a feeling things were about to get very interesting.

CHAPTER 9

SINCLAIR

"So, about the rubber chicken." Coast handed me a coffee and lowered himself into the chair beside the couch where Phoenix and I sat.

"What about it?" I sat back, crossed my legs at my knees and gave him an innocent look like I didn't know why he was asking.

"Let's start with... Was there really a rubber chick-en?" Phoenix said.

"That's a good starting point," Coast agreed.

We had a lovely dinner at Gianna's. The food more than lived up to the hype. We left right before closing, to go to Phoenix's. He lived in an apartment a couple of blocks from Coast. We all agreed we'd be safer here. At least for now.

"Yes, the rubber chicken was real," I said. "Sort of. It was really long. You know, the kind dogs play with?" I held my hands apart. "One of my father's associates sent someone after me. They woke me up when they stepped on the chicken. Just in time to grab a gun and shoot them in the chest. Don't ask me why I had a rubber chicken lying around. That's a whole other story. It worked better than my alarm system." The toy squeaked louder than my would-be attacker. I'd never looked at rubber chickens the same way since.

"I can't decide if that's the funniest thing I've ever heard or the coolest," Coast said with a grin. "The fact you can stand up for yourself like that is fucking awesome. And the rubber chicken as a warning system… It's innovative."

"I'm starting to feel unprepared," Phoenix remarked. "I have three or four guns hidden around here." He gestured around him.

I presumed he meant the whole house, but he might have meant in this room alone.

"Along with a couple of rolls of duct tape, some rope and a staple gun," Phoenix added. "But no rubber chicken. I'll have to order one tomorrow."

"A staple gun?" I asked.

"I know, a nail gun would be better," he agreed. "I prefer not to let anyone who's trying to attack me get close enough to use a staple gun anyway."

I wasn't sure if he was joking or not. Stapling someone would be painful, but not as effective as a bullet between the eyes.

"I see you're questioning my sanity," Phoenix said.

"Not your sanity," I said quickly. "I was wondering if you're serious. I mean… Staples…"

He leaned over closer to me. "Trust me when I say threatening to staple someone in the nuts is very effective."

Coast winced and pressed his thighs together.

Phoenix nodded towards him. "See what I mean? I didn't even have to threaten him and he reacted. Sometimes it's not about what you do, but about what people think you'll do. And then sometimes, you have to go ahead and do it."

"You've actually stapled a guy's balls?" This conversation had me ready to press my thighs together too.

Phoenix leaned back. "Personally, no. But I've seen Ice Miller do it. The guy's screams—" He winced. "I try to avoid getting on his bad side."

"That's someone whose sanity is questionable," Coast said. "But he gets the job done."

"For the record, I don't actually own a staple gun," Phoenix said. "But I'm starting to think I should. Seeing Coast's reaction would be totally worth it."

Coast flipped him off. "I'm sure Ice won't mind recreating the ball stapling if I ask him to do it to you."

"You wouldn't do that," Phoenix said. "You like me too much." He smirked at Coast.

"Says you," Coast retorted.

"Fucking right I do," Phoenix grinned. To me he

said, "He tries to deny it, but everyone knows the truth."

Their banter was adorable, but it begged the question, "Are you two..." I flicked a finger back and forth between them. "I'm not judging if you are, I just..."

I wanted to understand the situation.

"Together?" Coast's gaze slid to Phoenix, then back to me. "Of course not. We're just friends, that's all."

That wasn't all, I saw it on both of their faces. Phoenix more so than Coast. Like he was ready to explore whatever it was between them, but he knew Coast wasn't.

"I don't want to get in the middle of—" I started.

Phoenix put a hand over mine. "You're not. There's nothing to get in the middle of."

"But you want—"

It was Coast who interrupted me this time. "Phoenix is right, there's nothing to get between. We've known each other so long we give each other shit, like we're brothers. That's all it is. That's the vibe you're picking up."

He placed his half drunk coffee down on the coffee table and moved to sit on the other side of me.

"You also might be picking up the vibe that we're both into you. If you couldn't tell, we're super competitive. We'll compete with each other to get your attention. Unless..." His gaze dropped to my lips.

"Unless?" My breath hitched in my throat.

Phoenix placed a finger on my chin to turn my face

toward him. "Unless you'll let us share you." He brushed his lips over mine.

And now my panties were wet.

I snaked a hand around the back of his head and drew him closer so I could kiss him back.

He made a sound of surprise at my eagerness, but quickly matched it with his own. His tongue swept across my lips, then slipped into my mouth, tasting mine and brushing over my teeth.

I was the one who broke it off and turned to Coast. I placed a hand on his shoulder and kissed him as deeply as I kissed Phoenix.

He tasted of coffee and bacon from the carbonara he ate for dinner, along with something else uniquely him. One hell of a delicious combination. Would his cum taste like bacon? I wanted to find out.

My other hand dropped down to the front of his pants. He was already hard.

Phoenix slid his hands up the back of my shirt and around to cup my breasts. He rubbed his palms over my nipples until they became as hard as Coast's cock.

I moaned against Coast's mouth and grabbed my hem to pull my shirt off over my head. I threw it roughly in the direction of the coffee table, hoping not to knock over the half empty cups of coffee. I didn't stop to look. That was a problem for future Sinclair.

Phoenix unhooked my bra and slid the straps down my arms.

Coast leaned back for a good look before Phoenix palmed my nipples again.

"You have gorgeous breasts," Coast said. He leaned in to kiss the top of one of them, just above Phoenix's finger. Then the other. Then my mouth.

I worked the buttons of his pants loose and pushed them down insistently. I wanted to see if what his pants hinted at was accurate.

Hands to either side of him on the couch, Coast lifted his ass high enough for me to work his pants down. He kicked them off the rest of the way, followed by his bright blue boxer shorts.

Holy fuck yes, his cock was even more than I hoped for. Long, hard and slightly slanted to the left. And elegantly decorated with a magic cross.

"You like what you see?" he asked with his customary cocky smile.

"Very much." I wrapped my fingers around his length and slid them up to his head and down to his balls a few times, savouring the feel of smooth skin over hot blood. The vein that ran along the underside throbbed in my hand.

He kissed me again while both of them helped me out of my pants and panties.

Coast threw his own shirt aside and took his turn caressing my breasts while Phoenix shed his own clothes.

His cock wasn't as long as Coast's, and wasn't pierced, but it was thicker.

I wanted him inside me right fucking now.

Phoenix pressed me back against Coast and draped my legs over his shoulders. He lowered his mouth to my pussy and started to lick around and over my clit.

I found Coast's cock and ran my fingertips over him and his balls, just lightly. I wanted him to stay hard, but not to come yet.

"This is hot," Coast said softly. His eyes were on Phoenix as he lapped at my folds, tasting my arousal and driving me quickly to bliss. He tore his eyes away and leaned down to run his tongue around one of my nipples. He drew it between his lips and started to suck.

Being the centre of attention for two hot hockey gods was something I could definitely get used to. I wasn't shy about sex, but this was next level.

"Very hot," I said breathlessly. "Don't stop, I'm going to come."

Coast sucked on my other nipple for a minute or two, then sat back, his eyes on my face. "I want to watch you come."

My eyes on his, I rocked my hips, grinding myself against Phoenix's mouth. Loving the way his stubble grazed against my inner thighs. The way he knew exactly where to lick and suck and nibble to make me feel incredible.

On the brink of orgasm, I closed my eyes.

"Open them," Coast insisted. "Look at me when you come."

I forced them open and concentrated on his face as

Phoenix nudged me over the brink and into an orgasm that swamped my entire body with pleasure. Pleasure that was heightened by the expression on Coast's face, and the way his cock hardened even further under my fingertips.

"That's the way," Coast said approvingly. "Enjoy every moment."

I made an incoherent sound in the back of my throat, roughly the equivalent of, 'oh, don't worry I am'. At the same time, I rocked harder, making the orgasm last as long as possible before coming back down to earth.

"You're even more beautiful when you come." Coast helped take my legs down from Phoenix's shoulders. He grabbed my hand and pulled me to my feet. "Since you're not shy…"

He gave me every chance to duck away, but led me over to the window and grabbed my wrists. He pressed my palms against the glass and bent me forward.

He stood behind me, hands on my hips and guided his cock to my pussy.

The idea that someone might be outside looking sent a thrill of excitement through me. I couldn't see anyone, just darkness, but I imagined they were there. That was enough to get me going. I popped my ass out and let him slide into me.

"Fuck yeah," he breathed. "You feel amazing around my dick."

"You feel amazing inside me." His magic cross massaged my insides as he slid out and back in again. So fucking good.

I watched our reflections in the window as he pounded into me with firm, even strokes.

"Phoenix," I said over my shoulder. "I want to taste your cock."

"Sunflower, you are something else," Coast said. "Come on, bro. I want to see your dick in her mouth."

"On it." Phoenix jumped up from the couch and stepped over to me. Bent as I was, I was able to turn my face and let him slide his cock between my lips.

"Mmm." I loved sucking cock and his was particularly tasty. Warm and thick and giving.

Coast set the rhythm, fucking my pussy while Phoenix fucked my mouth.

"Holy shit," Coast ground out. "That is…" He had no more words after that, just groans and thrusts. He came first, filling my body with his cum and drawing another orgasm out of me.

I was lost in a rush of bliss when Phoenix came, spilling his sweet, salty release down my throat. I swallowed quickly, still in the middle of coming. I sucked and licked, milking him for every drop while Coast went on thrusting, making my orgasm last as long as he could.

Finally, I sagged forward, Phoenix's cock sliding out of my mouth.

"I like your idea of sharing," I managed to say while still trying to catch my breath.

"Me too," Phoenix said, his eyes taking in me and Coast.

Yeah, there was definitely something there, and if they'd let me, I'd help them to explore it.

CHAPTER 10

JAVEY

Sinclair didn't see me outside her house when she got back from work. Didn't see my car parked across the road, between a dark SUV and a car that looked like it should be towed to the wrecking yard.

My silver hatchback blended in like it belonged here. It didn't. Neither did I, or her... She belonged with me.

I watched her get out of her car as her friend, Wren, arrived. They hugged and disappeared inside.

I should leave, or knock on the door, but instead, I waited until Wren left. I put my hand on the door handle to open it when another SUV slid into the spot she just vacated.

Coast fucking Riggs and Phoenix fucking DiMarco. What were they doing here?

They both got out of the SUV and approached

Sinclair's house like they belonged there. Coast knocked on the door.

She wouldn't answer it. If she did she'd tell him to piss off. I should do that. I should get out and tell them to get lost before she even got near the door.

She opened the door. She looked fucking gorgeous with her golden blonde hair pulled back at the sides, light makeup accentuating the blue of her eyes. She laughed something one of them said and actually closed the door behind her.

What the fuck?

She followed Coast to his SUV and got inside.

I shook my head. I was seeing things. She wasn't actually going out with either of them, was she? She couldn't be. She was *mine*. She had better taste in men than that. So I thought.

Both were excellent hockey players, but they were as arrogant as fuck. Coast acted like the sun shone out of his ass. Phoenix seemed to take his name too seriously, believing he was some kind of second coming.

I bet if I set him on fire, he wouldn't really come back to life afterward.

Fury burnt hot inside me. If they did anything to her…

I started the engine and pulled out a couple of cars behind Coast's SUV. Where were they taking her?

I followed at a distance until they pulled up outside Gianna's. They'd be there for a while. I circled around and found somewhere to stop to grab a sandwich and a cup of coffee.

I should go home, but I couldn't bring myself to leave, not while she was in there, with *them*.

I watched the entrance to the restaurant while I ate my sandwich, sipped my coffee and scrolled through social media.

I liked a couple of posts on the Demons' Instagram page, even though Coast and Phoenix were in the centre of most of the photographs.

I was on there too, always off to the side. The shy, awkward guy who did his best to stay out of the spotlight. I didn't have to try hard. Plenty of my teammates were happy to bask in it. They took their roles as hockey gods too fucking seriously. Their days were filled with hockey and glory, and their nights with puck bunnies.

They had no excuse *not* to leave Sinclair to me. They needed to know, *she* needed to know, she belonged to me. They needed to back the fuck off.

I tossed my phone aside as they walked out of the restaurant and got back into Coast's SUV. They were talking and laughing like they were all old friends.

Friends was fine. I'd allow Sinclair to have them as friends. Anything more than that…

I started the engine and followed them, once again keeping at a distance. I thought they'd return to Sinclair's house, but instead they stopped outside Phoenix's apartment building.

I was too late to stop them from going inside.

Shit.

The building would have a doorman. I wouldn't get past without them informing Phoenix I was there.

Shy and introverted or not, I was still a Dusk Bay Demon. A lot of the city recognised me on sight. I couldn't step foot inside without being noticed.

I slammed my hand down on my steering wheel. "Fuck."

I circled the block and found a parking space where I could see right into any of the apartments with open curtains or blinds.

Which one belonged to Phoenix?

It didn't take long before Coast walked past the window, coffee cups in hand.

A friendly cup of coffee, that was all right. She'd drink her coffee and they'd take her home. Or better yet, they'd step out of the building and I'd take her home from there.

Yes, that would work. She didn't need to be with them any longer than necessary.

I grabbed my phone again and resumed scrolling until movement in the window caught my eye.

The next thing to be caught was my breath, in my throat.

Sinclair was naked, Coast behind her.

I watched with rising fury as he slid inside her.

She closed her eyes, clearly enjoying the way he felt in her pussy. Her breasts swung back and forth as he thrust into her. She turned her face and said something I couldn't make out. A moment or two later, Phoenix stepped over and started to fuck her mouth.

I undid the front of my jeans and grabbed out my dick. I wrapped my fingers around my length and jerked hard, in near-perfect unison to the movement of Phoenix's hips.

It should be me pounding into her pussy or her mouth. She should be taking *my* cock into her wet heat. I should be the one giving her that expression of rising need. It should be me coming down her throat and letting her swallow my cum.

Above all, it should be me making her come. And come. And come. And come.

My breath was ragged, my balls tighter than iron. I couldn't hear anything, but I imagined Coast moaning as he came inside her body. She and Phoenix were next, quickly followed by me, spilling hot cum over my hand.

It took the edge off the pressure and my fury, but I still had to talk to her. She needed to know how I felt.

I'd tell her, but that would have to wait.

I wiped my hand on my jeans, started the engine and pulled away from the curb.

CHAPTER 11

SINCLAIR

I pushed out of the glass doors leading out of the arena and headed across the parking lot.

I fumbled in my bag for my keys. Where were the bloody things? How did they always end up right down the bottom? I swear, one day—

Someone barrelled into me from behind. Shoved me forward and pressed me against the side of my car.

"Fucking hell." I curled my hand around one of my keys, ready to jab when Javey growled in my ear.

"You went out with Coast and Phoenix." He sounded furious.

I caught my breath and forced myself to calm.

Don't panic, he's not going to hurt me.

I hoped.

"Yes, I did," I said. "I had a date with Coast, but Phoenix came along with us." In both meanings of the word, but Javey didn't need to know that.

Although... I had a feeling he already did.

"Why would you go out with them?" He seemed genuinely confused and angry.

"Why wouldn't I?" The front of me was pressed against the cold car, but his body was warm against my back and ass.

"Because you're mine." His hardening cock poked into my hip. "I want to be with you."

"They want to be with me too," I said. How was my voice even right now? I was somewhere between fear and arousal. Was Javey armed? I might be very wrong about him not hurting me.

"Neither of them deserve you." He pushed his cock harder against my hip. "Can you feel what you do to me? I want you." He pushed my cardigan aside and slid a hand up the front of my blouse to cup my breast. His thumb brushed over my already hardened nipple. "I know you want me."

"How do you know I went out with them?" I managed to speak in spite of my rising need. The air was frigid, but I was burning up, tempted to let him fuck me up against the side of my car.

"I was outside your apartment," he said. "I watched you leave with them. I saw you go to Gianna's." He stroked my nipple. "I waited until you left. I saw you go to Phoenix's. The curtains were open."

"You saw us," I whispered.

"I saw Coast fuck you up against the window. It should have been *me*. But it wasn't me. I was in my car with my hand around my cock while his cock was inside you, making you come. Him coming inside you." He pinched my nipple.

I jumped. "You know there are laws against stalking, right?"

"I don't give a fuck about laws," he whispered. "I give a fuck that you're mine and you let them fuck you." He slid his hand out of my blouse and fumbled with the buttons on my charcoal, wool trousers. He pulled them open and pushed them down far enough to slide his hand inside and down to the front of my panties.

I moaned when he brushed over my clit. "We shouldn't do this here." It was almost dark, but the air was cold and quickly getting colder.

"You're right." He pulled his hands out of my pants and wrenched open the door to the back seat of my car. He pressed me inside, face first, before climbing in behind me and closing the door. He pressed a hand to my back to keep me down and tugged my pants to my thighs.

"Tell me you want me." He knelt in the seat well, running his fingers up and down the gusset of my panties.

"I want you," I said breathlessly. "But you can't tell me who I can and can't see."

He slapped a hand down on my ass. "Yes, I can."

He gripped my panties and tore them away. He parted my legs and rammed his fingers inside me. "This belongs to me. I was the one who watched out for you.

Who took the time to learn everything about you. Not some guys who just want you for your pussy. I want every part of you." He slid his fingers in and out of me, relentlessly fucking me with them.

"What if they want every part of me too?" I asked breathlessly. Was I deliberately provoking him? Yes I was.

Angry, possessive Javey was hot as hell and I was loving every minute of it. Not of his anger, but his taking control. I was usually the assertive one. The one who took the lead on things.

"They. Don't. Deserve. You." With every word he rammed his fingers in harder and harder. "You belong to *me*."

I was already close to coming. So fucking close. His fingers must be wet as hell from my arousal. A sucking sound filled the car when they slid in and out of me.

"What if I refuse to stop seeing them?" I asked. "What if I keep fucking them?"

His furious growl sent me over the edge, into a violent whirlpool of bliss that rocked me from the top of my head to the tips of my toes. I shouted his name into the upholstery of my car seat, one hand gripping the corner so tight my nails dug in, threatening to leave permanent dents.

I came down, gasping for breath, my chest heaving in time with his continued thrusts with his hand. Only when I was all the way down and his hand was drenched with my release did he slide his fingers out of me and roll me over onto my back.

"Sin." He looked halfway to regret. Like his being rough with me was slowly sinking in and he'd realised what he'd done.

"Javey." I sat up to undo the front of his jeans and release his erection. "I liked this side of you." I kicked my pants off the rest of the way and angled myself so I could wrap my legs around his hips and press the tip of his cock to my slick heat.

"I don't want to hurt you, but I need you," he whispered. "Are you really going to keep seeing them? Are you going to fuck them again?"

"I don't know. I want to," I said. "Are you going to keep following me around and watching?"

"Yes, I am." He pushed himself until his cock was fully seated inside me. "I'm going to stay close to you until I convince you you're mine. After that, we can be together all the time." He pulled back and rammed in again.

"Except when you have away games," I reminded him.

He stopped still for a moment. "Except then," he agreed. "That's only for another couple of years, until I retire." He resumed thrusting into me. The car moved with every stroke, no doubt letting anyone who walked past know exactly what was going on inside.

"I'll still be working," I said.

"I'll get a job at the arena." He seemed to have thought of everything.

"What if I want to be with you, Coast and Phoenix?" I rolled my hips to match his thrusts as best I could in the confined space. "What if I want to fuck all three of you?"

He growled softly. "I won't give you up. No matter what, you're mine."

"Even if you have to share?" His face was half-hidden in shadow, but I looked at him intently, trying to gauge his reaction. He was much more in control now. I wasn't goading him as much as I had before. Or he was covering it better.

His only response was to thrust into me harder and faster, while he gripped my hip with one hand and the side of the car seat with the other.

I decided to put the conversation aside for now and enjoy the way his cock felt inside me. With every thrust, he filled me all the way inside, as deep as he could go.

"You feel so good," I said softly.

"You feel so fucking good too," he said. "So fucking mine. So..." He groaned. He was right on the verge of coming.

"Come inside me," I whispered.

His eyes snapped open. "I *will* come inside you," he said. "I'll claim you by filling you with my cum."

"Yes please," I groaned. The pressure was starting to build again. Even harder this time. More frantic, more desperate. I needed to come so badly it almost hurt. "Come with me."

"Fuck, Sin... Yes." He cried out the same moment I came again, our bodies slamming against each other, driving each other higher and higher, muscles clenching. Breath coming in ragged pants. Calling out each other's names as we claimed each other, bodies entwined. Sweat-soaked skin slid together, lost in bliss, in fireworks and heat.

Then we were sagging down together, catching our breath and coming back to reality.

"Holy shit," I breathed. "Javey, I—"

He'd ducked his head, but he raised it now. "You don't need to say anything if you don't want to." The shadows couldn't hide the troubled expression on his face.

Not because of us fucking. He was worried that when I stopped to think about him following me, watching me with Coast and Phoenix, then him getting rough with me, I may reconsider letting him anywhere near me.

Most women would run at the very idea of it. Maybe there was something wrong with me, because I didn't want to run.

"I do want to," I said quickly. "It's complicated, but I do want to."

Complicated didn't even scratch the surface.

I had feelings for him and I wanted to explore them,

but I also wanted to explore them with Coast and Phoenix.

Maybe, we'd all end up nothing more than friends, but I wanted to see where it might go.

I already knew Phoenix and Coast were up for sharing, but where, if anywhere, would Javey fit into all of it? If he was going to get angry any time either of the other guys touched me, someone was going to end up stabbed, or worse. I didn't want at any of them ending up in Ice Miller's torture room with a staple or three through his balls.

"Me too," Javey whispered. He slid out of me and gathered me into his arms to hold me while our hearts slowed.

CHAPTER 12

SINCLAIR

Elenna winced. "That is a complicated situation. What are you going to do?"

"I don't know," I admitted. "I mean, I need to talk to all three of them. I'm just not sure how they're going to take it. Javey seems really sweet, but the more I see of him, the more I realise he's volatile."

I exhaled softly. "Phoenix is volatile around everyone else, I can only guess how he might react. I don't know if his angry facade in public is the real him or... Or not. As for Coast, you know what he's like. Does he seem like the sort to settle down to you?"

"No," she admitted. "But I would have said the same about Aidan, Finley and Orion. none of them were the settling down type, until they were."

"Until they met you," I said. "And fell head over heels in love." I tilted my head at her and fluttered my eyelashes.

She flushed slightly. She didn't seem to realise how gorgeous she was. She was even cuter when her face was as pink as it was right now. "If it wasn't me, it would have been someone else."

"That's bullshit and you know it." I waved my pass at the panel beside the door leading into the arena. The light flashed green and the doors unlocked.

"None of those guys would have looked twice at anyone else." I stepped aside to let her in, and closed the door behind us.

"Finley and Orion might have looked twice at each other." She shrugged.

"I doubt that, but that's another thing." I gestured for her to follow me to the PR office. With any luck, we'd be in there first.

"Should I be worried?" She pushed her bag higher up her shoulder, and gave me a smile.

"Not at all." I stepped in through the doorway and glanced around. Only a couple of people were here, but they were busy on their laptops, or with phones to their ears. We wouldn't be overheard for now.

I slipped my bag under my desk and spoke in a low voice. "How did you know Finley and Orion were interested in each other?"

She frowned. "It was Aidan who realised it first. He encouraged them to explore their feelings. He likes to… guide the three of us."

There obviously was more to it, but I didn't pry. I was probably overstepping as it was.

If Coast and Phoenix knew I was even alluding to any attraction between them, they could be pissed off. Whatever may develop between us, might be over before it began.

"So they needed some encouragement?" I asked. "Do you think they would have come together without it?" I realised what I just said, and made a face. "No pun intended."

She laughed. "I'm not sure that you *didn't* intend that pun, but I don't know. I feel like Aidan gave them —I don't know—permission to be themselves. Does that make sense? It was something they had to choose to do, and to know that we weren't going to judge them for it."

"Right," I said slowly.

That made sense. Coast and Phoenix were judged on a daily basis for their skills on the ice and their behaviour off it. People would definitely judge if they were in a relationship with me and with each other.

I'd seen how the press treated Aidan and Elenna, wanting to know about their relationship, and that was before Finley and Orion were also involved. Now, they were even more voracious.

So far, the four of them managed to avoid the worst. Would that be different with two players? Or three? Fans were more invested in them than they were in the head coach or equipment manager. Especially those who harboured secret desires to become involved with them.

I saw it all the time after games, when the guys were

out celebrating. Puck bunnies would swarm them the moment they stepped into Hazards, offering them everything from blow jobs to having their babies.

If they got involved with me, that would put me in the firing line. I could deal with that. Having their relationships with each other put under the microscope? That was a different story.

Elenna sat on the corner of my desk. "Do I want to know who we're talking about here?" she asked cautiously. There was a fine line between satisfying curiosity, and being too nosy.

I glanced around. "You can probably guess. Just don't go saying anything, all right?"

"Of course not," she said quickly. "When have I been known to spill anyone's secrets?"

I gave her a quick hug. "Never. That's what makes you such a good friend. I can tell you anything, and you won't judge me, or run off and tell anyone. Including Aidan, right?"

She chewed her lip. "If it impacts the team in some way that I think he has to know…"

"I'd tell him myself," I said firmly. "It doesn't, I promise." I leaned my hip against my desk. "Although—"

"Although, what?"

"Please don't read any more into this than there already is." I cocked my head and silently begged.

"Sinclair, if you're in trouble in some way, you know you can come to me. Whatever you need, I'm here for you."

"I'm not in trouble," I said quickly. "Not exactly."

"Are you pregnant?" she asked.

"What? Fuck no." That would be a whole other complication I didn't need any time soon. I sucked in a breath and told her how Javey was following me, including him watching me with Phoenix and Coast.

"Sinclair," she said slowly. "He's stalking you? He seemed so, I don't know. Shy and sweet."

"He is," I said. "There's just…a whole other side to him."

"Evidently," she said dryly. "He doesn't sound sweet at all, he sounds dangerous."

"He's not dangerous," I argued. "Not to me, at least."

"What about to Coast and Phoenix?" she asked. "What if he gets jealous of them, and decides to go after them?"

"I'm starting to think I shouldn't have told you." I sighed.

"You definitely should." She put a hand on my arm. "I'm just worried about you, that's all. Stalkers aren't usually known for being reasonable or rational. Or hinged, for that matter. It sounds to me like he needs some professional help."

For some reason, her words made me angry.

"You don't know him," I snapped. "He's not like that. He's just… Intense."

Not to mention obsessive and possessive. But not in a way that would put me in danger. "He's harmless, I promise."

"I don't want those to be famous last words." She squeezed my arm. "It's not wrong for me to be worried about you, is it? If you thought there was nothing to worry about, you wouldn't have been hesitant to tell me in the first place. Maybe you should stay away from him and, I don't know, come, and stay with me and the guys."

"The last thing I want is to be your fifth wheel," I said. "If I feel unsafe, I can go and stay with Wren."

"Please do that," she said. "Or stay with Coast or Phoenix."

Now things were about to get awkward.

"About Coast and his apartment," I started slowly. "He might have been attacked there and had to kill a couple of men."

She tilted her head at me. *"Sinclair…"*

I waved her down, "I know, I know. He can take care of himself. And so can I. You know that. Not long ago, you were in exactly the same position, getting involved with Orion. And Aidan, for that matter."

"I remember, and then there was that whole attack on the arena," she said. "The last thing I want is for that to happen again. While the Fiorellis are after Coast, it's a possibility. They won't stop coming until he's dead, or they are."

"All the more reason for him to be around Phoenix and me," I said. "And Javey. Safety in numbers and all that."

I put a hand over hers. "I know you're worried about

me. I love you for that. Believe me, I'm worried about me, too. And you. And Wren, because she's associated with us. And..."

I stopped and frowned. "Maybe we should lock ourselves away somewhere and hide until the Fiorellis are all gone."

She smiled softly. "That was what we used to say. Finley wanted us to run off to some remote island and spend our days in the sun, drinking cocktails and fucking."

"Finley is a redhead, that wouldn't end well for him," I said. It would go about as well for me. "That does sound very enticing, though. If you decide to do that, can I come? I wouldn't mind being the fifth wheel if the island is big enough."

"I have a feeling we need an island with an ice hockey rink, so we can bring everyone," she said. "Wren will want to come along too. And, in spite of them dancing around each other, I think she'd want to bring Tiger along and fuck knows who else."

"This island is sounding very crowded." I took my hand off hers and pulled out my laptop to boot it up.

She laughed. "It is, isn't it? It might be easier to deal with the Fiorellis. How many of them are left?"

I counted them off on my fingers. "Nicholas, Celine, Sawyer, Kaya. Amity if you want to count her, but she stays right out of the family business now she's with Lucas Brantley."

"And all of their associates," she said on an exhale.

"Assuming they have loyalty to their employers. They may jump ship the moment it's sinking hard enough."

"I would have thought that's already happening," I said. "Not enough to stop people from attacking Coast. I assume he's filling Aidan in on all the details as we speak."

"If he hasn't done it already," she agreed. "Aidan will want to know. He's going to be pissed off. He hates it when people go after his players."

I smiled. "For someone so angry a lot of the time, he's such a teddy bear, isn't he?"

"He really is, but don't say that to his face." She smiled softly, like a woman madly in love. "He sees himself as big bad Coach Draeger. Scourge of hockey players everywhere. Not to mention the opposition. I think he likes to imagine them lying awake at night, shaking in their skates."

"I'm one hundred percent certain, that's exactly what happens," I said jokingly. "I'm quaking just thinking about him yelling at me."

I'd probably yell back at him. I didn't take shit from anyone, not even the Demons' head coach. Sinclair Rooney wasn't that easily intimidated.

Although, if I *was*, it would be by Aidan. He was a daunting man. He'd softened slightly around the edges since he got together with Elenna. Soft, like a meat cleaver.

Okay, not very soft, but slightly less inclined to be as hard on the players as he used to. Of course, that could also be attributed to the fact that, under his leadership, they were actually winning. Whatever he was doing, it was clearly working.

"I can tell," she said, with a smile. "Do me a favour and be careful, okay? And if you need anything, any time, day or night, you have my number. Use it if you need to. I'll come and help you or send the guys. If you need all four of us, that's what you'll get. All right?"

"You're the best," I told her. "I will definitely call you if I need you."

I hoped never to need her.

CHAPTER 13

PHOENIX

"So then, I drove my skate into the asshole's throat, and shoved it in, nice and hard until he was nice and dead." Coast grinned.

Prick was going to dine out on the story for as long as he could. Why the fuck not? It wasn't every day you killed someone with an ice skate. Not even for us.

I'd personally used several different methods, but never an ice skate. I wouldn't let on that I was envious of his creativity. I was creative in my own way.

Coast did what he had to do at the time. That was all. Not all that impressive, when you think about it. That's what I'd tell him anyway, if he bothered to ask my opinion. His ego was fucking big enough as it was.

"They were definitely sent by the Fiorellis?" Aidan asked. He didn't look particularly impressed either. Not like he was going to condemn Coast for his methods, but he was more interested in what, who and where, than in the how.

"That was what they said," Coast agreed. "Who else would come after me?"

I snorted softly.

He flipped me the finger. "I'm not so unpopular that I have dozens of people who want me dead."

I gave him a sceptical look, but didn't say anything.

Coast Riggs was good at getting into trouble. I'd be surprised if it was only the Fiorellis after him. There were probably a bunch of angry husbands and boyfriends too. Granted, it wasn't his fault if women decided to cheat with him. For some reason, they seemed to find it hard to resist him.

Yeah, okay, I understood why. He was tall, attractive, confident, muscular, and a fucking good centre.

For all of those reasons, except the last, I should be fending women off as hard as he was. Being a goaltender should make me twice as appealing as being a centre. All he had to do was get possession of the puck and keep it away from the opposition. I had to stop the fuckers from scoring goals. It's definitely harder than it sounds.

"Where did you dispose of the bodies?" Aidan directed the question at me.

I wasn't just a goalie, I was also one of the go to guys for disposing of evidence. As a DiMarco, I had contacts, including my brother, Ric and my cousin Rose.

Between the three of us, I could make anything or anyone disappear. Was it something I was proud of? Not always. I wanted to spend my life on the ice, defending the bucket.

On the other hand, if I didn't help Coast, he'd be fucked more often than not. Not in that way, I was totally *not* thinking about fucking him. No way.

He was like a brother to me. I didn't want to screw things up between us. So I talked myself out of any attraction when it tried to rear its ugly head.

I had a feeling that was going to be more difficult with Sinclair involved. She was the sort of woman who'd encourage us to embrace all our inner shit, no matter how difficult it might be to face.

She'd be shit out of luck if she thought she could force me into anything I wasn't ready for, no matter how amazing her mouth was. The memory of coming down her throat made me hard. I wanted to be in her pussy next time. There would definitely be a next time, I'd make sure of that.

"Returned to sender," I said, with a smirk. "Celine Fiorelli would have had a nice wake up call this morning."

"You didn't put dead bodies in her bed again, did you?" Coast seemed amused at the idea.

I grinned. "No. I didn't have time on this occasion. Shame, because waiting outside to hear people scream is pretty fucking fun."

Aidan gave me a look like I was sick in the head, but he would have enjoyed it, just as much as I would. He liked to pretend he was slightly more civilised than the rest of us, but he was one of us at heart. If anyone tried to do anything to Elenna or her other partners, he'd do a lot worse than putting bodies in beds.

I gave him a look back that said I had his measure. Whatever he might do or say, he wasn't fooling me.

"Coast is crashing at my place for a while," I said. "Between us, we'll keep the fuckers away."

Aidan nodded. "Good. Make sure you keep an eye on each other. I'm trying to gauge what the Fiorellis-slash-Mancinis might do next. Until we worm out who's telling them our every move, our hands are more or less tied. We can't do anything without them knowing about it."

"I assume we have someone on the inside with them?" Coast said. "Someone telling you their every move."

"Why would you assume that," I asked. "Aidan didn't know they were coming after you two nights ago."

"That's true." Coast looked at Aidan through narrowed eyes.

Aidan looked back at him, unflinching. "Even if I have someone on the inside, they won't be privy to every piece of information. Obviously, I had no idea that was going to happen, or I would have warned you. The fact it did has pissed us both off. As does the fact I didn't hear about it straight after it happened."

"We had it under control." Coast raised his shoulders. He dropped them down again, and cocked his head at Aidan as though daring him to contradict him.

Aidan granted. "You're missing the point. We're a team. I'm not just the head coach. I'm also the one watching out for you and trying to keep you alive. I can't do that if I don't have all the facts."

He pointed accusingly at Coast. "Next time anything like that happens, I want to hear about it straight away. If I don't, it better be because you're dead. But don't fucking be dead."

"I have no intention of being dead any time soon," Coast said. "Next time, I'll shoot you a text. For the record, I had a date. Excuse me if my personal life is important to me."

"No pussy is worth risking your life for,"Aidan said.

Coast scoffed. "First of all, that's bullshit. Every pussy is worth risking my life for. Second of all, you don't believe that for a fucking minute. You'd risk your life all day every day for Elenna, and we all know it."

"She's more than just a pussy," Aidan growled.

"So is Sinclair," Coast argued. "Look me in the face and tell me you disagree. She's one of Elenna's closest friends. What would she think if she heard you call her that?"

"She'd be surprised a woman like Sinclair would go on a date with someone like you," Aidan retorted.

"Because I'm not good enough for Sinclair?" Coast's face was slightly pink now. Anger flashing in his eyes.

"Elenna will never think anyone is good enough for any of her friends," Aidan said. "She's very protective of them. But we all know what you're like. You'll get bored soon enough and move on to another pussy."

I grabbed Coast before he could take a swing at Aidan.

"Arguing amongst ourselves won't help anyone," I said. "I know we're all on edge, but didn't Aidan just say we are supposed to be a team? No wonder we keep fucking losing."

Coast shook me off. "We've been winning," he snapped.

"Yeah, so let's keep on winning," I said. "Being a pair of fucking dickheads won't help anyone."

Aidan looked ready to take exception to me calling him a dickhead, but he pressed his lips together in a tight line instead.

"Enough," he said. "I don't give a fuck where you stick your cock, but if you get her killed, I won't be responsible for what my wife does to you. Chances are, Finley and Orion will happily hold you down for her."

"I might help them," I said lightly, hoping to diffuse the anger in the moment.

"It would take more than three of you to hold me down," Coast said with a grunt.

"I'll help them," Aidan said darkly. He crossed his arms over his chest. "I appreciate your confidence,

Coast, but if you get too arrogant, you're going to make a mistake. If you think the Fiorellis or the Mancinis won't be there to take advantage of it, think again. You can never get too fucking complacent. If you do, it will get you killed, and I, for one will be fucking pissed off if that happens."

"So will I," I agreed.

"No one will be more fucking pissed off than me," Coast said. "I have no intention of—"

"It has nothing to do with intention," Aidan snapped. "Do you think Geneva came in here with the intention of dying? Or Jamison? Or any of the people with them? No, they came in here for one reason. They intended to take us all out and walk away. They had a plan, they had the numbers. They had the element of surprise. And they still. Fucking. Failed."

"Because I was here to take out Geneva," Coast said, smugly. "And if I hadn't, Phoenix would have." He jerked his head towards me. "And if not him, then Tiger or someone else. Because taking care of shit is what we do. If someone comes after me again… When someone comes after me again, I will fucking deal with the shit they throw at me. Me and Phoenix and whoever else is with me. Including Sinclair. She's just as much a badass as Elenna, or even you."

"At least you acknowledge I'm a badass," Aidan said with a grunt.

"Of course you bloody are," I said. "How many head coaches are there in the AIHL who know how to kill a man, and wouldn't hesitate to do it if they needed to?"

"Probably more than you imagine," Aidan said flatly. "But we're the exception. Most of them have no idea what it's like to be involved in any sort of mob activity. Unless you're talking about the kangaroo kind of mob." He rubbed a hand over the back of his neck and half smiled at his own joke.

I snorted a laugh. "Sometimes, I think they're the lucky ones. It must be nice not to know about all the shit that goes down."

I wished I didn't know about half of it. Some days, all I wanted to do was walk away. I could ask to get traded to another team where I could live my life playing hockey and not having to worry about dead bodies, and solving other people's problems. I could focus on, stopping fuckers from scoring goals.

Why didn't I? Partly because my life was too embedded here, partly because of my attraction to Sinclair.

In the back of my mind was a very faint admission that part of it was because of my attraction to Coast as well. Even if he never returned the sentiment, I wanted to be around him. He was like a magnet or a flame. Between him and Sinclair, I'd be lucky if I didn't end up burnt to a crisp. If that happened, while her mouth was around my cock, at least I'd die a happy, satisfied goalie.

"You'd be bored if you lived like that," Coast told me. "At least our life is never dull."

Aidan and I both gave him a look, like maybe he was the unhinged one. Once in a while, dull didn't sound so bad.

"You boys should be getting ready for practice," Aidan said. He stepped aside as the rest of the team started to roll into the locker room.

Grateful to have something else to think about, I started to pull on my padding.

"I love this place right before a game. It's always buzzing with people and noise." Wren followed Elenna and I through the door leading from the garage, into the arena. Strictly for staff and players, she was only allowed there when she was with one of us. Or in this case, both.

"It does have a good atmosphere," Elenna agreed. "I don't mind it during the week too though, when it's quieter."

"It's certainly a lot more hectic like this," I agreed. During the week, the arena was little more than a glorified office. Or not, so glorified, depending on how you look at it.

People seemed to think working for a professional hockey team was glamorous in some way, but it was work like any other. Harder, in some ways, given the egos I had to deal with.

Yeah, it's ironic that I'd want to get involved with any of the players, much less three of them. What could be better than dealing with egos at work and then going home to them? Not to mention what someone like Coast would think he could get up to if I was his girlfriend.

So I got drunk and slugged some guy in a bar; Sinclair will fix it.

That was something I was going to have to address at some point. There was no way he was getting away with shit like that, no matter what we were to each other. If he did, he'd make me and himself look bad.

Honestly, I doubted he gave a shit about making himself look bad, but hopefully he cared about not embarrassing me and making me lose my job.

Yeah, now I was wondering if dating any of the players was such a good idea.

We took the elevator up to the main level, and stepped out into a flood of people making their way towards the rink.

A buzz of excitement filled the air. Most wore Demons jerseys and hoodies, but plenty also wore the Sugar Gliders' colours: brown and yellow.

Of course, we wore jerseys with the Demons logo on the front.

Elenna's had Orion's number on the back.

Wren, being Wren, had the number sixty-nine on the back of hers, with her last name, Valentine.

Mine had no number or name. Any other choice

would have raised comments with one of the guys. I had a feeling Javey would lose his mind if he saw me in Coast's or Phoenix's numbers. I was down for that in private, but in public... It was better not to push that button.

We ducked into the staff area so Elenna could put down her things and get to work.

"I didn't think it was possible for this amount of laundry to exist." She grabbed the handle of a full hamper from outside the locker room and wheeled it to the laundry, and dumped the contents into a washing machine.

"It's a never-ending cycle," I said. "Just think how much worse they'd stink if not for you." One of the more unglamorous aspects of being a professional hockey player was how much they stank after a game. Think of smelly socks, then times it by about a million. Sweat and testosterone will do that to a guy.

"Not all heroes wear capes," Wren said lightly.

Elenna gave her a look, then cracked up laughing. "I don't think there's much heroic about doing washing. It's not as exciting as sharpening skates." She glanced at me meaningfully.

"Now we have extra reasons to keep them nice and sharp," I said, lighter than I felt. Truthfully, the idea of someone killing someone with an ice skate was both horrifying and hot at the same time.

"Absolutely," Elenna agreed. "I—" She stopped as Aidan stepped through the doorway.

"Judging by the fact you're talking about keeping ice skates sharp, you know what happened to Coast." He regarded us all like we were children caught doing something wrong. Even Elenna, but for her, he had a faint smile and a hand on her cheek.

"Sinclair just told us," she said. "I feel bad for him, attacked in his own home. He'd barely moved into the place too."

"Better him than you," Aidan said.

He glanced over at me, his eyes narrowing. "I trust you're not going to cause any trouble with my players?"

I didn't imagine the accusing look in his eyes, it just took me a moment to realise what he was accusing me of.

"It wasn't my place to tell you," I said. "It was—"

"I should've been told immediately, regardless of who did the telling," he said coldly. "You of all people should know how difficult it is to clean up a mess once it gets out of control. If the press got wind of this, they'd have a field day and you'd be right in the middle of it. How long do you think your job would last then?"

"Don't threaten me," I growled. I didn't give a shit if he was with one of my best friends, he didn't get to make suggestions like that. If he thought he'd get to me in some way…

Yeah, he was right, but I didn't have to put up with it.

He tangled his fingers in Elenna's hair like he might

bend her over the washing machine and fuck her, taking his frustration at me out on her pussy.

"I'm not threatening you," he said. "I don't need to. You know exactly how fucked you'd be if this got out. Coast would plead self-defence and probably walk away. But you, knowing what happened, and not coming forward, would be right in the proverbial firing line."

He emphasised the word proverbial, as if to accentuate the fact, I'd also be in the literal firing line. If I started pointing fingers at anyone named Fiorelli or Mancini, I'd end up on their shit list before I could blink. Being associated with Elenna and the team, I was probably on there already.

"I get it, you're pissed off I didn't come to you," I said. "But to be fair, I didn't realise it would take Coast so long. He could have called you before he came to my place to pick me up. He could have—"

"He could've done a lot of things, but he didn't," Aidan said. "Neither did Phoenix. As far as I'm concerned, you're all as bad as each other."

"Aidan." Elenna grabbed his wrist and glared at him. "We all know you're worried about the team and that they might attack the arena again. But we can't be at each other's throats. That's not going to help anyone."

"Elenna's right," Wren said. "Fighting amongst ourselves is not going to achieve anything. Especially not team unity." She raised a perfectly shaped red eyebrow at Aidan, clearly aware she was aiming right at his heart.

His grunt in response suggested she hit her target bang on. He'd talked so much about team unity, especially after the attack, he'd be a hypocrite to do anything to jeopardise that. Whether he cared about being a hypocrite or not, was another thing.

Sometimes I wondered how Elenna put up with him. At times, he could be a stone cold asshole.

"If the result is that more people are forthcoming with important information, then perhaps some altercations are necessary," he said coolly.

"That's bullshit, and you know it," I said. "I'm sorry I didn't come to you and tell you what happened to Coast, but if I had it to do over again, I'd do the same thing. It was up to him or Phoenix to tell you, not me. This may come as a surprise to you, but I'm not their nursemaid. I'm not even their girlfriend. I'm someone who works in the same place they do, that went out on a date with them. That's all." And fucked them, but that was none of his business.

"As someone who works in PR, that's even more important than if you were their girlfriend," Aidan said. "Being forthcoming with information about them is your fucking *job*. Next time, do it or I won't need to threaten. I'll explain the situation to the GM and you can find yourself a new fucking job."

"Aidan," Elenna snapped. "She's my friend. She did what she thought was right."

"She was wrong," he growled. "No matter who she is, it doesn't excuse..."

He rubbed his other hand over the back of his neck. "I'm trying to keep us all safe. I can't do that if I don't know what the fuck is going on. The Fiorellis are going to find two dead bodies, courtesy of Coast and Phoenix. What do you think they're going to do with that? Smile, laugh and walk away? No, they're going to come back at us harder than before. they're going to come back at Coast harder than before." He sucked in a sharp breath.

"As soon as I know this shit happens, I can put measures in place to keep him and the rest of us safe. I can have people watching him and protecting him. I can put extra security on the arena. And I have," he added. "But none of this is based on guesswork. It's based on information. If I don't have all of that, I can't do my job. None of that is rocket science."

He was starting to make me feel bad. He was right, Everything he'd done was to protect all of us. If he didn't know what was going on with one of us, it would be like trying to put together a puzzle with missing pieces. This was an important piece. We all knew Coast was at the top of the shit list. If they were going to come after anyone first, it would be him. And then they did exactly that.

I sighed. "You're right. Kind of. I should have made sure he told you. I didn't think to ask him if he had or not. I didn't think to ask Phoenix either. I assumed they were all over it and they weren't. That put all of us at risk." Especially Coast.

"You could have told Coast to contact Aidan, but do you seriously think he would have listened?" Wren asked.

Aidan gave her a look like she wasn't helping matters. His shoulders dipped.

"The problem with working with hockey gods is they take the *gods* part a bit too seriously. Especially guys like Coast and Phoenix. They think they're invincible. But they're fucking not. Coast could have been killed the other night. If they sent three or four, we'd be having a different conversation right now, and the Demons would have a different centre."

Elenna slipped her arms around his neck and pulled him close. "Lucky for all of us that didn't happen. And it won't. Coast can take care of himself and we're taking care of each other. You're making sure of it. We all know that. Right?" She glanced around at me and Wren."

"Yeah," I said, with some reluctance. Aidan was being such a dick right now. I didn't agree with the philosophy that someone could get away with being a dick just because they cared. Not when it came to Aidan.

Javey... Okay, maybe now I was the hypocrite. There was a difference between following someone around and growling at people just because you can. I knew which I preferred.

"The game should be starting soon," I said. "I'm sure we all have places to be."

I smiled sarcastically at Aidan who gave me a dark look in return. The conversation wasn't over, just over for now.

CHAPTER 15

SINCLAIR

"A shut out." I smiled as Javey slipped into the chair beside me. "You guys did amazing tonight."

He leaned over to kiss my cheek, but his eyes seemed to be everywhere.

Hazards was packed with players, families, and fans. And, yes, puck bunnies. Many of who were eyeing Javey speculatively. A few even gave me a dirty look when I leaned my shoulder against him.

I ignored them and gave him a brilliant smile.

He put an arm around me. "We did okay."

I looked at him in mock horror. "Did I hear you correctly? Are you suggesting you're actually a humble hockey god?"

The smile he gave me was the shy one I'd come to expect from him. Awkward and almost uncomfortable. Like he couldn't quite believe I was sitting with him, touching him.

"Not all of us have egos the size of Jupiter," he said. "Just most of us."

"Not you though?" I asked, half teasing.

"I've never been one to brag. Mostly because if I did, my siblings would tease the shit out of me." He took a sip of his beer.

"You should brag once in a while," I said. "Especially when you win against a team as tough as the Sugar Gliders."

"I'll leave the bragging to guys like Tiger and Coast." He scowled as both walked through the door followed by Phoenix, Bray and the rest of the guys.

Coast scanned the room before seeing me and striding over like he owned the place. Phoenix wasn't far behind.

"Hey, Sunflower," Coast ignored Javey's arm around me and leaned in to kiss my mouth.

Javey growled, a full throated sound of pure irritation. He could have put Aidan to shame.

"Hey, Jav," Coast said lightly. "How's it hanging? Good game tonight."

"What about me?" Phoenix moved around to the side of the table, and slipped into a stool. "Have you forgotten I didn't let a single puck get past me tonight?"

He glared at Coast, his angry, public expression on display. If I hadn't seen him being sweet, I'd buy that this was the real him.

"Yeah, you did okay," Coast said, clearly baiting him.

"Fuck off," Phoenix snarled. "I'm getting a drink." He stalked off towards the bar.

"So," Coast drawled, "do we have a problem here?" He flicked a finger back-and-forth between himself and Javey and me.

"Not if you fuck off." Javey looked as though if he had an ice skate in his hand, he'd use it on Coast's throat.

Honestly, I was getting the same vibe from Coast.

This wasn't the time or place I planned to have this conversation, but it had to happen. It might as well be here and now.

"In case you hadn't figured it out, Javey is interested in me too," I said. "I don't want you, *either* of you, to fuck off."

Coast leaned back and looked at both of us. "So you're proposing a sharing situation? Including him too?" He jerked his head towards Phoenix, who was leaning against the bar.

"That's what I'm hoping for," I agreed.

Javey was still glowering, but keeping it more controlled now, like he was trying to keep up his outward appearance of being a shy guy. He couldn't be shy and stabby at the same time, apparently.

These guys were nothing if not complicated. Did Coast also have layers he was keeping hidden? I suspected he did. Guys who hid behind bravado always did. He might be a scared little boy under it all.

Why did guys have to be so complicated? We weren't like that, were we?

"If that's the only way I can be with Sin, then that's what I'll do, I guess," Javey said reluctantly.

"Sin?" Coast grinned. "That's cute. Appropriate too." He winked at me.

My heart did a flip in my chest and only just stuck the landing.

"You think so?" I asked. "There I was, thinking I was sweet and innocent."

That made his grin widen. "You might be sweet, but not innocent. You're way too hot to be innocent."

"Are you saying I can't be both?" I cocked my head at him. I might have even fluttered my eyelashes.

"Of course you fucking can," Javey said, giving Coast a filthy look. "You can be whatever you want. It doesn't matter what he thinks. Just what you think."

"I feel like you're trying to provoke me," Coast said slowly. "But as it turns out, I agree with you. Sunflower here can be whatever she wants. Whatever that is, I'm here for it."

"For how long?" Javey sat up higher in his chair. "Until you get bored? How long is that usually? A night? A whole week? Maybe even two weeks?"

Coast propped his elbows on the table and leaned towards Javey. His expression was congenial, except for the snap of anger in his eyes.

"You should know me well enough by now to know, I don't like people insinuating things about me. Yeah, in the past, I've had a different puck bunny every night. Sometimes literally. That was before Sinclair. People can change. It's me, I'm people. Let me tell you right now, you will be on my shit list if you do anything to hurt her. And before you say I'll be on yours, I already got that message loud and clear. From you, from Phoenix, from Aidan and from her. It's sunk into my brain." He tapped a finger against his temple.

"So, I won't be fucking off any time soon. If you want to get rid of me, you'll have to be the one to leave. Understood?" The smile he gave Javey was distinctly unpleasant.

"I'm not going anywhere," Javey said simply. "Not as long as Sin wants me around."

Coast leaned back. "I'm glad we understand each other. Have fun having the same conversation with Phoenix, because he's not as nice as I am."

"Are you talking about me?" Phoenix stepped back to the table, just in time to hear Coast's last sentence.

"Of course we are," Coast told him. "Who else are we going to talk about?" He spread his hands to either side.

Phoenix stared at him, like maybe he was out of his mind. "I can think of plenty of other people you can talk about. None more interesting than me, but they do exist. That's a start."

"We could talk about Aidan, and how pissed off he is you didn't tell him about the attack sooner." I told them all about the conversation in the laundry.

All three of them look equally furious.

"If I knew he was going to say anything to you, I would have..." Coast started.

"You would have done what?" Phoenix asked. "Told him to back the fuck off? I'd like to see you try to tell him that. You wouldn't be first string centre for much longer if you did."

"I'm not scared of Aidan Draeger," Coast grumbled.

"Then you're dumber than you look," Phoenix said, half-teasing, at least. "Which is saying something."

Coast flipped him off. "I'm nowhere near as dumb as I look." He realised what he said, and shook his head while Phoenix and I laughed.

Javey rolled his eyes, like he was in complete agreement with the words, if not the intention.

"You don't look dumb at all," I assured Coast. I gave. Javey a quick, sharp look.

I really wanted them to get along with each other. If he was going to continue with the antagonism, this was going to be difficult and painful. Not to mention short and ultimately doomed.

Was I silly for trying to do this? I should choose one of them and make the other two get over it. Which one would I choose anyway? And would the other two actually back off and walk away?

I already knew Javey wouldn't. I suspected Coast and Phoenix wouldn't either. They'd have to learn to tolerate each other, or this could literally end up with them duelling at dawn, or some other ridiculous man thing.

"Not that dumb," Phoenix agreed. "Mostly you're pretty tolerable."

"That's the sweetest thing anyone ever said to me," Coast said sarcastically. "Pretty tolerable. That's almost as good as marginally better than meh."

I laughed. "Who referred to you as marginally better than meh?"

He grinned, completely self-deprecating. "Just me. Who else would dare to call Coast Riggs meh?"

Javey started to raise his hand.

I grabbed it and pulled it to me, so he wouldn't get into any trouble with it.

"I can think of a lot of words to describe you, but meh isn't one of them," Phoenix told him.

"Let me guess." Coast rubbed the stubble on his chin with his thumb and pointer finger. "Smart, talented, sexy, incredible."

"Humble," Phoenix said.

"Eh, humble is overrated," Coast said.

"Not that you'd know," Javey said, glaring directly at him.

"No, I wouldn't. Why don't you tell us all about it?" Coast cocked an eyebrow at him, not backing down for a moment.

"You could watch and learn," Javey retorted.

Phoenix snorted a laugh. "He's got you there. If anyone knows how to be humble and all that shit, it's Javey."

Javey gave him a look, like he couldn't understand why Phoenix would say anything nice about him.

"He's trying," I said. "Maybe we can all do that?"

"Yeah, I guess," Javey mumbled. He was clearly still deciding if it was a backhanded compliment or not.

Phoenix might not see humility as a good thing. Or he was trying to get Javey off guard.

Personally, I didn't think Phoenix was that sneaky. He liked to pretend he was an asshole, but saying nice things when he didn't mean them didn't seem to be his style. He was more likely to dispense insults, even to his friends. To tease and give them shit as much as possible.

"Phoenix can be very trying," Coast agreed.

"Fuck off," Phoenix told him. "I'm awesome and you know it."

He gave me a look which started out like he hoped I'd agree and quickly became heated.

I could almost see him thinking about his cock in my mouth. Yeah, now I was thinking the exact same thing. I'd lost count of the amount of times I've thought about it since. And fucking in front of the window.

At the time, I'd sensed someone was watching, it wasn't until right now. I realised I was right. Javey was.

Should I tell the other guys that? At some point, I was going to have to, but right now this was all too fragile.

They didn't care about being seen while they fucked me, but knowing Javey was following me around, that was something else. Something they may take exception to.

When the time was right, I'd tell them and make them understand. If I was okay with it, they'd have to be okay with it too. Whether they liked it or not.

If they were going to share me, they'd have to learn to compromise. This wasn't going to be easy for any of us, but if Elenna could make it work with someone like Aidan, then I could make it work with these three guys.

Yeah, okay, that was one hell of an assumption, but I was determined to make it reality.

CHAPTER 16

SINCLAIR

"My place is closer," Phoenix declared.

"Mine is closerer," Coast said. He draped an arm around my shoulders and pulled me against his body. He felt like rock covered in warm skin, softened by several beers and a few shots of tequila. Not enough to make him sloppy drunk. Even he couldn't get away with that during the season.

"Is not," Phoenix argued. "Mine is." He frowned. "Maybe it's about the same." He was also clearly buzzed, but not to the point of falling over.

"We should let them go to… Wherever," Javey said. He took my hand, encouraging me to step away from Coast. "We can go to your place or mine."

"We can't go to mine." Coast cocked his head, clearly, finally, remembering what happened. a loud whisper he added, "People died there. It's okay, though, they were bad people."

"Bro, you can't go saying shit like that, people might hear." Phoenix punched him on the arm, narrowly missing punching me as well.

"Ouch, the fuck, dude?" Coast rubbed his arm. "If people hear me, I guess I gotta kill them too." He peered at my face and grinned. "Not you, though, you're pretty." He kissed my mouth.

"It's good to know you have some limits," I said, dryly. I kissed him back quickly, but then said, "Let's get a ride to Phoenix's house."

Phoenix laughed. "Coast has limits? That's hilarious. Next thing you'll be saying he has boundaries too."

"Fuck off." Coast shook his head at him.

"You fuck off," Phoenix retorted. "I don't have to do what you say. I don't gotta do what anyone says."

"We should call them a ride share, " Javey said. "They can find their own way from here."

"Nah, we might get lost," Coast said jokingly.

"With any luck," Javey muttered.

I patted his hand and pulled out my phone to order a car to take us all to Phoenix's apartment.

If we were going to make this work, we might as well start right now. Besides, the two of them had enough to drink, I wouldn't leave them to fend for themselves. It might be just the opportunity the Fiorellis were looking for. Their reflexes would be slower right now, especially if they were drunk enough to pass out.

Javey sighed, but we all knew what was at stake here. If anything happened to either of them, he'd regret letting them go off alone. No matter what he might say, he wasn't a bad person, and didn't hate either of them. Once he realised they weren't a threat to him, and our growing relationship, he'd chill out.

I hoped.

The car pulled up to the curb a couple of minutes later. I opened the door and stuck my head in.

"Rooney?" The driver asked. "Hop on in."

I nodded to the guys to get in, and slipped into the front passenger seat.

Phoenix and Coast tumbled into the back, followed by a very unimpressed looking Javey.

I did my seatbelt and looked back over my shoulder. The three big guys were pressed together tight in the small backseat.

If that didn't help their team bonding, nothing would.

"Get your hand off my dick," Coast growled to Phoenix.

"That's your hand," Phoenix told him.

Coast raised his hand and stared at it. "Oh yeah. It fucking is too." He squinted. "Fingers are weird." He wiggled them. "Just look at them. They're like octopuses, or some shit."

"Your fingers are weird, 'cause they're attached to you," Phoenix told him. "My fingers are normal." He held up his hand to demonstrate.

I caught Javey's eye and smiled while he rolled his. A faint smile tugged at the corners of his mouth. He was almost as amused by their drunken antics as I was. This might be just what we all needed.

I turned back around. How far were we from Phoenix's place?

I frowned. "Is this a shortcut I don't know about?"

"Yeah," the driver said with a grunt. "Much quicker."

I turned to get a good look at him. I didn't recognise him, but I didn't know everyone who lived in Dusk Bay. I did, however, know all the roads.

"This is not the way to where we want to go," I said.

He didn't respond.

I looked back over my shoulder.

Javey's lips were pressed together tight, his gaze intent on the back of the driver's seat. He clearly heard what the driver said. He elbowed Phoenix in the ribs.

"What the hell?" Phoenix turned to stare at him.

"Sober the fuck up," Javey told him. He gestured out the window.

Phoenix stared. "This is not the way home." He looked and sounded very, very sober.

"'Course it is," Coast said. It was his turn to peer out the window. "Where the hell are we?"

He leaned forward, grabbed the driver's seatbelt on either side of him and yanked it up to his throat.

"You might want to reconsider your life choices right now." He, too, sounded sober now.

The driver took one hand off the steering wheel and tried to tug the seatbelt away from his neck. The car swerved, narrowly missing an oncoming truck.

"Pull over to the side of the road and let us out," Coast ordered.

"Bad idea," Phoenix said. He leaned forward and spoke to the driver. "Pull over, and *you* can get out."

"Yeah, that is a better idea," Coast said.

"I have them once in a while," Phoenix said. "Nothing is getting past me tonight."

"I'd offer you a fist bump, but my hands are kinda busy right now." Coast pulled the seatbelt tighter.

"That's okay, I'll take a mental fist bump," Phoenix said.

"We need to get this car stopped," Javey said urgently.

I looked out the front windscreen and realised he was right. The road we were on led to the top of the cliff. Veering off would suck. If the driver knew he was going to die, he might be content to take him with us.

Hard pass.

I grabbed hold of the bottom of the steering wheel with one hand, and, with the other, put the car into neutral. The engine screeched in protest, but gradually began to lose power.

The driver, apparently desperate, tried to wrench the steering wheel back as we approached the top of the cliff.

His eyes protruded from his face, which was getting redder and redder. His laboured breaths were coming out in gasps.

"He's a stubborn fucking asshole," Coast ground out.

"Die, already, motherfucker. I'll settle for you passing out. I'm not that fucking fussy."

I had both hands on the steering wheel now, pulling as hard as I could towards the side of the road that didn't end with a sheer drop down to the ocean. Not to mention a bunch of rocks that wouldn't make a soft landing.

I caught movement beside me. Javey threw himself over the centre console and helped me to wrench the steering wheel hard to the left.

Phoenix uttered a muffled, "Fuck."

The car finally slowed to a little over a walk.

Javey grabbed the handbrake and tugged it up. We came to a stop slanted across the road, the driver finally slumped in his seat. Dead or alive, it didn't matter too much to me right now. We weren't lying dead at the bottom of a cliff, in a tangle of metal.

I shoved open the car door and slid out, sucking mouthfuls of fresh air to combat the nausea swirling through my belly. I didn't usually get carsick, but there was something about potentially dying that didn't agree with my stomach.

It was Phoenix who came to put his arms around me, while Javey and Coast pulled the driver out of the front of the car and laid him down beside the road.

"Is he—" I peered over tentatively.

"Dead?" Coast asked. "No." He looked up at me and gave me a dark smile. "Not yet."

His expression and tone sent shivers all the way through me.

To Javey he asked, "How do you feel about a little extra team bonding?" He gestured down to the driver.

"I'm game," Javey said. He grabbed the driver by his upper arms, while Coast took hold of his ankles. Together, they picked him up, carried him over to the rear of the car and tossed him into the boot.

"I have to admit, I would have loved to throw him off the cliff." Coast closed the back of the car with a thud. "But knowing Aidan, he'll want to have him questioned." He looked regretful.

"Your restraint is admirable," I said without sarcasm. Killing the driver was no more than he deserved. Honestly, he'd probably wish he was dead once Ice Miller got a hold of him. I almost felt sorry for him.

Almost.

"Isn't it though?" Coast grinned, all of his bravado back in full force. "That cliff is incredibly tempting. "He clapped Javey on the back. "Thanks for the lift, buddy."

"Yeah." Javey eyed the cliff like he wasn't sure if they shouldn't throw the driver over after all. That was a step up from wanting to throw Coast and Phoenix over it. It seemed nothing brought people together more than attempted murder.

Was it a man thing, or was it about our mobster lifestyle?

Maybe both.

"Let's get out of here," I said. "I'll drive." I hadn't had

much to drink, not compared to the guys. The last thing we needed was to survive an attack only to die from driving drunk. That would be horrifically ironic. I didn't need that kind of irony in my life.

"I'm sitting in the front," Javey said quickly. He moved over to slide into the passenger seat before either of the guys could argue. Judging by the weary looks on their faces, neither of them could be bothered.

Without another word, Coast and Phoenix slipped into the backseat and closed the doors behind them.

"Where are we taking this asshole," I asked.

"Let me find out." Coast had his phone to his ear.

I couldn't make out the words, but the male voice on the other end sounded angry, and very much like Aidan. Presumably he didn't like receiving phone calls at nearly two o'clock in the morning. At least he couldn't complain about being left out of the loop.

Although it was Aidan, he'd complain if he wanted to.

Coast eventually got off the call and gave me an address. "He's going to meet us there."

"Goodie," I said under my breath. "I can't wait."

I very carefully turned the car around and headed back into the city.

CHAPTER 17

SINCLAIR

As I expected, Aidan looked half asleep and pissed off. But he wasn't alone.

"This just keeps getting better," I muttered to myself, as I parked the car outside what looked like a warehouse.

I knew the area, but not terribly well. It was usually limited to industrial activities. Automotive mechanics, carpet and kitchen sales, things like that.

Of course, that made it the perfect place to bring a semi-alive attacker to be dealt with.

I turned off the engine and slipped out of the car after the guys.

"Caleb, this is quite a surprise," Coast greeted Caleb Brantley like he was an old friend. Then again, he probably was, even though Caleb was at least a decade older.

Caleb grunted in clear annoyance. "This better be important."

Coast grinned, apparently undeterred. "Of course it is. What could be more important than someone trying to kill three of your best players?"

"And the best member of the PR Department," Phoenix said.

I wasn't sure about that, but I managed a smile, albeit at a faint one, for the Demons' owner.

Aidan looked as pleased to see me as I was to see him, but he basically ignored my presence and addressed the guys.

"You managed to not kill your attacker this time?" he asked.

"He was alive the last time we looked," Coast said. He popped open the back of the car and gestured inside.

The driver groaned, a good indication there was life left in him.

For now.

"Perfect," the third man said. Ice Miller stood beside Caleb, looking all too eager to get his hands and torture devices on the driver. He wore his dark hair up in a bun that looked like he got out of bed as hastily as Aidan and Caleb must have.

"Good work, "Caleb said.

That was the first time I ever heard him say anything nice to anyone. Usually, he didn't have much to say at all, but when he did, it was all business. Never praise. He must have a soft spot for Coast. The centre did have a way of getting under people's skin.

"Thanks, Cal," Coast said. "You need a hand to get this asshole out of here?"

Caleb gave him a look, like he didn't appreciate the shortening of his name, or the suggestion he'd get his hands dirty. If his pressed trousers and blue polo shirt, under a wool coat that looked like it cost more than I made in a year, were an indication, he kept them as clean as possible.

Of course he did. He was one of the two older Brantley brothers. Why would he get messy when he had people to do it for him?

"Go ahead," Aidan said. He also stayed back while Phoenix and Coast, with help from Ice, picked up the driver and carried him into the building.

"You can't say we didn't tell you straight away," I told him as the guys disappeared inside.

Aidan's gaze slid to me. "I was wondering how long it would take before you said something like that."

"Because it's true?" I asked. How much would I have to pay Ice to deal with Aidan too? Yeah, I know, Elenna would never forgive me, but maybe I'd be doing her a favour.

Fortunately, for everyone involved, I didn't have that kind of money, just a sarcastic, sweet smile for Aidan.

He rolled his eyes at me.

"I liked it better when we were on the same side," I told him.

"We're still on the same side," he said. "If you weren't on my side, you'd know about it."

Caleb was watching and listening to us, both, his expression unreadable. "Is there a problem?"

The look he gave us both gave away nothing of what he was thinking. He might be intending to get rid of me if I was an annoyance to Aidan, but he might be thinking the exact opposite.

Men like him, they always had an agenda. Siding with Aidan might not be on his. The Demons were winning because of Aidan, but no one was under the illusion they were Caleb's priority.

I knew for a fact, Finley was involved in smuggling when the team played away. I'd helped to make some of those arrangements on several occasions. I also knew Elenna helped Finley and I wasn't going to do anything to jeopardise her. Not if I could help it.

"I don't have a problem," I said. "All I'm doing here is what Aidan requested. If he has a problem with it—"

"No problem," Aidan said quickly. "I had to make myself understood, nothing more. Evidently, I was successful."

It sounded like he single-handedly took credit for Coast calling him to fill him in and ask where to bring the body.

"You made yourself crystal clear," I said coolly. Anything else I might have said was interrupted by the sound of screaming. I cringed. I didn't need to see to imagine what was going on inside.

Javey slipped an arm around me. "He's getting what he deserves," he said softly.

"I know," I said. "It's just..." The driver screamed again, with even more agony this time.

"I don't know about anyone else, but I could use a coffee," Aidan remarked. When Caleb nodded, he gestured for him to step inside in front of us.

Only because the idea of coffee sounded so good did I let Javey guide me inside.

I found myself in a harmless-looking room containing a kitchen, which included a fridge, coffee machine and a wide double sink. To the side of the room, stairs led down.

"Ice's workroom," Javey said.

I looked up at him in surprise. "You've been here before?" I'd heard of the place, we all had, but I'd never been here. Never wanted to.

"Once or twice." He stepped over to the coffee machine and got it started. "Only on the delivery side, never on the receiving end."

"I figured," I said. "People don't tend to survive being down there."

He offered me a faint smile and reached for coffee cups. "That's true. Ice is good at what he does, but he doesn't leave people to go and blab about him.

"It's unfortunate people like him are necessary," Caleb said.

I translated that as, *'If people just fucking did what they were told, I wouldn't need to resort to torture.'* I had a sneaking suspicion Ice would be very disappointed if Caleb stopped letting him work with people like the driver. He might resort to practising on other people, for shits and giggles.

Yeah, it was just as well people didn't always do as they were told. Fuck only knew how discriminating Ice would be. Not to mention, he may be influenced by Aidan. I didn't *think* he'd suggest I should be tortured, but who knows what Aidan might do when he was in one of his moods? Since that was most of the time, it was better to stay the hell out of his way.

"It comes with the territory," I said. "Can I ask why you're here?" Caleb had people to deal with situations like this. Why come in person?

His eyebrows twitched. "The situation in Dusk Bay is escalating. I'm concerned it may end up out of control."

That was a legitimate concern. "What will you do if it does?" I asked.

"I hope to stop it before that happens," he said. "Aside from that, if anything happened to any of you, much less all of you, it wouldn't go unnoticed."

Now we got down to the real matter at hand. If players and staff from the team he owned ended up dead, it would draw attention to him and his activities.

I wouldn't have much sympathy, but that would extend it to Finley and Elenna. They'd be the ones to take the fall for Caleb if the police came sniffing around. He'd make sure of that.

"It would be a PR nightmare," I said, as if I didn't know exactly what he was referring to. "Not to mention potentially jeopardising the team's position in the AIHL."

That made Aidan twitch. He was up to his eyeballs in the same shit as Caleb, but he was passionate about the Demons. The team was his second love after Elenna. If they lost their place in the league, he'd be devastated. That was, if he had the time to be. Elenna's arrest would be his primary focus. Or getting her out of the country before that happened.

"The result would be undesirable all around," Caleb agreed. "Whatever we can do to circumvent it, we'll do it."

"Yes, we will," Aidan agreed. He accepted the coffee Javey handed him and glanced towards the stairs. "Whatever it takes."

His words were punctuated with another scream. Louder, now we were closer.

Javey handed me a coffee. "Do you want to go down and hear what he has to say?"

"So far, it sounds a lot like agony, not confessions," I said softly.

"It will be a confession soon enough," Caleb said. "No one lasts long down there without admitting everything. We already know who he works for. With any luck, he'll be privy to their plans."

"No offence, but it seems like their plans are to kill Coast, even if it means taking other people with him," I said.

The knowledge I could have died, was slowly sinking in. With that came a measure of anger, and a sliver of desire to get revenge. I was usually all about defending myself, and the people I cared about. Being on the offensive was new for me, but right now, maybe that was the best defence.

"Then we need to figure out what method they may try next," Caleb said evenly. "While at the same time, making plans against them."

His piercing blue eyes on Aidan, he asked, "Any word on who is working against us from inside the Demons?"

"We're getting close," Aidan said uncomfortably. "I have someone on the inside with them too. That should get us closer to what we need to know."

"Good," Caleb nodded. "I'm sure Sinclair will be amenable to helping you in any way you need."

"Happy to help," I said lightly. "Trying to kill the guys and me is kinda personal."

"I'll give you a list of names, and you can feel them out," Aidan said. "It's a short list, but when you see it, I'm sure you'll agree they all have grounds to be on there."

The look in his eyes suggested I also did, but wasn't because he knew I'd never do anything to jeopardise the team or Elenna. Him not liking me didn't matter right now. What mattered was figuring out who was betraying us and dealing with them.

"I'll help," Javey said. "People never suspect the quiet, shy guy." He glanced down at the floor, embracing that persona again.

Now I'd seen more of the real him, it was almost funny. He played the role so convincingly. He was right, no one would suspect he was up to anything.

"Between us, we'll figure this out," I said.

Footsteps sounded, coming up the stairs. A moment later, Coast appeared. His expression was one of grim satisfaction.

"We didn't get much out of him other than he was hired by Sawyer Mancini. He was supposed to take us to his house. The downside is, he's dead. Anything else he might have known is going with him to his grave."

"He was never leaving here alive anyway," Aidan said.

Coast's gaze slid to him. "Right. Aidan, a word." He jerked his head back towards the stairs.

CHAPTER 18
COAST

I avoided looking in the direction of the dead driver.

Ice and Phoenix had removed him from the chains and lowered his body to the ground. I already knew his face was a mess of incisions, and his throat was swollen from where I wrapped the seatbelt around it.

Was I squeamish? Fuck no, I just hated waste. The asshole didn't need to die. All he had to do was stay the fuck away from us. He made his choice when he worked for Sawyer. If you work for dubious people like that, they'll make you do fucked up things.

Yeah, okay, the people I worked for were little better than Sawyer Mancini, but I was alive, and the driver wasn't. That counted for something.

I moved away from the stairs and turned to watch the expression on Aidan's face as he took a good look at the body.

He was unmoved. He'd probably seen and

dispensed more death than I ever had. He hid behind a mask of respectability, like we all did. More so.

There was something less suspicious about being the head coach of an ice hockey team, than there was being a centre. A certain amount of testosterone fuelled stupidity was expected of a guy like me.

"Anyone you know?" I crossed my arms over my chest and leaned back against the wall. Let him think I was accusing him. I watched him carefully for his response.

In true Aidan fashion, he gave very little reaction. He squinted at the man's face, and shook his head.

"Never saw him before." He looked from the driver to me. "What's this about?"

"I heard the way you were talking to Sinclair," I said. "And the way you look at her. I thought it best to inform you in advance, that if you ever talk to her that way again, I'll rip your fucking face off."

I kept my tone friendly, conversational. My words spoke for themselves. I meant every one of them. I didn't care who he was, who he was connected to, or what might happen to me as a result. Sinclair deserved better than to be spoken to like she was the criminal.

I didn't expect Aidan to look impressed, and he wasn't. "Interesting. I should issue the same warning to you if you flirt with Elenna."

I raised a hand to concede the point. "That only happened before you reaffirmed your commitment to her, and before she was involved with Finley and Orion."

I *might* have done it to get a rise out of Aidan, but I respected Finley and liked Orion as much as anyone could like a guy who doesn't seem to like anyone, including himself.

"Consider yourself warned," he said coldly. "I will put my wife before the team."

"Good for you," Ice said approvingly. "A guy should always put his woman before everything else. I always do." He moved over to the sink and started to wash blood off the knives he'd used on the driver. He definitely seemed to get enjoyment from his work.

Good thing he was on our side. I wouldn't like to get on the bad side of someone like him.

One of Aidan's eyebrows twitched, but he nodded and headed back up the stairs, effectively dismissing me and ending the conversation.

"That was badass," Phoenix said.

"Thank you," Ice and I said at the same time.

All three of us chuckled.

Phoenix rolled his eyes. "Nice to know you both have your egos intact." Apparently he wasn't going to elaborate on whom he was trying to compliment.

"Always," I said lightly. "Hey, Ice, how long have you kept someone alive down here?"

Ice started to dry his knives with a towel covered in pictures of pink kittens.

While he dried, he looked thoughtful.

"I think the record is two weeks and six days," he said finally. "We were going for three weeks, but the guy just gave up. I guess he didn't have the commitment I do."

"Yeah, that doesn't surprise me," I said. "I'm not sure if I have the commitment it takes to be tortured for three weeks either."

"And you call yourself a big bad, hockey player," he said teasingly.

"If that's what it takes to prove myself, call me a big, soft marshmallow, instead," I said.

"That sounds more accurate," Phoenix said. "A big pink marshmallow. "

"You can throw insults at me all you like, but it's still better than being tortured." I gave him a sarcastic smile. I loved bantering with him. He was like a brother to me. Closer than that maybe.

Yeah, I knew he wanted more, but I didn't know what I wanted. Feeling things and acting on them were two different things. Especially when people had expectations of me I was happy to live up to. That was easier than stepping out of my comfort zone.

I was Coast Riggs, I got my dick wet in any pussy I could get it into. I've lost count of exactly how many that was. None of them meant anything. Just a quick fuck and a quicker goodbye. I'm not saying I don't last, I do. I'm just saying I take what I want and then I leave.

What I felt for Sinclair and Phoenix was confusing all of that. Between them, they grabbed a deck of Kink or Drink cards and threw them up in the air, scattering them everywhere. I didn't know where to start to pick them up and put them back in a neat pile.

So I did what I always do. I teased Phoenix and threatened Aidan. And killed people who try to kill me or the people I care about. Not to mention, killing it out on the ice. These were all the things I did best. Things I should stick to because I knew I could nail them.

Sinclair already threw my life for a loop. I'd always thought she was cute, but the more I got to know her the more I realised there was so much more to her than that.

The way she grabbed that steering wheel, and even knew to throw the car into neutral to slow it down… She was hot as hell. Smart as hell too.

She saw right through my bullshit and still liked the guy underneath it. Most women never got that close. If they did, they tended to run in the other direction. Not her. The better she got to know me, the more she wanted to know.

Not to mention, she had the most perfect pussy on the face of the planet. Thinking about it made my cock want to jump right out of my jeans and slide into her panties.

"It might surprise you, but some people like being tortured." Ice opened a drawer and placed the knives away.

"Don't you mean you enjoy torturing people?" Phoenix asked.

"That too," Ice agreed with a grin of pure glee. "But some people genuinely enjoy pain. I've had a couple down here like that. They're absolutely fascinating. I get a kick out of working out exactly what turns them on and what doesn't. It's a fine line for some of them."

"For the record, I'm not one of them," I said. Okay, maybe I was, but not for his intents and purposes. If I was going to be chained up in here, I'd want Sinclair with a paddle in her hand, not Ice with blade in his.

"Me, either." Phoenix raised his hands to either side, as if trying to ward off the very idea.

Ice pouted playfully. "I thought you guys were more fun than that."

"We're lots of fun," I argued. "We just don't want to end up as toys of yours. I think that makes us sensible."

"Definitely makes us sensible," Phoenix said with a grunt. "Anyone who thinks torture is a party out of their fucking mind."

"That's what Ares always says," Ice said. "For some reason, he thinks I'm crazy for enjoying being on my end of it, too. As if he doesn't get a kick out of it as well." He shrugged one shoulder, obviously not too worried.

"Ares is one of Ice's girlfriend's other boyfriends," I said to Phoenix.

He gave me a look like he already knew that. I figured he would, but I wasn't entirely sure. We didn't follow the love lives of the other residents of Dusk Bay for shits and giggles.

"No shit," Phoenix said. "Sometimes I think you think I was born yesterday."

"Of course you weren't, bro," I said. "The day before that, maybe, but not yesterday."

He flipped me off, which, under the circumstances, was totally fair.

"You two are so cute," Ice said. "Are you together? You, Sinclair and Javey?"

I didn't meet Phoenix's glance, even though I knew he was looking at me.

"Not exactly," I said. "We're just good friends."

"Ah." Ice nodded and gave us a knowing look. "Gotcha. That's often where it starts. Where it ends, is up to you. Unless you fuck up, then you may end up here." He pointed towards the chains attached to the ceiling.

"You could look a bit less like you'd savour that," I told him.

He grinned. "I could, but where would the fun be in that? I like what I do and I'm good at it. If it means I get to throw around threats once in a while, that's an added bonus. Although, I usually leave threats to Mannix and Ares. They're better at that than I am. Given they're both crankypants."

I opened my mouth.

Phoenix pointed a finger at my nose. "If you're about to tell me Mannix is also one of Kennedy's boyfriends, don't. I already fucking know."

"I was going to say that Phoenix was a crankypants,"

I said, with a grin. "You had to go and illustrate my point for me."

"You fucking suck," he growled. His gaze dropped to my groin.

"You wish," I told him.

He wouldn't meet my eyes.

"You know, I have a very special form of therapy," Ice said. "It's called, chaining both of you up here until you admit what you feel."

"I feel like I've left Sinclair alone with Javey for long enough," I said. "It's time to get the hell out of here, take her somewhere more private."

"Yeah, what he said," Phoenix grunted. "If we don't get back up there, Javey will run away with her. Then we'll be forced to hunt him down and bring him down here for you to play with."

"Which I suspect you'd do, except it would upset Sinclair," Ice guessed.

I scrubbed my chin with my hand. "Probably. I guess he gets to live a while longer yet."

Honestly, I liked the guy, but for some reason he didn't seem to like me or Phoenix.

That shouldn't be too hard to remedy. I was, after all, me. I could charm just about anyone if I put my mind to it.

A number of times before, I'd even charmed people before killing them. None of them ever saw it coming. Neither would he.

"Just a bit longer," Phoenix agreed. "Lucky for him

he's a Demon, or he might be that much more dispensable."

Being a member of the team wouldn't keep them safe from me if I needed to act against them. Whatever I had to do, I'd do. I wouldn't like it, because I considered the guys my brothers, but I put myself, Sinclair and Phoenix before any of them.

I know, I know. Team unity. There was a tiny sliver of truth to the rumour that some things were more important than hockey.

For fucks sake, don't tell anyone I said that. I have a reputation to uphold.

CHAPTER 19

SINCLAIR

"I don't know about you, but I don't think I'll trust a ride share again any time soon." I shut the car door and rubbed my temples with my fingertips.

"Don't let one of them put you off the rest," Coast said. "It's still better than drinking and driving."

"Since when are you the responsible one?" Phoenix closed the back door of the car with his elbow.

"Since forever." Coast grinned. He took the keys from my hand and dropped them into his pocket. "Tomorrow I'll figure out if the car is stolen. Um, later on this morning. It'll be daylight soon."

I didn't bother to hold back a yawn. "Yeah it's almost four in the morning." No wonder I was tired. I'd been up for almost a day. The guys must be wiped out. I hadn't played a game of hockey only a handful of hours ago.

"Almost my bedtime," Phoenix said with a smile.

"It's way past your bedtime," Coast told him. "If the goaltender coach knew you were up so late, you'd be verbally eviscerated. Or physically eviscerated. He gets the shits if you let anyone score a goal past you because you're tired."

"That's why I have you," Phoenix said. "To stop the puck from getting anywhere near the goal. If you do your job, I can have a snooze in the basket."

"You two are the kind who act drunk when you're tired, aren't you?" Javey observed.

Coast glanced over at him sideways. "In case you hadn't noticed, we're always like this."

"Yeah, I had, now you've mentioned it." Javey looked at me like he was going to suggest we go to his place after all, but then finally shook his head.

It was too late to get back in the car and go anywhere else.

Instead, he placed a hand on the back of my neck. We followed Phoenix through the front door of his building.

"If there's anyone in there trying to kill us, I'm going to be pissed off." Coast covered a yawn with his hand.

"If there's anyone, we'll deal with them," Phoenix said.

It must have been an indication of how tired he was that he didn't suggest Coast or Javey go inside first and look around. He just unlocked the door and flicked the light switch, illuminating the entryway and living room of his apartment.

If anyone was waiting there for us, they didn't immediately jump out.

I followed the others in and locked the door behind me.

"I only have three bedrooms, so some of us will have to share." Phoenix stepped deeper into his apartment, flicking on light switches until it became evident the place was empty apart from us.

"Dibs on sharing with Sinclair," Coast said.

"No way," Javey growled. "I'm not letting her out of my sight."

"Unless you're planning to sleep with your eyes open, then that's not going to happen," Coast said. "Also, if you're in any way insinuating I can't take care of her, then you can piss off."

"Are you planning to stay awake?" Javey retorted.

"Can you guys all stop?" I said wearily. "It's been a long night. I could do without you arguing with each other."

"Me too," Phoenix agreed.

Before anyone could argue further, he grabbed my hand and pulled me towards one of the bedrooms. "If they can't agree, then I get you."

Both Javey and Coast growled behind us, but I let Phoenix drag me along.

Right now, I was too exhausted for any more conversation, or anything else for that matter. If I wasn't lying on a bed in about three seconds, I'd be sleeping on the floor. I wouldn't even care, as long as I got to sleep.

Phoenix pressed me down to the side of the bed, and crouched to pull off my shoes.

It was all I could do to lift one foot and then the other to help him. He dropped them aside, and I flopped back onto the mattress.

I let out a long, tired breath out my nose and closed my eyes. "Are your nights always as crazy as this?"

His laugh sounded as tired as I felt. "I was going to ask you the same thing." He flopped down beside me, his hand touching the back of mine.

"No, my nights are usually exciting," I joked. "Drinks with the girls can get wild sometimes."

I sat up just enough to unhook my bra and slide it out the armholes of my shirt. I tossed it away and slipped off my jeans, so I was lying in my shirt and panties.

"You look fucking hot in my bed." He lifted up the covers and helped me under. He was down to his boxers, his muscular chest bare.

"You look pretty hot yourself," I murmured. With what energy I had left, I kissed his mouth.

Our lips still touching, I fell asleep.

***

I didn't know what time it was, but when I woke, my body was already on fire.

I was vaguely aware of the rub of stubble against the inside of my thighs. A skilled tongue was working on my clit. My hands were curled around fistfuls of sheet, my body rocking in time to the attention that was being lavished on my pussy.

I glanced down to see Phoenix's head between my legs, only his dark hair visible. All of my nerve endings quivered as I came, rolling my hips and grinding against his mouth. I was very horny, or he'd been at it for awhile, as I slept.

Either way, I arched my back and let my orgasm roll over me, hard and fast.

I managed to suck in a couple of mouthfuls of air as he pulled his face away from me, moved up to kneel between my legs and slid his cock into me.

I gasped out with the sudden pleasure of him filling me, waking me further.

"Morning." He leaned down to kiss my mouth. His lips tasted of my release. "I saw you lying there so fucking gorgeous, and I couldn't help myself. I needed to have you. "

"There are worse ways to wake up," I said. His face between my legs was definitely one of the better ones.

He looked relieved. "Thank fuck for that." He thrust into me a couple of times. "Can I tell you something?"

"Of course." His cock sliding in and out of my pussy suggested a certain level of intimacy. If he couldn't tell me what was on his mind now, I didn't know when he could.

His tongue swept over his lips.

"I kind of have a thing for it." When I looked

confused, he added, "Fucking while you're still asleep or waking you like that. It's…"

He seemed nervous, scared I'd judge him. I understood why. Consent was a big deal and fucking someone while they were asleep…

"Would you ever do it to someone who was certain they didn't want to fuck you?" I asked carefully.

"Never," he said strongly. "But I should have spoken to you first."

Yeah, he probably should. If I woke up with his cock in my pussy, I might have freaked out. But now I knew, what did I feel about it?

"I like you a lot," I said slowly. "I consent to you fucking me, on the condition you don't give me anything to put me to sleep so I don't know about it." If he tried to drug me, we were over before we began.

"I promise never to slip anything into your drink," he said. "Or your food or anything. Asleep is one thing. Out cold and unable to wake up and stop it is another. It's more of a kink than it is about power." He thrust a couple more times.

"I consent to you touching my cock at any time, whether I'm awake or asleep." He grinned. "I will absolutely never object to waking up with your mouth around my dick."

That thought was as arousing as hell. I made a mental note to do that at some point. For both of our enjoyment.

I also made a mental note to have the same conversation with Javey and Coast. Just because Phoenix was into it, didn't mean either of them were. That was totally fine. I'd find out what they were into and we could do that instead.

I already knew Coast was into some exhibitionism. I was here for that as well. And Javey, he was aggressive and submissive, depending on the situation.

I wouldn't be bored with the three of them around.

Slightly more awake now, I rolled us over and straddled his hips. My hands on his chest, I rose and fell, lifting myself almost all the way off his cock before lowering myself back down.

"Holy shit, you feel good," he groaned loud enough for the other two guys to hear, if they were still in the apartment.

I assumed they were, and that he was doing it to get their attention. Was it to brag or to entice them to join us? Possibly both.

"Not as good as you do." I rubbed my clit against him with each movement, driving myself back to the edge. My breasts swung until he cupped them with his hands, and palmed my nipples.

"We could argue this point all day," he said, "but you should know right now I'm not conceding, even a little bit. And I can cling onto an argument for hours. I'm good at a lot of things, but letting go when I know I'm right isn't one of them."

I actually giggled in response. "It's cute that you think that will deter me from disagreeing with you. I deal with difficult hockey players all day long, not to mention coaches and staff. I know how to get you guys to do what I tell you. "

"That's both hot and a challenge at the same time." He thrust faster. "You've never had to deal with me professionally before. That's because I know how to stay out of trouble when it counts. But now, I think I'm going to do something to get into trouble. Will you put me over your knee and spank me?"

"Tempting as that is, there's laws against assaulting players to get them to behave," I said, with a grin.

"It's not assault if I consent." His grin matched mine.

"It's not exactly *punishment* if you consent," I said. That depended on the context. "Besides, I don't punish players, I work with them to improve their reputations by encouraging them to do charity work."

"I could volunteer at an animal shelter," he said. "I'm very good at washing pussies."

I laughed and focused on riding him harder. Neither of us had any breath left for words. Everything went into driving each other, flesh slapping on flesh with each stroke.

I closed my eyes and came again, harder than before. My muscles clenching around his cock drew an orgasm out of him too.

I felt him come, spilling his release deep into my body.

We both shouted out loud enough to be heard

through the whole building. Coast and Javey would definitely hear us.

I was vaguely aware of movement behind me. The opening of the door.

I didn't look back over my shoulder until I came back down to Earth. When I did, Coast and Javey, stood in the doorway, with matching erections.

"What took you so long?" I asked teasingly.

They glanced at each other, and stepped inside to join us.

CHAPTER 20

SINCLAIR

"Getting a head start, were you?" Coast drawled. He slipped his boxers off his hips and let them drop to the floor. His cock was thick and hard, his magic cross glistening in the sliver of light that shone between the curtains. His erection bobbed as he stalked toward the bed.

He knelt down on the edge beside us, his eyes raking up and down my body.

"We figured you could use all the beauty sleep you could get." Phoenix leaned back against the pillows and looked at Coast the way the centre was looking at me. Hungry, eager. Wary at the same time. Coast could as easily tell him to fuck off as he could join in with us both.

"I don't need extra sleep to look this hot." Coast kissed my thigh, right above my knee. He slowly worked his way up past my hip and over my belly.

Javey stepped out of his boxer briefs and knelt down on the other side of me. He showed no sign of interest in the other guys at all, barely acknowledging their presence. His eyes were for me and only me.

While Coast kissed and licked my stomach, Javey lowered his mouth straight to my nipple, drawing it between his teeth and sucking.

Phoenix stayed up near my head, stroking my hair and kissing my mouth. He let his tongue slide between my lips, tasting my mouth and grazing over my teeth.

I sucked on his tongue before letting it dance with mine. He still tasted faintly of my release, as well as his own unique flavour. Something warm and spicy that made me want more. My body was singing, as though I hadn't come twice already.

Coast moved further up my body, gaze on me and occasionally on Phoenix. He captured my other nipple and sucked, his head almost touching Javey's. He traced slow circles around my nipples with the tip of his tongue, then continued his slow journey up over my chest to my neck.

Phoenix sat back, making room for Coast to kiss my mouth. Before he did, I saw him glance down at Coast's cock. His eyes were wide, curious, and anxious at the same time.

I slid my tongue into Coast's mouth and reached down to wrap my fingers around his erection.

I worked him up and down a couple of times before pulling my face back and locking my eyes on Coast's.

Moving slowly, I took Phoenix's hand and guided it down towards the centre's cock.

I waited for one of them to object, for Phoenix to pull away, for Coast to move back.

Neither spoke a word or twitched a muscle. Not until Phoenix's hand closed over Coast's erection.

"Holy shit," Phoenix whispered.

I expected Coast to say something sarcastic, but he didn't. Instead, he shivered slightly, as though a jolt of electricity passed through him. Moving as slowly as I had, he moved his hips, thrusting himself into the goalie's hand. At the same time, he closed his eyes. His lips dropped apart.

Javey rolled me onto my side, facing the other guys and parted my thighs with his warm hands. He lay behind me, and positioned his cock before slamming into my pussy, all the way to his balls.

I let out a soft groan, aroused at the sight in front of me, and the feeling of the man behind me, his thick erection pulsing inside my body. These guys were going to be the end of me, right here, right now. I couldn't fucking wait.

Phoenix slowly, carefully, touched Coast's balls, massaging them with his calloused fingers.

Judging by the expression of tentative enjoyment on Coast's face, he'd never been touched like that by another man.

Javey started to move inside me slowly. "Fuck, Sin, you feel incredible."

"That's what I told her," Phoenix said. He was looking from me to Coast and back again.

"You want to taste him?" I asked softly.

Phoenix swallowed audibly and looked directly at Coast. His tongue darted over his lips. "Yeah, I do."

We all held our breath, waiting for the centre to respond. Even Javey stopped moving inside me, his fingers tense on my hip.

"Do it." Coast's whisper was hoarse, like he hardly dared to say it out loud. "Suck my dick."

His hand at the base of Coast's cock, Phoenix lowered his mouth slowly and let his tongue tease the very tip, sliding over the drop of pre-cum which leaked from the slit.

"Holy fuck," Coast breathed. "More. I want to feel the back of your throat."

Phoenix glanced up at him before he obliged, sliding his lips all the way down until he gagged.

"Yeah, just like that." Coast tipped his head back and groaned. "I should have known your mouth was good for something other than bullshitting."

Phoenix snorted and went on sucking and licking.

"That's so hot." I was going to come again just from watching. When Javey started moving again, he drove me even closer.

Coast pressed a hand to my belly before sliding it with teasing, decadent slowness, down to my pussy. He swirled his fingers around my clit, making me quiver.

He glanced down, blue eyes wide again.

I suspected his fingers brushed Javey's cock as he thrust into me. I couldn't tell what he thought, but he didn't pull away.

"It's okay to want to touch," I said, my voice low. "No one here is judging you." I couldn't see Javey's face, but he made no sound of disagreement.

"Yeah." I'd never seen Coast appear as vulnerable as he did right now. Conflicted and cautious, but real. Much more so than his usual cocky, hockey god bravado.

He closed his eyes and thrust into Phoenix's mouth. "I'm going to come."

He slid himself out from between Phoenix's lips, turned his body and pumped himself a couple of times before spilling himself over my belly.

His cum was warm and sticky on my skin. The sight and sensation made me come again, rocking against his hand and squeezing Javey's cock until he also came.

The entire world disappeared, replaced by the pleasure of both my orgasm and being surrounded by three incredible guys. All that existed were fireworks, fingers stroking my clit and cum inside and outside my body. It was a moment of pure, blissful sex. One that could have gone on for the rest of eternity as far as I was concerned. Nothing else in the world mattered right now. Nothing else in the universe.

Too soon, I drifted back down to earth like a leaf on a warm breeze. Like a feather landing on a pink marshmallow. Warm, soft, sticky and content as fuck.

"That was something else," Phoenix said softly.

I looked over to see him exchange a glance with Coast. Something had shifted between them. After this, their relationship would be different. Hopefully for the better.

We couldn't afford to be ripped apart now.

"They're all staff who work here at Demons arena?" Wren whispered.

"Staff, one coach, and a couple of second string players." I glanced around the team's private box, but no one was paying us any attention. Not openly, anyway.

I leaned over to Elenna. "Are you sure none of these people are on the list because they pissed off Aidan at some point?"

She kept her eyes on the ice, where Orion was warming up with the rest of the team. "It's possible, but not likely. I mean, we both know what he's like, but this goes beyond his ego."

I made a sound in the back of my throat.

She turned to look at me. "I know it seems implausible that anything is beyond his ego, but I promise you, it is."

She smiled and turned back toward Orion. It wasn't

often she got the chance to watch a game with us instead of working. She was determined to enjoy it, which I couldn't blame her for. Hockey in general, and Orion, in particular, were good to look at.

Not, in my totally *un*biased opinion, that he was as attractive as Javey, Coast and Phoenix.

They were also warming up.

Phoenix was doing the groin stretches that mesmerised hockey romance lovers all over the world. And me. There was something compelling about a guy who looked like he was humping the ice.

In my mind, I saw the way he looked when he fucked me, and my face warmed. How would it feel to wake up with his cock in my pussy? I was both intrigued and aroused at the idea. That he would want me so much, he wouldn't be able to wait until I woke before fucking me. If that was wrong, I didn't care. It turned me on to think about him parting my legs, sliding into me, while I dreamed. Taking me because he wanted to, needed to. And me doing the same to him.

I cleared my throat. "If you say so, I believe you. I know Aidan's put a lot of work into putting this list together." How did he have time to do his *actual* job? Trying to find a mole was a job in itself.

"I've lost count of the amount of times I've gotten up in the middle of the night to find him at his desk, reading over information and trying to figure out who it is before something happens again. There isn't a single person who works here, or anywhere near the Demons, that hasn't been under consideration. Including me."

My eyes snapped back to her in surprise. "Even you? Why would he think you had anything to do with it?"

I'd consider *him* before I considered *her*. Yeah, okay, I'd consider him before I considered a lot of other people too, but especially her.

"I work here," she said softly. "He'd be negligent if he didn't think there was a possibility I might be involved in something. However slight."

"He'd be crazy if he thought that," Wren said firmly. "He knows you better than that."

"For a while, they thought my brother was working with the Fiorellis," she said. "If they thought that, they'd at least take a moment to assume I was as well."

"Yeah, I guess so," I said, reluctantly. "But he knows you're not, right?" Things might get really ugly if I had to kill Aidan on her behalf. I knew he loved her, but sometimes love isn't enough. Not where loyalty is concerned.

"Definitely," she said. "The point is, no one is above suspicion. Not even Aidan. But the chances are, whoever betrayed us is on that list." She nodded toward the phone in my hand.

"Can we rule out any straight off?" Wren had her face almost pressed against the glass, her breath misting it before it cleared and misted again. She sat back and turned to us.

"I'd like to rule out all of them." I admitted. "But not yet. Javey is feeling out the players and coaches. We're going to keep an eye on the staff."

I was slightly surprised, but relieved at the same time, that Coast's name wasn't on the list. I heard him talking to Aidan down in Ice's work room. Torture chamber. Whatever you wanted to call it.

To begin with, threatening the head coach wasn't necessarily the best career move a player could make. Doing it where Caleb might overhear, could have easily ended up with Coast dangling from those chains. Or worse.

Either way, it was a quick way to end up on Aidan's shit list.

It occurred to me he might have more than one list. One for us and one for— I didn't know who else. He might want to distract me and my guys. The more I thought about it, the more I didn't think that was the case. If that was, Elenna had no idea.

Of all the things I might accuse Aidan of, I didn't think keeping secrets from her was one.

"I'm surprised Bray isn't on that list." Wren grimaced down toward her stepbrother.

Braylon Ellis seemed nice enough to me, if a bit of an asshole at times. He and Wren never got along. From what I gather, they'd both been violently opposed to their parents getting married. Naturally, their parents did it anyway.

Now, Wren and Bray barely spoke to each other,

except to glare within intense dislike. And a fuck ton of repressed sexual tension. Which Wren would deny with something bordering on horror and disgust.

"Should he be?" I picked up my phone and held my finger over the screen, like I was about to tap in his name and add it to the list.

"Only because he's an asshole," she said. "But for all I know, he's up to his helmet in whatever Sawyer Mancini is into."

"I'll tell Javey to keep an eye on him," I said. "You never know, you might be right. I mean, whoever it is, they're going to do their best to stay under the radar."

"That's true. Aidan might not even have them on this list." She frowned.

"We can't worry about that now," I said. "We need to deal with who actually is."

"It might be more than one betraying us," Elenna pointed out. "It might be *everyone* on the list."

"That's a disconcerting thought." I wrinkled my nose. "But you're right, it could be."

I'd watch my back, no matter where I went. The whole arena could be full of people ready to turn on us.

No, if that was the case, they would have succeeded in killing us all when Geneva attacked the place. Right?

Shit, what if they started working here after that? What if Geneva was so convinced she'd succeeded that she left them out of it?

What if…

I was going to drive myself crazy with the speculation.

"I can see it on your face, you're thinking what I'm thinking," Wren said, in a stage whisper. "If we keep thinking it, we're going to jump at every shadow."

"Wren is right," Elena said. "Be careful, but not paranoid. Don't forget, you're here for the game tonight. You're meant to be enjoying yourself."

I grinned and laughed like she told me a joke. "I am enjoying myself. What could be more fun than sitting with my two best friends, getting ready to watch the Demons kick some pucking ass?"

"And look good doing it," Wren said, with a jerk of her head toward the rink, where the guys were getting into position, ready for the starting whistle.

"I can't argue with that." I sat back, looked down and caught Coast's eyes.

He gave me a wink and a cocky grin before he skated over to say something to Javey.

Javey scowled, but looked up at me and nodded. He turned away quickly like he was awkward. Like a guy looking at a crush he knew he'd never get.

My heart skated a breakaway in my chest and scored a goal of its own.

It beat even harder when Phoenix skated over to stand in front of the goal and gave me a salute with his glove.

I gave him a finger wave back.

He nodded and turned his attention to the ice.

If anyone was watching the exchange, they'd think Coast was flirting, and the other two barely knew me. They probably wouldn't guess we all shared each other a couple of mornings ago.

I blushed at the memory. All the pants, moans and groans were tattooed onto my brain. My clit throbbed. If I lingered on it too long, I was going to have very wet panties.

I was so lost in thought, I missed the puck drop, but Coast got possession and drove it in front of him, before the opponent's power forward closed in on him, stick snapping out to knock it away.

Javey was right there, blocking the winger and taking possession from Coast. He sent it back, right before the opposition's leftwinger took it from him.

Coast was about to slam it back when the opposition's power forward crowded Javey, pounding him into the boards.

He hit hard, pushed himself off and gave the other player a filthy look. He looked like he wanted to punch the snot out of him. In keeping with his shy guy persona, he skated backward and away, keeping his eyes on the player and the puck.

Bray, the Demons' enforcer, who had an eye on the puck and another on the player, returned the favour a few moments later, complete with an elbow to the other guy's face. That got him sent off for five minutes in the sin bin. Bray grinned, clearly not regretting a moment of it.

Wren groaned, her forehead pressed against the glass. "I wish I didn't find that so fucking hot. He's a dickhead and he's my stepbrother. What the hell is wrong with me?"

I patted her on the back. "The clit wants what the clit wants."

She looked over at me sideways, and made a face. "That's *not* what this is about. "

I raised my eyebrows.

"Okay, maybe it is what it's about, but I'm not going there," she said.

"No one would judge you if you did," I said.

"I'd judge me," she said. "I'm the worst at judging myself."

"I feel that deeply," I said. Weren't we always worse at judging ourselves than other people were at judging us?

She sighed and turned back to the game.

I exchanged glances with Elenna. She shrugged and so did I.

Life was too short to deny yourself what you really wanted. I knew she felt pretty much the same way. We never knew when life might come to a screeching halt. We might as well live our best lives as much as we could for as long as we could.

If that meant spending time with three hot as fuck hockey players and having lots of orgasms, then I was here for it.

For every precious moment of it.

CHAPTER 22

JAVEY

"So, we're doing this?" I kept an eye on Sinclair, who was playing pool with Elenna and Wren.

Elenna was beating them both, like she always did, while looking as though she didn't understand the game at all. I knew better than to play against her. Or bet against her. She was a better actor than I was. Most of us had cottoned on to her by now, but her friends humoured her. It was worth it to see her take money from opposition players when they came to drink at Hazards after a game. I saw it a handful of times now, including tonight.

The Koalas' power forward stood back a bit. He still looked smug, even as the realisation he'd been taken slowly sank in. He wasn't giving up without a fight. Guys like him never did.

He'd lose this game, the women would suggest double or nothing. He'd accept. None of us would say a thing. If he wanted to be a dumbass and lose his money, that was up to him, he had plenty to spare.

"This could be several things," Coast pointed out. "Care to elaborate on which one you're referring to?" He toasted me with his glass of water before taking a sip. None of us were going to drink to excess tonight. Not after what happened the last time.

I responded by jerking my head to the side, to indicate the second string players at the table beside ours. Two of them were on Aidan's list. The third was Bray, who seemed a decent enough guy to me. The fact he was sitting with the others made me suspicious, but if he wasn't on the list, then I'd focus on his companions.

"No time like the present," Coast said. After a moment he added, "Don't take anything I'm about to say personally."

I snorted as though I'd give a shit about anything he might throw at me. I had much thicker skin than that. Thicker, I suspected, than his.

"Don't make Javey cry," Phoenix teased.

Coast laughed like that was actually funny.

I gave them both a 'fuck you' look. As if they could make me cry. I'd sooner make them bleed.

Coast propped his elbow on the table and rested his cheek on his palm.

"The fact is, I don't think you're good enough to play first string." He said it loud enough to be heard at the table over. "Ice hockey is a growing sport here in Australia. I understand when they signed you, they couldn't do any better. Now they can. They have the money to hire people from the US and Canada. It's only a matter of time before they tear up your contract, and you're done with the Demons."

I didn't suppress the flare of anger at his words, even knowing they were bullshit. They'd be crap even if he meant them. I was better than that. We all knew it.

"You can talk," I snarled. "The reason we've been losing so badly for so long is mostly because of you."

I turned to Phoenix. "And you. You couldn't stop a goal in your sleep before Aidan got his hands on you. And Tom." The goaltender coach was new too.

"Yeah, he was pretty fucking hopeless," Coast agreed. "I did all that work, keeping the biscuit away as best I could. If it got anywhere near him, that bitch went right in the basket."

Phoenix flipped him off. "If that's your idea of the best you could, then you need to try fucking harder. Maybe you should have taken up figure skating instead of ice hockey. You might do better with a tutu, doing a pretty dance, than trying to handle a stick that isn't in your pants." He raised his arms and mimed a dance move in his seat.

We might have done too well at flinging insults at each other. People at the other tables were starting to listen and stare. That was the point, but this was getting too personal.

"I'd look better in a tutu than you would," Coast retorted. "I could out dance you any day of the week."

He pointed a finger gun at Phoenix. "In fact, I'm prepared to put my money where my mouth is. I challenge you to a dance-off, on the ice."

Phoenix leaned forward. "You're on. I'm going to whip your fucking ass."

"You're both a pair of idiots," I told them. "But I'll be there to watch your dance-off. You should be encouraged to find a career once the Demons realise how badly you both suck."

"If that's the case, you should join us," Coast said. "Because you suck way more than I do. "

I caught Phoenix's swallow on hearing Coast say 'suck.' That was a subject we hadn't discussed yet. That and our relationship with Sinclair. Or maybe they had and didn't include me.

I glanced over to see her watching us, a slight furrow of worry in her brow. She must have overheard part of the 'argument' as well.

I turned back to Coast. "You suck so hard, you don't even know how much you suck."

Yeah, I was deliberately stirring up Phoenix, as I was insulting Coast. He really needed to tell the centre what he was feeling. If I had to provoke him to get him to do that, then I would. He could thank me for it later.

"You can fuck all the way off," Coast told me. "Maybe you should go and see if the Koalas need a winger. They're more used to losing than we are."

"That's bullshit," Phoenix said. "No one is more used to losing than we are. It's practically our motto."

"You might be used to it, but I'm not," Coast said. He paused and frowned. "What the fuck am I doing sitting with a pair of losers like you anyway?" He picked up his half empty water, slipped off his stool and stalked away.

"I was just going to say the same thing." I picked up my own glass, gave Phoenix a quick glance and stepped away from the table.

"Fuck you too," Phoenix growled behind me.

His tone shouldn't have sounded hot. Yeah, he might not be the only one with unresolved feelings.

"Hey," Bray called out. "You okay, Jav?" He waved me over.

Pretending to be reluctant, I stepped up to the table and stood in the empty space between two stools.

I shrugged. "I'm okay. I should know better than to listen to those assholes."

"I'm surprised they know one end of the stick from the other." Tank lived up to his nickname, being both wide and tall. He was one hell of a goalie, if not quite in Phoenix's league. Being so big, not a lot got past him. Any bigger and he could stand there, blocking the basket.

In spite of what I said to Phoenix, he had skills Tank was still developing. Our losing streak was because of all of us, not just him, and not just Coast. I was equally to blame, but not more so.

If they actually thought that, they could fuck all the

way off. If I didn't know the argument was bullshit, I could have let it get right under my skin.

"They only know which end of the stick is which, because of where the cum comes out when they play with it," I said.

Tank laughed. He did that like he did everything else, big. Loud.

The defenceman sitting beside him, BJ, gave him a look, but chuckled. "That sounds about right. They both think a lot of themselves. They can't do anything we can't."

If he really thought that, he needed a reality check, but I nodded like I agreed with him.

"There's only one reason you're not on the first string." I glanced towards Elenna, as somehow she influenced Aidan to place Orion in a spot BJ deserved. If BJ actually believed that, he was a bigger idiot than I thought he was.

Elenna would never try to get one of her boyfriends into a position they didn't deserve. Aidan wouldn't listen to her anyway, not in this. And Orion deserved his position more than most. He was a prickly prick, but he was a fucking good hockey player. One of the best I've ever seen.

BJ grunted. "Some people will do anything for pussy."

I couldn't stop my gaze from sliding over to Sinclair, and then down to her pussy. I'd do anything for her and hers. The fact I was here, talking to these guys, was proof of that.

At face value, they seemed harmless enough, but Aidan's list suggested otherwise. If Tank and BJ were up to anything, the last place I wanted to be was here. But if they were working against us and planning something that might get Sinclair hurt, then this was a sacrifice I'd make.

"Right?" Tank said. "I mean, she's cute and all, but if we lose because of her tits, that fucking sucks for all of us."

"To be fair, it's Aidan's decision," Bray said. "Some of us know how to say no." His own gaze lingered on Wren. Weren't they related? Whatever, that was their business.

"Is he one of them?" I asked. "You're right though, the problem is with him, not Elenna. He's the one who keeps Orion, Coast and Phoenix where they are."

"Some might suggest he's the problem." BJ looked at me mildly.

"They might," I said, just as mild. "There's not much we can do about it though. He's head coach, we're not."

"Who would be head coach if he's gone?" Tank scratched the side of his head with his massive hand. He and BJ seemed to be insinuating something.

"They might promote Lex Stone," I said, with a shrug. "Or bring in someone from the outside." Replacing Aidan would be bad for the team and for us personally.

Bray looked like he was here for the conversation, but I could be misreading him. I didn't think so, though. His brow was furrowed, like he didn't like what he heard.

"They'd be hard pressed to find someone as good as Aidan," he said uncomfortably.

Tank shrugged his shoulders. "I don't know about that. Don't get me wrong, he's okay as a coach."

"But not okay, in what way?" Bray didn't seem like he wanted to know the answer.

Tank and BJ exchanged glances.

Yeah, whatever was going on, they were both in it up to their eyeballs. They weren't sure if they could trust us.

"I've heard he's into some shifty things," I volunteered. "The same shifty things Coast and Phoenix are into."

BJ leaned forward eagerly. "You were sitting with them, what did they say?"

"The usual bullshit," I said with half a shrug. "They suggested I help them on some job for Caleb. When I said no, they got all pissed off. You heard the rest. Coast was telling me I should help them because clearly my career as a hockey player is not going to last much longer. Apparently Caleb pays well."

There was that glance between BJ and Tank again. I almost missed it because Bray spoke.

"Caleb does pay well, if you don't mind leaving your morals at the door." He smiled lopsidedly.

"Some people don't have morals to begin with," I remarked. I looked pointedly where Coast was apparently trying to teach Sinclair to play pool against Elenna. He had his arm around her, his groin against her ass. She laughed at something he said.

I resisted the temptation to grab the pool cue and beat him over the head with it. If I was going to be with Sinclair, I was going to have to deal with my jealousy. Still, watching the other guys touch her was difficult.

"You can say that again," Tank said. "Anyway, I'm done here for the night. I'll see you guys tomorrow for practice." He gave us a nod, slipped off his stool and stepped away.

"Me too," BJ followed him a moment later.

Neither player spoke to each other. They slipped out the door a minute or two apart.

I wouldn't bet on anyone beating Elenna, but I *would* bet on those two meeting up outside and planning something.

CHAPTER 23

Coast sat on the couch and propped his feet on the coffee table. He leaned back and laced his fingers behind his head.

"I'm not surprised those two are up to something. They should spend more time worrying about their game and less time getting up to shit."

He hadn't even questioned Javey's assessment of BJ and Tank. He'd listened along with Phoenix and I, and nodded. Evidently, he trusted Javey more than he let on. That was a good sign.

Right?

"I could say the same about a few others." Phoenix gave him a dark look. He seemed salty about what Coast and Javey said about his game, even though it was a ruse to make the other players sympathetic towards Javey.

Fair enough, I supposed. Ruse or not, coming after a

guy's professional skills was always going to cause tension.

Coast grinned. "I thought it was Javey who was going to take that shit personally."

Phoenix flipped him off. "The ends better justify the fucking means."

Javey slipped into the seat beside him. "You never heard it from me, but your skills are fucking awesome. I've never seen a goalie as good as you. The Demons are lucky to have you."

Phoenix shifted uncomfortably. He may even have adjusted the front of his jeans. It wasn't just Coast he reacted to. Interesting.

"Yeah? You think so?" It wasn't just ego that made Phoenix ask, it was the electricity that crackled between them. I hadn't noticed it before, but it was definitely there.

I watched Coast watching them, in the corner of my eye. He sat forward slightly, listening intently. He must have picked up on the same vibe. I wondered what he thought about it, but I couldn't take my eyes off them to look at him properly.

"Yeah," Javey said softly.

He was a better actor than I thought he was. Or much better at denial. He hadn't shown any interest in either of them in the bedroom. Not that I'd seen. Hadn't made eye contact. Of course, I couldn't see his face when he was behind me, fucking me.

When Coast's fingers touched his cock, he might

have reacted. I remembered the way he stopped thrusting and watched Phoenix decide whether or not he was going to suck Coast's cock. I'd assumed it was curiosity, but now I wasn't so sure.

Evidently, the four of us sharing a bed like that affected all of us. It wasn't just a shift in the relationship between Coast and Phoenix. Javey was different too.

Had the three of them been suppressing their feelings for each other for that long? Were they guarding their masculinity or their hearts? Or both?

"We're lucky to have you too," I said to Phoenix. "Not just the team."

The tips of his ears turned pink.

"You're going to give me a big ego to go with my big dick," he said.

"I think I speak for everyone in this room when I say it's too late for that," Coast teased.

"Yes, my dick is already big." Phoenix grinned.

Coast snorted. "I was talking about your ego, dickhead. That thing is about ready to swallow up the room. Along with mine. I'm starting to think Javey might have one too."

The warmth in his tone was a far cry from the argument in Hazards. If they weren't careful, they might end up friends. Or more.

"Not compared to either of yours," Javey said. "Mine is a blip on the radar."

Coast chuckled. "Keep telling yourself that, bro." He paused for a few moments. "You know all that shit I said isn't true, right? You deserve to be on the first string as much as any of us. Maybe more so, because you put up with assholes like me."

"I know," Javey said lightly. His tone was more humble than his words. "Someone has to put up with you. It might as well be me. But—" He drew the word out. "I still want to see that dance-off."

Coast threw back his head and laughed. "Seriously? Because I'd totally do that." He looked over at me and cocked an eyebrow. "What do you think, Sunflower? We could make it a charity thing. Raise some money for sick kids at the hospital. We could get the rest of the team to take part too. "

"I love that idea," I said. "We might even convince Aidan and Finley to participate."

Aidan had played hockey at a professional level in North America before retiring. He could still skate circles around most people. Even some of the players. Watching him try to dance would be hilarious.

"Finley would," Coast said. "Aidan would have to get the stick out of his ass first."

"Finley and Elenna can work on him," I said. "I bet between them, they can convince him. If not, Orion can glare at him. That should do it." The D-man could out glare most people I knew. Including Aidan.

"As exciting as this is, shouldn't we be worrying about Tank and BJ?" Javey asked.

"I don't know about you, but I can worry about more than one thing at a time," Coast said. "I'll tell

Aidan about them, and Sinclair can organise the dance-off." He looked thoughtful.

"You think they assume we'd be distracted by holding a charity event, don't you?" I asked.

I wouldn't be able to have it organised before the end of the season, which was weeks away yet. Things like this took time and the guys needed to concentrate on winning. They'd beaten the Koalas, but they still had several games to go before they could even think about making the finals and taking out the Goodall Cup.

"Exactly," Coast agreed. "If we look like we're focusing on this, they'll think they have the opportunity to make a move. If they try to bring Javey in on whatever they're up to, even better. We'll be ready for them."

Javey shifted uncomfortably at the idea of pretending to work for Sawyer Mancini.

I got that. It didn't work well for Elenna's brother, Ike. It wouldn't end well for Tank and BJ either.

"It would be easier to take them out now," Phoenix said. "It's not like the team needs them."

"The team might need them in the future," I said. "But it's Aidan's call. If he wants them taken care of, they will be."

I could imagine the look on his face if we acted without speaking to him first. He'd be furious. It was well established that he didn't like being undermined. The last thing I needed was for him to have an excuse to get rid of me.

Phoenix looked like he wanted to disagree, but

instead he flopped against the back of the couch. "I guess so."

Coast looked at his watch. "I'll give him a call now and let him know." He pulled his phone out of his pocket and disappeared into another room.

I was going to point out how late it was, but this was Aidan we were talking about. If we called in the morning, he'd say we should have called right now. If he complained about being woken up, that was too fucking bad. He couldn't have it both ways.

I nodded and rubbed a hand over my eyes. "At least organising this dance-off will be fun."

"Do we have to wear tutus?" Phoenix asked, his lip curled.

"Now that you mention it, yes," I said with a smile. "Remember, it's for sick kids. They'll get a kick out of seeing you all dressed up. I might even get some of those unicorn horn headbands for you to wear."

He groaned. "This is getting worse by the minute." But he was trying hard to hold back a smile.

"If you think that's bad, picture Aidan in a tutu and a unicorn horn," Javey said. "Complete with a built-in grumpy face."

I choked back a laugh. "That would totally be worthwhile." Finley would ham it up for everyone, as would Coast, but Aidan, Orion and Phoenix would all have their built-in grumpy faces on.

"I'm starting to regret that whole conversation,"

Javey said. "We should have let them come after Coast and stayed out of it." As if he would have done that.

"Think about the team unity," I told him. "The Demons and us."

Bit by bit, we were becoming more of a family. Slowly, but the incident in the car the other day developed a bond between us that was growing more and more. Nothing brought people together better than narrowly avoiding dying.

"I am thinking about that," he said. "That's the only reason I'd wear a tutu. That, and for kids."

"Notice, he doesn't need to be talked into wearing a unicorn horn," Phoenix observed.

"I'm only human," Javey told him.

Phoenix snorted. "I'm starting to think your life's goal is to wear a unicorn horn, and this is your opportunity to do it."

"I think you're projecting," Javey replied. "Don't worry, none of us will judge you." He patted Phoenix's knee.

"You will totally fucking judge me," Phoenix said.

Javey smiled. "Yeah, we will. But we'll look just as fucking stupid as you will."

"Speak for yourself," Coast said as he re-entered the room. "I've never looked fucking stupid in my life, and I don't intend to start now. I'm going to look so good I'll put all of you to shame and start a new fashion trend." He pretended to fluff the back of his hair.

"Unicorn couture," I said.

"Coasture." He grinned.

"You're such an idiot," Phoenix said. He rolled his eyes and shook his head, but smiled at the same time.

"That's what you like about me," Coast said. He glanced at Phoenix, then at me, his gaze lingering on both of us.

"Keep telling yourself that," Phoenix said, once again, shifting in his seat, and adjusting his jeans.

"Do you think you guys should talk about it?" I asked softly. "It's obvious to everyone in this room that there's something between you two. Sooner or later, you should address it, and…" They could either end it once, and for all or see where it would go.

"I care about you," Coast told me. He glanced from me to Phoenix and back again. "I don't want to—" He stopped short on a deep exhale.

"This doesn't have to be either-slash-or," I said. "The three of you want to share me, I don't see why that means you can't share each other too, if you want to."

Coast scrubbed a hand over his forehead.

"It's okay if you don't," Phoenix said. "What did Aidan say?"

Relieved at the change of subject, Coast sank down onto a chair. "He was pissed off. I caught him in the middle of something." He grinned. "He was a bit breathless."

I grimaced. I didn't want to think about him and Elenna in the middle of anything.

"Apart from that, what did he say?" I asked.

"He agreed that BJ and Tank's behaviour sounded suss as fuck. He wants us to keep an eye on them. No killing. Yet." He shrugged and tossed his phone onto the coffee table.

"Good, I'm comfortable here." Phoenix leaned back and crossed his legs at his knees.

No doubt if Aidan sent us out to kill both players right now, Phoenix would be just as happy to get up and do that. More than anything else right now, he looked frustrated that Coast wouldn't have that conversation with him. Not frustrated enough to bring it up again though. And not, apparently ready to broach the same subject with Javey.

I'd have to give them time and space to decide for themselves when and if they'd discuss it. Hopefully they would, and sooner rather than later. Otherwise, it was going to cause tension between us, and that was something we couldn't afford right now. We needed to be as unified as the Demons were. If we weren't, it could get us all killed.

"I don't know about you, but I'm tired," I said.

Javey was on his feet like a shot, faster than the other two. "I'll tuck you in."

I thought the others might offer to join us, but it seemed the tension was too great right now. For the sake of avoiding any awkwardness, they'd leave Javey and I to fuck by ourselves.

I took his hand and let him lead me out of the room.

CHAPTER 24

Javey left the door open behind us. I wasn't sure if that was an open invitation or a way of taunting the other guys. Maybe both.

If they decided to join us, they were welcome, if they didn't, they'd have to suffer hearing us pant and shout.

Honestly, my clit was throbbing and my panties were so wet I wanted, needed a cock inside me right now. Javey's cock.

He guided me to the bed and lay me down on my back, before lowering himself to his knees and crawling up beside me.

"How are you so fucking gorgeous?" He nibbled on my lower lip before making his way down my cheek, to my neck and throat.

"I could say the same about you." I tugged up the front of his shirt and ran my hands across his abs. His skin was warm and smooth over rock hard muscle. "In fact, I *will* say the same about you."

I could barely get my head around one of these guys being interested in me, much less three. If this was a dream, I didn't want to wake up. Not until I had all the orgasms.

He chuckled and teased my throat with the tip of his tongue. "You always smell so good." He inhaled deeply. "I don't know what it is, but I could get drunk on it."

It was probably nothing more than a combination of soap and shampoo. I rarely bothered with perfume. My mother used to sneeze whenever anyone around her wore it. Ever since then, I've been wary of inflicting it on anyone else. Shame, because I love the shape of perfume bottles.

Almost as much as I loved the shape of his body.

He worked his hands up under my shirt and caressed one lace covered nipple. It became a stiff peak in a matter of moments. My whole body quivered at his touch, begging for more.

He tugged his shirt off over his head and threw it aside. It barely hit the floor when he was helping me with mine. He undid my jeans and dragged them down my hips and off my feet.

He sat back to take a good look at me lying in only my pink lace bra and panties. Both sheer enough to see my pussy and nipples through them.

"Like I said, absolutely fucking gorgeous." He licked his lips like I was a tasty meal he was about to devour.

"You're overdressed," I told him.

He gave me a lopsided smile and shed his jeans and boxers. "Better?" He knelt beside me, his cock erect, pointing at me. His piercing glittered in the light from the lamp beside the bed.

I propped myself up on my elbow. "You're a work of art. If I could paint, I'd paint you just like that. On a nice big canvas I could hang in the living room for everyone to appreciate. Except, then if they looked at you I'd have to poke their eyes out." I grinned.

He chuckled. "I don't think I could sit still long enough to have a portrait painted of me. But if you want to take a photo with your phone…"

"You'd let me do that?" I said in surprise. "I'd never share it with anyone." That should go without saying, but trust was a precious commodity and sometimes relationships didn't work out. I couldn't imagine being the kind of person to post revenge porn on the Internet, but that was the risk in doing something like that.

He brushed hair off the side of my face. "Of course you wouldn't. For one thing, you'd be the one having to explain to the world why a naked photo of me is out there. That sounds like a PR nightmare to me."

I laughed softly. "You're so right. That's exactly why I wouldn't show anyone. It would make my job more difficult." That was another good reason not to do it.

I grabbed my phone off the table beside the bed, tapped on the screen and held it up in front of me. The image of him naked on my screen made my heart leap and my clit pump like crazy.

"Are you sure? I don't mind if you change your mind."

He held out a hand. "Go ahead. I trust you. Unless you want me to pose."

He pressed a hand to the back of his head and puffed out his chest. He raised his chin and looked at me with a 'fuck me' expression on his face.

Holy shit.

I took the picture, but then said, "Relax. Just be yourself." What would Coast or Phoenix do if I made a suggestion like that?

Coast would probably do something silly like stick his tongue out.

Phoenix was more likely to scowl.

I wouldn't mind capturing either of those in a photograph. Maybe both in the same photo.

Javey relaxed and even gave a hint of a smile.

"You should be a model." I took another couple of photos, then put the phone aside.

"I wouldn't want the kind of recognition that comes with that," he said. "It's difficult enough being a professional hockey player. You'd know better than anyone what kind of fan mail we get."

"Yeah I do." I put my arms around his neck and drew him down with me. "Used panties, marriage proposals, teddy bears." Lots and lots of teddy bears. It was a hockey tradition. One that kept the kids hospital in lots of soft toys.

"The only used panties I'm interested in are yours." He hooked his fingers in the waistband of mine and pulled them off. He raised them to his nose and sniffed while smiling at me.

"Now this is something that should be illegal. The smell of your pussy is addictive." He dropped them down on top of his jeans, like he intended to keep them. He confirmed that suspicion by saying, "I'll wear those under my uniform from now on. I mean, in my pocket."

I swallowed down a laugh. "I'd never judge you for wearing pink, lacy underwear."

He shook his head and rolled me over so he could unhook my bra and slide it off. He held it up in front of himself. "I don't think it's my size." He tossed it to the side.

I giggled. "My breasts might be slightly larger than yours."

He placed his hands on both of mine and cocked his head. "They're the perfect size. A handful and then some." He rubbed his palms up and down, and around my nipples, making them both as erect as his cock. "I love your nipples. They're so perfect and responsive." He leaned down to kiss one, then the other.

"I love your breasts." He kissed all around them both, from the top to the underside. "I love your belly." He kissed his way down my stomach to the curls of hair at the base.

"I love your pussy." He opened my legs and pressed a kiss right to my clit, then one to either side of my thighs.

"I love the way your tongue feels on my pussy," I said.

"Like this?" He demonstrated by licking all around my clit and folds.

I shivered deliciously at the sensations his touch sent all the way through my entire body. "Exactly like that. More of that, please."

He looked up at me, locked his eyes on mine and said, "I love you," before lowering his head back down and devouring my pussy like it was his last meal.

Had I heard right? The blood pumping in my ears was loud, but I could have sworn he said he loved me.

I didn't know how to answer that and right now, I wasn't capable of words. Just moans and groans and the rolling of my hips against his mouth. Gasps and pants, and finally shouting out his name when I came.

I shattered right down to my core. I could have sworn I left my body for a minute or two. All I knew was the way his mouth felt on me and a combination of fireworks, sparks and blood hotter than lava.

His face was shining when he lifted it away from me and kissed his way back up my body. He rolled me over and pulled me up to my hands and knees. Gripping my hips, he guided me onto his cock.

I groaned as he filled me all the way to the hilt

before keeping still for a handful of minutes. The only movement he made was to slide one hand from my hip to my breast. He palmed my nipple and started to move, thrusting into me oh so slowly.

"Javey," I whispered. I could never get enough of the way he felt when he touched me, inside and out.

"Sin," he whispered back. "I've decided that's ironic, because you might actually be an angel."

"You're the first person who thought so," I told him. I'd been called a lot of things before, but never an angel. I didn't feel very angelic. That might be a better description of Elenna than me.

"I doubt that." He thrust a little faster. "They just didn't tell you, that's all." He breathed heavily through his nose. "You feel so fucking amazing. The way your muscles hold my cock. It's pure heaven."

"Heaven is the way you fill me," I said.

I rested my weight on my knees and one hand as I rubbed my fingers over my clit in rhythm to his thrusts. Slowly at first, then more quickly the closer I got, but always taking my time the way he was taking his. Enjoying every moment and trying to make it last.

"I'm going to come again," I said after what was still not long enough. I could have done this for hours. Apparently my body had other ideas. That was just what he did to me. Him and the other guys, they all drove me wild.

"I want you to come inside me," I said. I loved the

idea of his cock being deep inside me when he orgasmed, knowing it was the friction of our bodies and the tight heat of my pussy that made him come.

He groaned. "Fucking yes please."

"Javey," I said when I was right on the edge. "I love you too."

Maybe it was saying those words, and maybe it wasn't, but I pitched right over the edge, coming harder than before, my fingers frantic on my clit, his cock pounding just as frantically into me. My muscles clenched around him, drawing out his orgasm as well.

His fingers tightened around my hip and pressed and he roared as he came, spilling himself into my body.

"Fuck… Fuck… Yeah… That's… Yeah." He groaned. "So fucking good."

We both sagged down at the same time. I just managed to stay on my hands and knees, keeping his cock inside me until we both lowered down to the mattress, him spooning me.

"I love falling asleep inside you," he said softly. "It's the only way I want to sleep from now on."

"I love feeling you there," I said back. There was something wonderful about being connected like that for hours. Something even more intimate than sex. More satisfying than orgasms. It was a closeness I couldn't get any other way.

"Perfect, because he's happy right where he is."

Javey nestled into me, one leg over mine, his arm draped over my waist.

Right before I drifted off to sleep, I heard Javey say, "I love you."

"I love you," I murmured back before sleep claimed me.

CHAPTER 25

"You're organising *what?*" Wren laughed silently, her hand pressed to her chest. Tears poured down her cheeks.

"I know, I know," I said. "A dance-off is silly, but it'll be a lot of fun. We'll raise a ton of money for charity and get a good laugh in the process."

Elenna eyed me doubtfully. "You really think I can convince Aidan and Orion to dress in a tutu and unicorn horn?"

"I'd like to think you can, but we can dial it back for their male egos," I said. "Team jerseys and track pants should be perfect. The guys who want to go crazy with their outfits can." At the end of the day, it didn't matter what they wore as much as whether they participated. People would pay to see them, regardless. Especially if it was for a good cause.

Wren wiped the tears off her cheeks. "Where's the

fun in not having them all dressed up in tutus? I'd love to see Tiger and Bray dressed up like that. I can just imagine the expression on their faces right now." She started laughing again.

"That's exactly why I don't think I can twist Aidan or Orion's arms to wear that," Elenna said regretfully. "Neither of them would appreciate if they weren't taken seriously afterward." She gave me an apologetic look.

"That's exactly why they should," Wren said. "Life is too short to be taken too seriously."

I lowered my voice so no one else in the café could hear. "Coast thinks it will lure Sawyer Mancini into acting against us, thinking we're distracted with this."

Wren stared at me for a moment, then started laughing even harder. "I'm sorry," she said between breaths. "I'm just picturing our guys, dressed in tutus and unicorn headbands, chasing Sawyer's minions down the street."

Elenna put her hand over her lips to suppress a laugh. "I have to admit, that would be funny. I might have to put that in a book."

Wren tipped her head back. Her whole body shook. "I'd read the hell out of that. Please write it."

"I think I might, but I'll have to change the names to protect the… Is innocent the right word?" Elenna smiled.

"Hardly," I snorted. "But we get you. Can you make the tutus, pink, purple and blue? Maybe one or two yellow."

"Absolutely," Elenna agreed. "Rainbow pastel, with matching horns. One or two could wear some angel wings as well."

Of course the mention of the word angel made my brain go in a completely different direction.

"Javey said he loves me," I blurted out.

Wren wiped her cheeks with the back of her hand and smiled. "That's terrific. Isn't it?" She cocked her head and frowned.

"It is," I agreed. "I… I said it back." Heat rose up my face.

"Awww, I'm happy for you." Wren leaned over and gave me a hug, almost knocking her coffee off the table. She pulled back and grabbed the handle of her mug at the last second.

"Me too." Elenna put a hand on her own mug and leaned over to give me a squeeze. "What about Coast and Phoenix?"

"I care about both of them too," I said. "The guys are starting to get along with each other better and they all seem to like me. I'm hoping we can survive long enough to make it work."

Elenna sat back in her own chair. "That's the tricky part, isn't it? I mean, relationships are difficult enough without having to worry about attacks from all angles. Are you doing okay, after the thing with the car?"

"Yeah, mostly," I said. "I'm nervous to let anyone else drive me, if I don't already know exactly who they are. I may never take another taxi or rideshare again.

For all I know, they could all work for the Fiorellis or Mancinis."

"It wouldn't surprise me," Wren said. "Given the way the family is dropping like proverbial flies, their employees are probably looking for other ways to make money."

I snorted a laugh. "That wasn't what I meant, but you have a point. Having your bosses dying can't be good for business."

"Excuse me if I don't have much sympathy for them," Wren said. "They should have gone into a different line of work to start with. Something more honest than hired muscle. Or hired gun, for that matter."

"To be fair, that's a side hustle for most of them," Elenna pointed out. "They usually have normal day jobs. Or night jobs, in the case of hockey players." Aidan must have told her about Coast's phone call.

"Did he say what he's doing about Tank and BJ?" I asked softly.

Elenna glanced around surreptitiously. "Nothing more than 'we're keeping an eye on them.' Finley said he thought they were as suspicious as fuck the moment he met them. As you can imagine, Orion thought he was full of bullshit. Finley has been as friendly to them as he has to any of the other players."

"It's his job to be friendly," I said. "The same as it is mine and yours."

"Yeah, but Orion thinks if Finley suspected them, he

would have said something sooner. Which is true. Finley has never kept secrets from Aidan." She ran the tip of her finger up and down the handle of her mug.

"It sounds like they give each other shit the way Coast and Phoenix do," I said. "And Javey too, to some extent. It must be a guy thing."

Elenna smiled. "Very much so. The truth is, Finley and Orion adore each other. As much as they adore me. They may not show it in public, but it's there. In private, they're different."

"It didn't take much for them to admit that about themselves, did it?" I asked carefully. "I mean, they didn't fight it."

"They did a little bit at first," she said. "But I think they were relieved to explore how they felt with me and with each other. The attack on the arena made us all realise how short life is and that we should grab it by the balls and enjoy the hell out of it. Sometimes literally."

"I love that for all of you," I said. "I'd prefer we not have another full on attack like that just so the guys can feel free to be who they want to be."

If it didn't take an attack on Coast's apartment, and the driver trying to abduct us, then I didn't know what it *would* take. Maybe it was just a matter of time and maybe it would never happen at all.

Either way, I'd be there for them whatever they wanted to do.

"I'd prefer not to have another full on attack no

matter what," Elenna said. She took her hand off her coffee mug and started to wring both of them together.

"You're still having nightmares?" I asked as gently as I could.

She glanced down at her hands, pulled them apart and rested them on the table. "Not as much as I was. But sometimes I dream about standing there in front of Geneva and all of those armed people. All of those guns aimed at me and the team. It's always so vivid that when I wake up I'm surprised I'm not there."

I pushed my cup to a safe distance and leaned over to hug her. "That must have been terrifying." It could easily have ended with her death and that of a whole bunch of others. Thanks to Coast, Aidan and the other guys, it hadn't come to that.

Of course not, Aidan wouldn't let anyone kill Elenna. Not unless he was dead first.

"It wasn't the highlight of my life." She squeezed me back, her head resting on my shoulder briefly. "But almost being driven off a cliff would have been a thousand times worse."

"I'm not sure how useful it is to compare trauma," I said frankly. "On a scale of one to absolute bullshit, they both suck." I didn't think I could have stepped through the doorway and faced Geneva the way Elenna did. All I did was grab the steering wheel and put the car into neutral. It was pure survival instinct, not bravery. Elenna should be given a medal. Not that she'd accept one. She preferred to keep a low profile.

"I admire both of you," Wren declared. "You've both been through horrible things and you're both still standing, smiling and planning to put big, manly hockey players into tutus. Both of you have bigger balls than any guy I ever met." She nodded to punctuate her statement.

"Even bigger than Bray's?" I teased, to cover the fact I was blushing like crazy.

She gaped at me for a moment. "What makes you think I know anything about his ball size?"

I grinned. "Just a hunch. Are you going to answer the question?"

"Not a chance," she said lightly. "I plead ignorance on the matter. Also, I don't want to think about my stepbrother's balls."

"Sure." I exchanged glances with Elenna.

Wren swatted me on the arm. "I'm serious. Bray is a massive asshole and I have no intention of going there, no matter how hot he is or how big his balls might, or might not, be."

Elenna leaned over and put a hand on Wren's. "Whatever you do, or do not do, we support you. We would never judge your choices."

"No, we wouldn't," I agreed. "We love you and want you to be happy and have lots of orgasms. Whether they're given to you by Tiger, your stepbrother or whoever."

Wren closed her eyes and exhaled. "I know you wouldn't. I love you both too. Maybe I should fix him up with one of you, to put him out of temptation's path."

"Three is enough for me," Elenna said.

"Me too," I said. "But honestly, if you're that tempted, maybe he's not so bad after all."

Wren rubbed the heel of her hand against her forehead. "He really is that bad. To me he is. He basically hated me on sight and he's treated me like shit ever since."

"I'm sure you give it back just as hard," I said.

She smiled. "Of course I do. And then some. He deserves every bit of it."

"I almost feel sorry for him," I said. "He clearly doesn't know what he's missing. Or does he?"

Wren scooped up a napkin from the table and threw it in my direction. It travelled a few centimetres before fluttering back down to the table top. "That was very unsatisfying," she complained.

"Maybe we should try paintball or laser tag next time," I suggested.

"That would work," she said, perking up. "I could cover you in orange paint."

"I thought you loved me." I grimaced. I couldn't stand the colour orange. Or the fruit, for that matter. There was something about it that made my skin crawl. Yeah, I know that's weird. It's just a colour, but I stand by my dislike for it.

Wren grinned. "I do love you, but if you tease me about Bray any more, then you deserve to be covered from head to toe in as much orange paint as possible. Right, Elenna?"

She raised her hand to either side. "I'm staying right out of this. The last time we played paintball, it took a week to get all of the paint out of my ears." She mimed scraping it out.

"I'm sure it wasn't that bad," Wren said.

Elenna arched a perfectly shaped eyebrow at her. "I should get to work. Finley wants me there for the morning skate, to help keep an eye on Tank and BJ."

"I should get to work too," I said. "There's a couple of staff in the office I need to watch."

I hoped like hell I wouldn't see anything suspicious from either of them, but there was little reason to expect they were innocent. The Fiorellis were getting desperate. If I was them, I'd infiltrate us as deep as I could.

CHAPTER 26

SINCLAIR

An hour into my work day and I felt as though I could have put 'stalker' on my resume.

When Charlotte went to make herself a cup of coffee, I had a quick look over her desk.

Like the rest of us, she knew to turn off her computer screen when she stepped away. Anyone would think we didn't work for the same team.

Apart from a photo of what looked like a new kitten, I saw nothing suspicious on her desk. The kitten was only suspicious because I could have sworn she was allergic to cats. Or was that Divina? Either way, without opening her computer and taking a look, I couldn't discern anything.

I barely managed to step away before she returned and found me looking suspicious as fuck.

I went back to my desk and back to work until Kylie stepped out from behind hers.

Under the guise of trying to find a pen—they did walk off on an almost hourly basis around here—I rose and went over to her desk for a good look there.

Again, her computer was turned off, but her workspace was strange because there was nothing personal there. No photos of partners, children or pets. No posters to remind her that Friday would come eventually. Not even a game roster. How long had she been here? At least a couple of months. Long enough to make some kind of mark on the space.

Granted, not everyone wanted to, but her space was strangely bare.

"Looking for something?" she said behind me.

Apparently I couldn't put 'good stalker' on my resume. I jumped and turned around, trying not to look as guilty as fuck.

"I was looking for a pen," I said. "The damn things seem to sprout legs and run off." I choked back a laugh that didn't sound genuine even to my ears.

She didn't look convinced, but she smiled. "I've noticed that. No matter where you work, there's never enough pens. Which is weird, because we do most of our work on computers."

I shrugged. "There's always some kind of paperwork to be done. Things that need to be signed by hand. Amendments to the roster that need to be made, but we have to scribble on it to save having to print it all out again."

I was babbling. A sure sign of nerves.

She looked at me funny. "Yeah, I guess so." She gestured towards her desk. "Help yourself."

She had a whole cup full of them, but the cup said nothing on the side of it. It was a plain white coffee cup that looked like it was never used.

Either she was the tidiest person in the world, or she really hated having personal things around her. At least the pens had the Demons logo on the side. Otherwise, I might have thought she was a serial killer.

Honestly, I wouldn't rule that out. She worked here, after all.

"Thanks." I smiled a little too broadly and grabbed up a pen.

"I'd say any time, but chances are they will have run away by this afternoon," she said with a smile.

The laugh I gave in response was higher than normal. I hoped like hell she didn't notice. She might think *I'm* a serial killer.

I hurried back to my desk and slipped back into my chair.

I wouldn't win any awards for my espionage skills. So far this morning, I'd learned nothing of any significance. Maybe I wasn't going to. I could very well be barking up the wrong tree here. Just because Aidan thought they were suspect, didn't mean he was right. Tank and BJ might be the only ones. Or they could be totally innocent too.

If I kept thinking about this too hard, I was going to

start to suspect myself. I was pretty sure I had no reason to. I'd always been loyal to the Brantleys.

I'd never tell, but I'd had a crush on Joshua Brantley at one point. Why wouldn't I? He was rich, smart and hot.

He was also as controlling as fuck, like his older brothers. Hot stopped being quite so hot when I couldn't do anything or go anywhere without the permission of a guy.

No thanks.

I turned on my computer and tried to focus on work, with half an eye for the goings-on around me.

People talked in low voices, moved around to get coffee or go to the toilet. Just the usual everyday sounds and movements in the PR department. Nothing out of place, but everything put me on edge. Every whispered word, every person who walked past.

I kept expecting someone to pull out a gun and started shooting, or for the whole place to explode.

Absolutely nothing happened. I booked some appearances for the players, making sure to include the children's hospital, and the junior Dusk Bay hockey team. The players were role models to kids like that and everyone got a lot out of those appearances.

Honestly, I wasn't sure who enjoyed them more, the players or the kids. Even the big, bad grumpy ones like Phoenix and Tiger seemed to like hanging out with kids who adored them. And the kids— They walked away sure they wanted to be professional hockey players someday. Most of them wouldn't make it, but one or two might and that made it worthwhile.

I was just looking into ice dancing when people started to step away from their desks and go to eat lunch.

One of the rules our office manager made was that no one should eat at their desk. It was a habit a lot of us had, but she was right. We needed to step away and take a break. It was good for us and gave us a chance to get to know each other better.

With that in mind, I grabbed my lunch out of my bag, closed my computer and followed Charlotte and Kylie without trying to look like I was following them.

After all, there were only so many places in the arena to eat lunch.

I was hoping they'd choose to eat outside in the winter sun, but instead they headed to the cafeteria.

They both ordered coffee and sat down separately. Charlotte with a group of other women and Kylie by herself. She sat with her back to a wall, facing the room. I couldn't blame her, that was always my preferred choice of seating. Trust was a precious commodity I didn't have much of, even before all of this started. When you grew up surrounded by criminals and dubious people, you tended to assume everyone was one.

Taking that as a cue, I slid into the chair opposite Kylie. "Can I sit here?" I placed my sandwich down on the table and started to peel back the cling wrap.

"It's a free country," she said.

I suddenly felt like I was back in high school. "That's what they want you to think," I said with a laugh. "Then you reach adulthood and start paying taxes, buying food and paying rent. Then you realise, maybe it's not so free after all."

"Right." She gave me the same funny look she had when I asked for a pen. "I just meant you could sit there if you want to."

"Oh, I know, I was just saying…" Shit, this just got really awkward.

I picked up half of my sandwich, cut diagonally of course, because I'm not a serial killer, and bit into one of the pointy ends.

I managed to swallow without incident. "So, are you enjoying working here? You've only been here for a few months, right?" I hoped that was the case. I'd look pretty stupid if she'd worked at the arena for years and I hadn't noticed her.

Of course, I didn't know everyone who worked here, but the PR department wasn't so big that anyone could fly under the radar for that long. We tended to know each other and each other's business pretty well.

"It's fine." She sipped her coffee and bit into a wholemeal wrap that looked full of vegetables. She was giving me absolutely nothing.

"Great," I said with enthusiasm I really didn't feel. If it wasn't for that list, I'd pick up my lunch and go and eat somewhere else. But we did have that list and I could have died the other night because of someone on it. Or someone not on it…

Either way, I had to do what I had to do to figure out if she was some kind of threat.

She set down her wrap and picked up her coffee. "What do you really want, Sinclair?" she asked bluntly. "You've been behaving squirrelly all day. I'm sure I'm not the only one who's noticed."

She didn't sip the coffee in her hand. Her brown eyes were focused on me. Full of suspicion and unease.

Her gaze probably mirrored my own. Between the attack on the arena and Aidan's list, we were doing a really good job of being suspicious of each other. Maybe there was no one here working for the Fiorellis, they just wanted us to think that was so we'd be divided and drive each other crazy.

If that was their plan, it was working way too well. I might be jumping at shadows where there weren't any. Honestly, that was preferable to having a traitor in our midst, but how would we know? Once a seed of suspicion was planted, it was difficult to kill off.

"I'm just trying to be friendly," I argued. "Is there a law against that?"

"That depends on why," she said. "Or what you're planning."

I sat back in my chair and looked at her in surprise. "I'm not planning anything. I'm just getting my work done and eating my lunch." I leaned forward again. "What makes you think I'm planning anything?"

She leaned forward too. "It's just a vibe I get. Like something is coming. I don't know what, but something. If you're trying to question my loyalty, don't. I have no agenda against anyone here."

I narrowed my eyes at her. "That's what someone would say if they do have an agenda." It's exactly what I'd say. Anything to put people off the proverbial scent.

Then again, the majority of people who were up to something weren't going to come out and admit it, were they? I mean, some people would, but not most.

"That's true, but I don't," she said. She glanced down at the table.

"But?" I prompted. There was clearly something else going on here.

"I know who does." She looked back up. "I don't expect you to believe me."

I frowned. "What are you talking about? You know of someone working against the Brantleys?"

"I don't know for certain, but I saw them talking to Geneva Mancini right before the attack on the arena. I didn't know who they were at the time, I'd only been here for three or four days. I didn't understand the significance until much later. So much later I didn't know who to talk to about it."

I wasn't sure if I should believe her, but she seemed sincere. If nothing else, I could hear her out.

"I see how that could happen," I said slowly. "It's difficult to know who to trust sometimes. But you can trust me."

"Can I?" she asked. "You haven't heard what I have to say yet."

"No, but you can trust me to listen and I can take whatever you have to say to someone who knows what to do." Whether that was Aidan, Elenna, Coast or one of the other guys, I wasn't sure. That depended on what she told me.

She bit her lip. "It was Phoenix DiMarco. They looked… Cosy."

Elenna winced. "You know I have to tell Aidan. Or you do."

"I know, I know," I said. "I just… Of all the people I thought she might say, Phoenix wasn't even on my list. He and Coast are tight. Friends," I added quickly.

"I can't believe he'd work with people who'd go after Coast. Not to mention that he was in that car right along with us." I leaned against the wall of the equipment manager's office and rubbed my forehead with my fingertips.

Finley had taken one look at the expression on my face and left Elenna and I alone to talk. It was probably just as well. If he heard, he'd be on the phone to Aidan already. Or with his head out the door, shouting for the head coach.

Neither of which I'd blame him for, but I needed to reason this out with someone else before it went that far. Especially given that Aidan or Finley might shoot Phoenix first and ask questions later.

Okay, neither of them were that rash, but I wouldn't rule out them taking him to Ice's workroom to torture the truth out of him. I wasn't ready to inflict that on a guy I cared about.

"Maybe he isn't," Elenna said. "Kylie might have pulled the name out of thin air. You know what people are like when they're under pressure. She could as easily have said Orion or Finley. Or Tiger, or me. Or anyone."

"I know," I said again. "She seemed genuinely sincere. And reluctant to tell me anything."

I rubbed my forehead harder. "Or she's a really good actor. She might have said that to put me off the scent. For all we know, she's plotting some shit as we speak."

Elenna leaned her hip against the desk. "I know you don't want to consider the possibility, but is there any chance he *was* working with them then? I mean, he might have been loyal to Geneva until she died. When he realised she wasn't going to win, he turned on her and helped take her down. If she was working against Nicholas and Celine, there's good reason for Phoenix to want to go after them and vice versa. There may be no one left who knows he was loyal to her."

I grimaced. "I guess it's possible. But wouldn't Sawyer have known?" I hated the fact that what she said made any kind of sense. The last thing in the world

I wanted to believe was that he was working against us, even if that was in the past tense.

"It's possible he didn't," she said slowly. "It's also possible he didn't intend for the driver to kill you. He said he was taking you somewhere, didn't he? Maybe they didn't want to kill Phoenix, they wanted to make it look like he was still on our side. Then when you got to wherever you were going…"

I frowned. "He seemed just as angry as Coast about getting into a car that was hijacked."

"Or their plans went wrong." Elenna stepped closer to me and put a hand on my arm. "I know you don't want to think any of that is possible. I don't want to either. But we have to consider the possibility it's true. And if it is, we have to deal with it. And we will. Together. You know, no matter what happens, I've got your back."

"I know, I've got yours too," I said weakly.

I shook my head. "I don't know what to believe anymore. If Phoenix was tight with Geneva, then maybe Coast isn't who I thought he was either. Or Javey for that matter."

Hadn't Javey and Phoenix been bailed up together? Coast might have killed Jamison and Geneva to keep them quiet.

Elenna ran a hand up the back of her hair and clasped her ponytail. "That wouldn't explain why someone broke into Coast's apartment and tried to kill him."

"Allegedly tried to kill him," I said in a small voice. "The only ones who saw anything were…"

"Coast and Phoenix," Elenna finished for me. She dropped her hand to her thigh with a slap. "You really think they made the whole thing up?"

"No? Yes? No? *Fuck*, I don't know anymore. I don't know what to think or who to trust. Javey said Tank and BJ were suspicious, but maybe they aren't. Maybe he is. Maybe they all are." I threw my hands up in the air and let them fall to my sides. "I might be going crazy here. I'm just so confused."

"What do you want to do?" Elenna asked.

"I want to talk to them," I admitted. "But we know what they're going to say. Either way, they'll deny all of it. They'll probably be pissed off I suggested they could be involved. I think maybe we have to talk to Aidan. He knows the guys well enough he should be able to rule out at least some of this."

Or I was clutching at straws? If they fooled me, they would also have fooled Aidan. Wouldn't they? If there was anyone who distrusted most of the people around him, it was the head coach. People wouldn't pull the wool over his eyes easily.

"They weren't on his list," Elenna said.

"Which either means he doesn't think they're working against us, or he's trying to put them off guard. Oh, fuck. What if Tank and BJ are completely innocent in all of this? Or Kylie and Charlotte?"

I frowned. "Wait a minute. Aidan gave the guys the

list and he gave one to me. If he thinks they're up to something, then maybe he thinks I am too." Anxiety was quickly turning to full-blown panic.

"Are you?" Elenna asked lightly.

"Absolutely not," I said as firmly as I could possibly manage.

I cocked my head at her. "You don't really think I'd be—"

My heart raced. Sweat broke out on my palms.

If she really thought that, I could be in serious trouble. I had no doubt Finley had weapons hidden around his office somewhere. Not to mention the not so hidden kind, like a couple of hockey sticks leaning up against the wall and a broken ice skate on his desk.

Was it broken? Maybe people were supposed to think it was, but if they tried to attack him, they'd find out he could use one the same way Coast had.

I eyed it doubtfully, but didn't inch away in spite of my instincts suggesting maybe I should.

This was Elenna, she wasn't going to hurt me.

"Of course not," she said quickly.

I exhaled in relief at her words and how fast she was to say them. There was absolutely no doubt or hesitation. Of course there wasn't. It was only my paranoia suspecting she'd respond in any other way.

Idiot, I told myself.

She went on as though I wasn't sweating like crazy and calling myself names. I knew she noticed, she was way too perceptive to miss me freaking out.

"I know you and Wren better than to think you'd be involved with people like Nicholas, Celine or Sawyer. You're a good person. You have a big heart and you're loyal to the people you care about. You'd never do anything to put any of us in harm's way. Not on purpose anyway." She smiled slightly to show she was teasing.

"Accidents happen," I agreed.

Not if I could help it. If anything happened to her or Wren, it would be accompanied with butt loads of guilt. Even if it only resulted in one of them breaking a nail.

They were like sisters to me, family. Found family. The people you choose to spend time with because you love them, not because you share blood.

I'd rather be with them than anyone I shared a last name with. Which was saying something, because I was close to my biological family. There was just something different between the two kinds of bonds. Something I couldn't explain, but I was grateful for every single day. Especially on days like this when I hardly knew if I was coming or going.

I could always talk to Elenna and she'd be the voice of reason. I could have come to her with just about anything and she'd hear me out and help me make sense of it.

Wren would do the exact same and I'd do it for both of them. Even though we teased each other, we were always there for each other. I hoped that didn't change. I didn't know what I'd do without them.

I leaned my head back against the wall and closed my eyes. "Let's talk to Aidan and see what he has to say. I'm almost certain he'll tell us we have nothing to worry about."

"And if he doesn't?" Elenna asked.

"Then we'll deal with it," I said. Even if I got my heart broken in the process. Right now, that seemed like all too real a possibility.

"Now I remember why I don't put myself out there." I sighed. "Because shit like this happens. I risk getting my heart stomped on, and shredded into a thousand pieces. Fuck that." Tears prickled at the corners of my eyes.

"This could all be nothing," she reminded me. "Didn't you just say you were sure Aidan was going to tell you there was nothing to what Kylie said?"

"Yeah, I did. It's the doubt that fucks with my brain. If it's not this, it might be something else."

I opened my eyes and looked back at her. "How did you deal with looking over your shoulder, waiting for the Fiorellis to get revenge for Oscar's death?"

"One day at a time," she said. "It wasn't easy, but in the end, trusted my guys," she said. "I love them and I had to put my faith in them and in myself. I had to learn how to communicate and not be scared anymore. And I know, no matter what happens, they would never do anything to hurt me. You don't think any of them would hurt you, do you? Because if you do, I will personally deal with them."

She reminded me of a mother tiger protecting her cubs, or her fellow tigress.

"Knowing you'd have nightmares after doing that, it means a lot," I told her. "You're sweet and I'm lucky to have you." I put my arms around her and gave her a squeeze.

"I'd do anything for you," she said. "Even if it means having nightmares."

"I believe you," I said.

Although, I had a hard time imagining her getting enough of an upper hand on all three of the guys before they disarmed her. I knew better than to think she wouldn't try though.

The thought of them doing anything to her cemented my resolve to speak to Aidan.

This wasn't just about me and the guys, this was about the possibility of Elenna or Wren becoming collateral damage. I wasn't going to let that happen, no matter what I had to do to prevent it. Even if I had to tear out my own heart and put a bullet in the middle of it.

"Let's go and talk to him now." She curled a hand around one of mine. "I have a feeling you won't sleep either until we get this sorted out."

"Probably not," I agreed. I let her pull me from the room, my senses on high alert for anything anyone out of place. Paranoia was alive and well.

I had a feeling it would be for a while.

CHAPTER 28

SINCLAIR

In typical Aidan fashion, he looked at me like he wasn't surprised I was putting a problem at his feet.

Since we all knew what happened if we didn't tell him things, I had to take the 'sorry, not sorry' stance.

As it happened, he also looked pissed when I told him what Kylie said.

"Phoenix?" He rubbed a hand over the back of his head. "Cosy with Geneva?"

"That's what she said." I shrugged.

I stood back while Elenna detailed our discussion. I thought he might have dismissed all our theories as nonsense, but he listened, clearly thinking them through.

He might have told us it was all nonsense if it was me talking, but he had more respect for Elenna. He was an asshole, but he adored her. That was obvious for everyone to see.

She could have told him the sky was bright yellow with purple polka dots and he would have considered it. Everyone had their soft spot and she was his.

"I agree it's possible, but I think it's unlikely Coast is working with them," he said finally. "Phoenix... He's a tougher nut to crack. Javey too. They both keep their thoughts to themselves."

"Maybe that's what Coast wants you to think," Elenna suggested. She looked like she didn't believe it either. Or it didn't want to.

"Coast is a dickhead, but I don't think he's on their side," Orion said. He and Finley had been so quiet until now I almost forgot they were there.

"I don't want to think any of them are," Finley said in his soft, Irish lilt. Even after so long in Australia, he still had an accent. "Not even Tank or BJ. We're supposed to be a team here. We shouldn't be working against each other." He gave Aidan a meaningful look, then tilted his head towards me.

Aidan grunted. "I'm not working against anyone here."

"I know you don't like me," I started.

"Of course he does," Finley said. "Aidan loves every-one. Right Aidan?"

Aidan raised an eyebrow at him. He would have told most other people to fuck off, but not Finley. He wasn't the soft spot Elenna was, but their friendship was as tight as Coast and Phoenix. Tighter maybe.

"The point is, we're all on the same side," Finley

concluded. "If we let them get to us too much, then they win."

"They don't get to win," Aidan said. "We're working together." He stepped out from behind his desk and put an arm around Elenna. "I'm glad you brought this to me. We need to figure out what we are going to do about it."

"I could ask," Orion suggested.

"What, just walk up and say *hey, bro, is there any chance you're betraying us*?" Finley grinned. "No offence, but I can't see them being inclined to give you a straight answer if they are."

Orion shrugged. "Just an idea. I'm one of them; they may open up to me."

"You're also one of us." Finley gestured to himself, Aidan and Elenna. "To them, that makes you suspect as hell. They'll know you'll go running off to tell Aidan or me."

"I don't think anyone is going to get a direct answer to a question like that, no matter who they are," I said. "Not until they're ready to admit to it. By then, it'll be too late."

"Then we try to get an indirect answer," Aidan said as though it was as simple as that. "Sinclair, keep planning your charity event, and keep an eye on Kylie."

He frowned in thought. "We need to figure out a way to set them up so they reveal themselves."

"We could feed them some false information and see who acts on it," Elenna said.

Aidan snapped his fingers. "Good idea. Let's get on to doing that. We can also feed some misinformation to Tank and BJ. Kylie too. Each bit subtly different, so we know exactly who was told what and who responded to it. But close enough that if they compare notes, they'll assume there was some kind of misunderstanding."

"I really am starting to feel like a spy," I said. "They didn't teach this at uni."

"That's a shame," Finley said with a smile. "Everyone should learn espionage one-oh-one. Followed by hacking one oh one, picking locks and tapping phones."

"Those aren't skills everyone should have," Orion said. "Especially hacking. People can stay the fuck out of my phone."

"No one would dare to hack your phone," Elenna told him fondly. "They'd be too scared to try."

Aidan cleared his throat.

She bumped her hip against his. "Yours either."

"I don't care if they hack mine," Finley said. "They'll find out I have a secret obsession with ducks."

I stared at him. "Ducks?" Did I want to know?

He grinned. "Yeah, I watch lots of videos of ducks doing funny things like chasing people. Also, llamas spitting. If I have anything to hide, I'm not hiding it on my phone. Not the phone you all know about anyway." He gave me a wink.

"I'm not sure what any of that says about you and it's probably best if I don't think about it too much," I said. Chances were, he was joking about the duck and llama videos. At least, the extent of them.

After all, everyone knew the Internet was designed for cat videos. And, to a lesser extent, weird dances.

"Anyway," Aidan said, drawing all of our attention back to him. "I'll put something together and get it out to you. You'll all have someone different to deal with." His gaze found mine. "Can you manage Coast, Phoenix and Javey?"

I only hesitated for a heartbeat or two. "Yes I can. If any of them wanted to do anything to me, they would have done it already."

"That's a big assumption, but someone needs to do it and you're in the best position," he said.

"So to speak," Finley said under his breath.

I felt my face heat.

"Don't be a brat," Elenna told him.

He chuckled. "Once a brat, always a brat. Nothin' I can do about it."

She rolled her eyes, but the look she gave him was as loving as the one she directed at Aidan and Orion.

Once, I envied her relationship with the guys. Now, I wondered if three was a complication that maybe I couldn't handle as well as I thought I could.

Somehow, they made it look so easy. I knew it wasn't; they'd gone through a lot to get where they were.

Would that be me with the guys at some point, or was everything just about to blow up in my face?

At times like these, I wished I had a crystal ball so I could see the future. Then I'd have some idea if I should ride this out or run the hell away, right now.

No, either way I had to stay and see this through. This was about more than just me. Fuck only knew how many lives were at stake if we got this wrong.

"So, about the tutus," I said to lighten the mood.

The eyes of everyone in the room turned to me.

Elenna's amused.

Finley looked like he was holding back a loud laugh.

Aidan and Orion looked like they were both holding back on throwing me off the roof of the arena.

"No tutus," Orion said. "I'll get out there on the ice and make a fuckwit of myself, but not dressed like that."

"You'll wear one if Elenna tells you to wear one," Aidan said.

We all looked at him in surprise, but probably shouldn't. If Elenna wanted him to climb up into the sky and hang a second moon, he'd try to do it.

If she wanted them to dress up in pink, purple and blue, then he'd make that happen too. Hell, if she insisted on naked hockey players, that's what we'd get.

Honestly, it was a shame I hadn't thought of that first. Not where children were involved, of course, but...

"We could put together a nude calendar," I blurted out.

"I'm in," Orion said immediately. "If I don't have to

wear anything silly, I'll be as naked as you want." He crossed his arms over his chest and gave Elenna the side eye, as though daring her to disagree. Not with the naked part, but with the whole tutu thing.

I had a feeling a tank, the vehicle kind, not the player, couldn't budge him on that. In the end, he'd do what he was told for his team, but no one was going to make him like it. Not even her. Not Finley either. Certainly not me.

"I vote we do that as well," Finley said. "The guys would line up to take part."

I doubted that, but some of them would. Coast would be at the front of the line, right behind Orion. I'd happily hang a calendar like that on my wall. Lots of other people would too, even if it wasn't for charity.

"I like that idea too," Elenna said. "Maybe some of the background people as well." Her sly gaze slid to Aidan.

"People want to see naked hockey players, not coaches," he told her. "I'd only bring down the mood."

Apparently he could tell her no after all, but in a more roundabout way.

He had a point though. People would pay to see the players. We could make a ton of money for charity.

"I'll look into it," I said. I was going to be busy planning all of this stuff. I knew just who to ask for help.

"Orion should be Mr December," Finley said. "He could wear a wreath around his cock." He wiggled his eyebrows playfully. His gaze dropped to Orion's groin, obviously picturing that in his head. And liking what he saw.

Orion snorted. "As long as I'm not Mr February."

"You'd make a perfect Mr February," Elenna told him. "You're very romantic."

His expression softened. "Only for you. I don't want the rest of the world knowing. I have a reputation as a coldhearted asshole to uphold. Having anything to do with Valentine's Day would completely fuck that up."

The side of his mouth pulled up in a very slight smile. That was all I'd ever seen him do. I wondered if he smiled in private, because he sure as hell didn't do it in public.

I knew he wasn't the cold asshole he made himself out to be, but he wasn't warm either. Elenna's guys couldn't be more different from each other.

"I'll make sure you're not February," I assured him.

He wasn't the one I wanted to see with a wreath around his cock. That honour went to Coast, Phoenix and Javey, equally. I might have to make sure that happened, if only for a personal photograph.

CHAPTER 29

PHOENIX

I wouldn't claim to be the smartest guy in the world, but I knew when something is off. And right now, something was *definitely* off.

I thought, since she got a lift in with Elenna, I'd surprise Sinclair by turning up at her office to pick her up and take her home. Her home, my home, whatever. Somewhere we could eat dinner and have some time alone.

The moment she lay eyes on me, her smile was— I don't know, forced.

She rallied quickly and chatted about her day, the weather, my practice and all that, but the moment stuck in my head the whole drive. In my experience, ignoring shit like that got you dead.

"You sure you don't want to go back to my place?" I asked. "You'd be safer there."

I glanced around her small cottage and noted the

lack of security system, cameras or decent locks. Anyone could smash a window in or kick the door down. That could get *her* dead.

"I'm perfectly safe here. I mean, you're here with me, right?" She placed her bag down on the table and picked up her phone. "Do you want to order something to eat?"

I closed the door behind me and sauntered over to her, my best cocky smile on my face. "I'd rather eat you."

She responded with a laugh just this side of nervous. A fraction too high to be normal. Was I the cause of that? I could be a handful, but I thought we were past that. Hell, I've been wrong before, it was bound to happen again.

"Maybe we should tell Coast and Javey where we are. They might want to… I don't know. Hang out." She went to touch the screen of her phone.

Without thinking, I snatched it from her. "Don't do that."

I was not prepared for her reaction.

Her eyes widened. She stepped back.

What the fuck?

"What the fuck?" I put a hand out to her.

She backed further away, until she hit the wall with her ass.

"Sinclair?" I raised my hands to either side. "Did I do something? I know sometimes I'm a dickhead, but whatever it was, can we talk about it?"

I'd had people scared of me plenty of times before. I practically made a living out of it. But never someone like her. Not someone I actually gave a shit about.

She blinked a couple of times and forced another smile. "Sorry, I'm just a little twitchy. It's the whole… The thing with the car."

"Bullshit," I snapped. "It's more than that and you know it. Something happened. What is it? Something has you freaked the fuck out."

I might scare her more, but I stepped forward and placed my hands on the wall to either side of her shoulders. I raised my eyebrows at her expectantly.

She swallowed audibly. "It's just…"

"The truth," I insisted. "What. The. Fuck. Happened?"

Shit, I *was* scaring her. I hated myself for it, but I had to know what was going on.

"The… The list," she stammered.

I frowned. "Aidan's list? What about it? I'm not on it am I?" I almost laughed, until the expression on her face didn't change. "What the hell? Why am I on his list?"

"Because of me," she admitted. "In a manner of speaking."

I narrowed my eyes at her. She better explain, or I was going to choke it out of her. Not in a way she'd enjoy either. Shit, I didn't want to hurt her, but…

I couldn't even finish that thought.

"I was talking to someone on the list," she said

quickly. Her voice quavered. "They suggested you might have been working with Geneva Mancini."

Now I *did* laugh, this time with disbelief. "They said what? Who would say something so fucking stupid?"

Her tongue slid over her lips. "It doesn't matter who."

I slammed the palm of my hand against the wall. "It matters. Who the fuck said that?"

She flinched. "Kylie. She—"

"Kylie was on the list," I said. "Not without reason, or Aidan wouldn't have put her on there. Now he's put me on there?"

"Not exactly," she said uneasily. "Do you want to back off or do I need to knee you in the balls?"

I chuckled and placed a hand around her throat. "How about you don't? Tell me what the hell is going on." I squeezed lightly.

"What Kylie said raised suspicions against you, and by association, Coast." She swallowed. "Now everyone is wondering if maybe we shouldn't trust you two, or Javey."

I closed my eyes and listened while she told me what she and Elenna discussed.

"You think Coast faked the attack on himself?" I could hardly believe what I was hearing. "I helped dispose of the bodies. There was nothing fake about it. But I guess that's what you'd expect to hear if he and I were in cahoots."

Did people really use words like cahoots? Whatever.

"He didn't fake the attack. I was not working with Geneva. I spoke to her a couple of times over the years, because my brother sent me to deliver a message. I was in the door and out the door as quickly as I could. That's the extent of any involvement with her. If you don't believe me, ask my brother, Ric. If he had suspicions, he would have had me killed and asked questions later. He doesn't have room for doubts when it comes to the people around him and their loyalty."

I leaned my head against the wall beside Sinclair's. "If Coast is working with them, I'll eat my helmet. I can't speak for Javey, but the dude is head over heels in love with you. I don't think you have anything to worry about there."

"I want to believe you," she said softly.

I lifted my hand and looked her straight in the eyes. "*Believe me*. I'll swear on anything you want me to, I'm not working against you, against the team or against the Brantleys. I am sure as hell not working with anyone named Fiorelli or Mancini."

I exhaled a frustrated breath.

"Does Aidan think I am?" The asshole should know better. Coast and I were right there during the attack on the arena, helping to disarm and dispose of the enemy. Not to mention the fact he was our coach. He should have fucking faith in us.

"I don't know what he thinks. He wants to find out exactly who is working for whom."

Reluctantly, she outlined the plan to give snippets of

different information to different people.

"Let him do it," I said. "When I don't act on it, he'll know I'm… Okay, maybe innocent isn't the word for me, but innocent in this regard." The smile I gave her was faint at best. I was still trying to get my head around anyone suspecting me.

I've done a lot of shitty things in my life, but I'd never work against my family or my team. I'd certainly never work against Coast or Sinclair. Javey either, now I thought about it.

"Except that I told you," she pointed out.

"Yeah, you did, but I don't intend to act on any information that would make me look like I'm doing something wrong." That might be harder said than done, but I'd try. "If you like, you can spend twenty-four hours a day, seven days a week with me and see that I'm the guy I say I am."

I wouldn't hate that. I liked spending time with her.

"I believe you," she said finally. "I'm sorry I thought you were… You know."

"I know," I said on an exhale. "I would never do anything bad to you." I shook my head. "I hate this. We shouldn't be fighting amongst ourselves or pointing fingers at each other. Team unity and all that shit."

I leaned in and roughly kissed her mouth. She tasted like pure heaven. When did she not? She was still trembling slightly, but she kissed me back. I was *almost* certain I wasn't going to end up with her knee rammed into my cock.

"Should we tell the others?" she asked between heated kisses.

"Naw, let them figure it out when someone is following them around," I said jokingly. "It could be good for a laugh."

Coast would probably find it hilarious.

Javey… He might try to stab someone between the eyeballs.

On the other hand, maybe he *was* involved. He'd said it himself, no one suspected the shy, quiet guy. He might have been referring to us all along, not the enemy. If he was, I was going to rip his fucking nuts off and jam them down his throat.

"Should we tell them to come over here?" She ducked her head and looked towards the window.

"What?" I asked.

That sense that something was up, tingled in the back of my mind again. "What is it?"

I lowered my hand from her throat and looked around for something to use as a weapon. I shouldn't have brought her here until I had the security upgraded. The house wasn't safe for her to be in. If anything happened to her, I'd kick myself for it. After I kicked the ass of anyone who dared to lay a hand on her.

"It's just that—" she winced. "Javey might already be outside."

"He—" She was trying to tell me something, but I couldn't quite grasp what it was.

"You think he's planning something?" I'd kick his ass if he was. I'd kick it so hard he'd be able to tell us whether or not we won the cup. Now I thought about it, that might be useful. I might do that anyway.

"No," she said quickly. "He likes to follow me. To, you know, keep an eye on me. That night at your place, up against the window, he was outside watching."

Her face was flushed with excitement at the memory. Her eyes were so dark I could have drowned in them. The woman was so hot I was ready to melt on the spot.

I leaned back and stared at her. "He's stalking you?"

"At first he was, but now he just—" She searched for the words for whatever he was apparently doing. "He's trying to keep me safe."

"Sounds like fucking stalking to me." I stomped over to the door and wrenched it open. I looked left and right, but saw no sign of him. Not until I looked out onto the street and saw his car, him sitting in it.

I marched over, yanked the door open and grabbed him by the front of his shirt.

"You're stalking Sinclair?" I growled. I yanked him halfway out of the car and got right up in his face.

"I was watching her and making sure no one was disturbing you." He tried to pull back. "Let me fucking go."

I kept my grip on his collar. "You were making sure no one disturbed me and Sinclair? Is that all?"

"No, I also want to keep her safe," he said. "If you

were distracted, someone had to be paying attention."

He seemed unsure if he should pull out a knife and stab me in the guts or not. He'd have to move fucking fast to do it. I could break his neck while he was still considering.

Fuck knows I didn't want to. I liked the guy, possibly too much. How well could I trust someone who was stalking my woman? Our woman, whatever. I wasn't going to argue over terminology as long as she knew part of her belonged to me.

I hesitated, then shoved him back into the seat of his car. "All right. I guess I can get behind that." It was screwy but I didn't want to be disturbed either. "I have my phone. Call if you see anything."

I started to turn away, but I turned back and said, "Unless you want to come in and join us."

I thought he might insist on staying outside and keeping watch. I half hoped he would.

My heart skipped when he climbed out of his car and locked it behind him.

"I'd much rather be in there than out here." The shy, awkward look he gave me was genuine. It wasn't about not knowing me well. No, this was all about our attraction to each other and the potential to finally give in and explore it.

My cock throbbed. Before he could burst out of my jeans and make me lose my load out here in the street, I turned and stomped back inside, leaving Javey to follow behind me.

"He was out there all right," Phoenix growled. "I figured he'd be better off in here where we could keep an eye on him." He carefully locked the door behind Javey.

Javey and I both gave him a look. We knew exactly what the score was. Neither of us called him out on it.

Squealing playfully, I let Phoenix scoop me up and carry me to the bedroom. Just inside the door, I kicked off my shoes. They landed on the floor with a plop.

Phoenix tossed me onto the bed. I bounced before I righted myself, hands to either side for stability.

Both guys started to pull off my clothes. I don't think I ever got naked so quickly. Or so aroused.

Every brush of their calloused fingers on my heated skin made me hotter. Every kiss or lick between unhooking my bra, or tugging down a sleeve made me wetter between my thighs.

"I've decided we're the luckiest guys in the world

right now." Phoenix sat on the side of the bed and looked down at me, his gaze only broken when he pulled his own shirt off over his head and threw it aside.

"Because you play for the Demons?" I asked teasingly.

He grinned and wriggled out of his pants. "Yeah, exactly. But this is icing on the cupcake. Wouldn't you say, Javey?"

Javey was already taking off his boxers, but he stopped for a moment to nod his agreement. "This is better than playing hockey. Sinclair is everything."

He gave me a soft smile that melted my heart a little further. A flutter of butterflies turned into a flock of flamingos when he turned that glance on Phoenix.

"You're both everything," I said carefully. Could they be everything to each other? Did they want that?

Phoenix caught Javey's expression and his face turned pink, right up to the tips of his ears. His eyes darkened. His cock seemed to get even harder. He really had been denying himself for too long.

"Yeah," Phoenix said softly.

"Do you want to touch each other?" I kept my tone light, gentle. My heart raced, eager to see what they might do, both with each other and with me.

"I want to." Javey's voice was barely more than a whisper. "I've never..."

"You've seen the extent of my experience." Phoenix was more awkward than I'd ever seen him. He'd kill someone without a second thought, but when it came to suppressed desire, that was something very different. More confronting, apparently, then death.

"What do you want to do?" I sat up.

Elenna told me how Aidan liked to tell her and her other boyfriends what to do and how to do it. Could I be that for them? I wasn't as bossy as Aidan. I didn't feel the need to dominate. All I wanted was for them to express themselves however they felt comfortable.

Phoenix leaned over and kissed my mouth. His tongue slid over my lips. He drew back and did the same to Javey. This kiss was light, exploring, testing boundaries.

He sat back and looked at both of us. "I want to do that again."

"Me too," Javey said. He placed a hand on the back of my neck and pulled me in for a deep kiss. His mouth was warm and soft on mine, his stubble grazing my cheek.

I could happily have kissed him all day long. When he finally drew away, it was to hook his hand around the back of Phoenix's neck and kiss him just as deeply.

I wrapped a hand around each of their cocks and worked my fingers up and down slowly. Just enough to make them harder, but not so they'd come too soon.

Both thrust up into my hand, bucking their hips almost in sync.

"Is this what you want to see?" Phoenix asked, some

of his bravado back in place. "You want to see us kissing?"

"I liked seeing it," I said. "You two together are hot."

He glanced over to Javey. "You hear that? We're hot."

Javey shrugged. "Of course we are. So is she."

"So, it takes one to know one?" I teased.

"Something like that." Phoenix kissed me again, one hand palming my breast, the other teasing the tip of Javey's cock.

I slipped my hand off, allowing him to wrap his fingers around the winger's erection. I pressed my opposite palm against Phoenix's chest, giving Javey the chance to run his fingers up and down Phoenix's length.

"You're so thick." Javey's tentative touch soon turned bolder, the pads of his fingers tracing up and down the vein of Phoenix's cock and lightly touching his balls.

"I can't decide which is hotter, your piercing or Coast's." Phoenix traced circles around Javey's Prince Albert. "I think it's a tie."

"Do you want to taste him like you tasted Coast?" I asked.

Phoenix looked intently at me, then at Javey. He licked his lips. "Yeah, I do."

Javey looked like he was going to say something, but wasn't sure how to speak the words out loud.

"What do you want?" I asked him. "You want him to suck you?"

He hesitated, his jaw moving back and forth. "Yeah. But I..."

"You what?" Phoenix asked. His eyes were intent on Javey's. There was no judgement in his tone, no mockery. He showed a hint of nerves, but mostly the desire to make Javey feel accepted. There wasn't anything he couldn't say that we wouldn't completely understand.

"I want to taste you too," Javey said in a rush.

I swallowed down a knot of surprise. My pussy was going to start dripping at this rate.

Phoenix nodded and guided Javey onto his back. He turned around so his face was in front of Javey's cock and his was in front of Javey's mouth.

Slowly at first, they teased each other's tips with their tongues, tasting each other's pre-cum, flicking and swirling around each other's head.

I dipped my hand down between my legs and traced slow circles around my clit while I watched them sucking each other. I couldn't remember seeing anything hotter than this; two burly, muscular hockey players with their mouths on each other's cocks, sucking, licking and thrusting slowly.

"You need a security alarm," Coast said as he stepped into the room and raised his eyebrows. "Looks like I got here just in time." He started to strip off his own clothes. "Don't stop on my account." His eyes were on me when he spoke.

Gaze intent on him, I rubbed my clit harder, slipping a couple of fingers inside myself.

"How wet are you?" he asked.

"Very wet." I didn't stop or slow, I kept stroking and rubbing myself.

"How close are you to coming?" He stepped out of his bright blue boxers and knelt on the end of the bed, his head tilted to the side.

"Very close." I glanced over at Javey and Phoenix. They were balls deep in each other's mouths. Eyes closed, blissed out.

"They look close too," Coast remarked. "Do you think they'll come in each other's mouths?"

"Do you want them to?" I asked.

"I think they should. I think you should come. Right now." Without taking his eyes off me, he lowered himself down onto his ass. "Come for me, Sunflower."

His words wrenched an orgasm out of me. I came hard around my fingers, back arched, my eyes still on him. The world disappeared in a kaleidoscope of colours and flashes of light. I rocked against my fingers, making myself last until my clit became too sensitive to touch.

"Perfect." He pushed me back against the pillows and sat facing me. He draped my legs over his thighs and pulled me until I slid onto his cock. "So perfect." He half-closed his eyes and began to thrust into me.

I grabbed hold of his biceps and held myself in place while I rocked against him. The room was filled with the sounds of sucking and moaning.

I didn't know where to look; right at Coast's face while he fucked me or at the guys while they fucked each other's mouths. There was no wrong answer. Everything was so incredibly right, I could barely get my head around it.

It was Javey who pulled his cock out from between Phoenix's lips and drew away from him.

"I'm going to come," he said breathlessly. He raised himself to his knees and knelt beside my face. He pressed his cock between my lips and thrust a couple of times before filling my mouth with his salty cum.

I sucked him as hard as I could, milking every drop of his release from his slit. When he sagged and slipped out of me, I tilted my head back and swallowed.

"Fuck," Coast said breathlessly. He glanced over at Phoenix whose hand was curled around his cock. "Let me taste you." He jerked his head to the side to tell Phoenix to come to him.

Phoenix's eyes widened, but he hurried to kneel beside Coast. When the centre opened his mouth, he slid his cock inside.

Coast made an appreciative sound and sucked as deep and hard as Javey had.

"I'm going to come," Phoenix whispered. His dark eyes were caught between ecstasy and worry. He clearly didn't want to push Coast any further than he was willing to go, but he very much wanted to follow this all the way through.

Coast grunted his agreement and sucked at the same time as he was driving into me. He made no attempt to pull away. He was as committed to this as the goalie was.

The sight pushed me over the edge into an orgasm at least a billion times more intense than the first. I tipped my head back and shouted to the ceiling. I didn't know what I shouted or if I was even coherent, but I shouted something.

Who cared if the neighbours could hear me? They could be happy I was having the time of my life. Why not? I wanted that for them too. Although, it didn't seem possible they could have as much fun as I was having right now.

Phoenix grunted and started to pull away, but Coast grabbed his ass and held him there while he came down Coast's throat.

"Fucking hell... Yes," Phoenix panted. "That's so fucking... Good." He slumped forward, puffing heavily for a few moments before finally sliding out of Coast's mouth.

His lips tight together, Coast smiled at me. He grabbed my shoulders and pulled me forward until he could press his mouth to mine. He squirted Phoenix's cum onto my tongue before sitting back and driving in harder than before.

The combination of Javey and Phoenix's releases was delicious. I swirled the cum around in my mouth, savouring the taste before I swallowed.

"You guys are tasty," I said. "Now, I want you to come for me." I rocked harder and faster against Coast, pushing him closer and closer until he couldn't have stopped himself if he wanted to. Palms pressed to the top of the bed behind him, he came, grunting and groaning out his release while spilling himself inside me.

"So fucking... Incredible," he moaned. "So fucking... Good." He finally sagged back and slipped his cock out of me.

"It's only fair," Javey said softly when Coast moved aside. He lay down with his face between my legs and started to clean up Coast's cum as it leaked out of my pussy.

"That's definitely fair," Phoenix agreed. He draped an arm over Coast's shoulder and the pair sat and watched, both looking comfortable with each other.

CHAPTER 31

"I should have known you assholes were here long before I was." Coast glared at Phoenix and Javey before leaning in to kiss my mouth. His hair was damp from the shower and he still looked half asleep.

I kissed him back, but stepped to the side to grab my coffee.

Phoenix grinned. "You really should, bro. Where else would any of us be?" He bit into the corner of his toast. He was standing in my kitchen wearing only track pants and a smug face.

I couldn't help admiring his chiselled body. He seemed absolutely comfortable in his own skin this morning.

"What he said," Javey mumbled. He was dressed the same as Phoenix, but had a banana in his hand instead of toast.

"You both suck," Coast said. "I don't mean dick."

Javey and Phoenix exchanged meaningful glances. Dick was exactly what they were thinking.

"We were going to call you," I started.

"No we weren't," Phoenix said. He shot Coast a lopsided smile, then nodded towards the coffee machine and the empty cup on the bench beside it. "We figured you'd show up sooner or later."

"Like a bad smell," Javey said.

Coast flipped them both off, a finger for each, but didn't stop smiling. He filled the mug and set it aside for a few minutes to cool.

"So, you assholes didn't run." He leaned back against the counter, took my hand and drew me to him so my back was pressed against his chest. He wrapped his arms around me and held me hard.

Javey frowned, confused.

Phoenix didn't even seem surprised. "Told you you're an asshole. Of course we didn't run. Do we look guilty as shit?"

I glanced back over my shoulder. "You knew?"

He squeezed me tighter. For a while I thought he was angry.

He huffed a laugh. "Of course I knew. Aidan trusts me. Apparently none of of you do."

"I trust you, I just had more important things to do last night." Phoenix casually continued eating his break-fast. We could have been talking about the weather.

Javey watched Coast with dark eyes but no words. He didn't need them. He didn't completely trust Coast.

Not even after the night we all shared. What would it take?

"I appreciate that fucking Sinclair is much more fun and a somewhat higher priority than telling me you're not sure whose side I'm on, but for the sake of team unity, you could have made a quick phone call. Or even a text." That was as pissed off as I'd ever heard Coast.

"We should have," I said quickly.

"For what it's worth, we didn't call Javey either," Phoenix said. "He turned up outside."

Javey gave him a 'thanks for throwing me under the bus,' look and shrugged. "I was keeping an eye out for trouble."

"For me?" Coast's tone was stone cold now. Could he feel me tremble? The way he was holding me should have been reassuring, but I was becoming more and more anxious.

"Not for you specifically," Javey said. "For trouble in general. If you're planning to cause any…"

"I could suggest the same of you," Coast said. "Both of you." Apparently that didn't include me. Or maybe he thought I was easier to deal with.

"We're all on the same side," I managed to say. "What did Aidan say to you?"

My mind was turning over and over. I had too many questions and not enough answers. Was this about Aidan trying to catch us out? Had he used Kylie to do that? Did Elenna know about any of this? I liked to think if she did, she would have come to me and told me. Her loyalty was with Aidan, but she couldn't possibly think I was the enemy.

Could she?

"He said someone from the list pointed a finger at Phoenix, and if Phoenix ran once he found out, that would confirm it. I saw you pick up Sinclair from the arena and I knew she wouldn't be able to resist saying something." He leaned forward, his breath stroked my cheek.

"I know how much you hate keeping secrets, especially from people you care about. And I know how good Phoenix is at getting secrets out of people. He's almost as good as Ice. A lot more subtle though."

"You knew I'd babble," I concluded. I sounded pathetic. He was right though. I was better at keeping secrets for people I loved, not secrets *about* them.

Wait, love? I'd said it to Javey, but the other two guys? That was something I'd have to think about later.

"I wouldn't call it babbling, just being honest," Coast said. "Something Phoenix apparently has trouble with."

Phoenix snorted around his last mouthful of toast. "You knew what was going on and didn't tell us either. Don't be a fucking hypocrite."

Coast tensed.

For a few moments I thought he was going to reach for a knife, or a rolling pin.

Finally, he relaxed and let out a breath that tickled my neck. "Yeah, I guess so. I let Aidan get into my head the same way you let Kylie get into yours."

Aidan also got into our heads, but now wasn't the time to bring that up. We didn't need more problems right now.

"So, we've all established that Kylie was full of shit," I ventured. "It seems likely she's working for the enemy."

"I wouldn't assume anything," Phoenix said. "I wouldn't put it past Aidan to plant her there to do exactly what she did, so he knew exactly who he could trust."

"That sounds like the kind of dick move he'd make," I agreed.

"My money is still on Tank and BJ," Javey said. He didn't seem to give a shit whether Aidan was setting any of us up or not. He knew where he stood with me and vice versa. As far as he was concerned, that was enough.

"Mine too," Phoenix said. "I think at this point, we've whittled that list down to only them and possibly Kylie. If Aidan has a list that had us on it, it doesn't now." He fixed Coast with a look that said he better make sure that was the case.

"I think we can agree on that." Coast loosened his grip on my wrist but brought my hand up to kiss my palm. "What's this I hear about a nude calendar?"

All eyes were on me now.

Javey almost choked on his last mouthful of banana.

"Um." I glanced down toward the hardwood floor. It could use a bit of sanding and re-staining. The whole house could use some work, to be honest. Phoenix and Coast were right about the lack of security, but it was home to me.

I forced my eyes back up. "Just one of those, you know, tasteful calendars featuring you guys. With strategically placed props in front of your junk, of course."

"Of course," Coast said smoothly. "Wouldn't want to shame the rest of the male population of Australia." He nudged the bulge in his jeans against my leg.

Phoenix snorted a laugh. "You said 'embarrass your-self' wrong."

"No, I did not," Coast said. "You already know I have nothing to be embarrassed about. None of us do."

"You really don't," I said, a flush creeping up my cheeks. "Does that mean you'll pose for it?"

"I will if you're there," Javey said. "If you want me to, that is…"

"Of course I do," I said quickly. "You three are the hottest guys on the team. You'd sell the most calendars out of any of them."

"That's the most truthful and correct thing I've ever heard," Coast said, with a chuckle. He pressed a hand to my belly and nuzzled into my neck. "Are you sure you want to share us with the world?"

"Now you mention it, that's a good point." I dropped my head to the side to give him better access. "I might have to poke out some eyes if people stare at your photos for too long." I was joking, of course.

The guys all had social media profiles and plenty of photos of themselves on the Internet in a professional capacity. In the case of Coast and Phoenix, in a personal capacity. Only Javey didn't have a personal social media presence, as far as I could tell. That wasn't surprising given how private a person he was.

"It would be worse if it was a calendar with a photo of you on it," Coast told me. "We'd have to hunt down and kill every single person who bought a copy. Starting with the photographer. That would quickly become a full-time job."

I didn't think anyone would pay for a calendar with me in it, but I had no intention of posing for one anyway, so the photographer was safe on that count.

"You're the famous ones," I said diplomatically. "You're the ones people want to see. I might organise some baby animals for the shoot as well."

"Can I have a snake?" Phoenix asked. "I love snakes."

Coast shuddered. "Bro—"

"What?" Phoenix shrugged. "They're cool. And not because they're long and thick." He glanced sideways at Javey, then back at Coast.

"I'll make sure you get a puppy," I assured Coast. "Unless you'd prefer a tarantula or something like that?"

"I thought you liked me," he complained. "Spiders are even worse than snakes."

Javey smirked. "What else are you afraid of?"

"I'm not afraid of anything," Coast retorted. "I just don't like them, okay? I'm fine with puppies. And kittens." He slipped his hand down my stomach. "And pussies." His palm rested over mine, heat radiating from his skin right to my clit.

"Are you going to pose with a spider?" Phoenix asked Javey, probably to goad Coast as much as out of curiosity.

"There are no spiders in this country big enough to hide my cock," Javey remarked.

Coast grunted. "Can you stop talking about spiders near your junk? That's fucked up in too many ways. Those things could latch on and make a web or some shit. Or bite your cock off."

"To be completely fair, a kitten could bite off your dick too," Phoenix remarked.

"I'm starting to think this whole calendar thing is a bad idea," Coast said.

"No it's not," I said. "It's a good idea. Nothing is going to bite your cock. I promise. Not unless you ask nicely." I looked back at him and smiled.

His tongue swiped over his lips. "I don't know about biting, but I could use some sucking." He turned me around to face him and gently pushed me down to my knees.

I smiled up at him and undid the front of his jeans to release his already straining erection. Balls cupped in my hand, I massaged them lightly while swirling my tongue around his tip and tasting the salty bead of moisture that leaked from him.

He wound my hair around his fist and held my head while he pressed himself deeper into my mouth.

"You feel so fucking good," he groaned. "I'm going to give this to you hard. You're going to tap my thigh three times if it's too much for you. Okay?" He looked down at me until I nodded around my mouthful.

"Good girl." He started to thrust hard and fast, touching the back of my throat and making me gag every few strokes. He wasn't gentle, but I loved every moment of it. Knowing I made him hard and that when he came it would be because of me. I was the one who did that to him. It was as arousing as watching the guys do the same to each other.

I hooked a hand around him and dug my nails into his ass cheek. The harder he thrust, the deeper I dug.

"Fuck yeah, this kitten has some fucking amazing claws," Coast gasped. "I'm going to come right down your fucking throat. You're going to take every drop like the good fucking girl you are. But don't swallow it yet."

He grunted and thrust a few more times before he came, spilling himself into my mouth with a burst of salty heat. "Yeah, that's so… Good." He arched his back and thrust in a couple more times before sliding out. He kept his hand in my hair, keeping me down on my knees.

"Phoenix, get over here." He jerked his head at the goalie.

Phoenix dusted toast crumbs off his hands onto the plate and rose. "Usually I don't take orders—"

"Get on your knees beside her," Coast snapped. "Take everything she has in her mouth."

"Unless I like the order." Phoenix knelt beside me and pressed his lips to mine.

I kissed him before squirting Coast's cum into his mouth. I leaned back far enough to watch him taste his mouthful and swallow.

"Not bad." He nodded like he'd sampled a fine liqueur. "I'd like to try it directly some time."

He helped me to my feet, led me over to the table beside Javey and bent me over the top. He rucked up my skirt to my waist and pulled aside the gusset of my already drenched panties. He slipped a couple of fingers inside me and pumped a handful of times.

"So wet already." He slipped his fingers out and undid his jeans. He gripped my hips with his hands and slammed his cock into my pussy.

I cried out and dug my nails into the top of the table, gripping on while he pounded into me. I raised my face to look at Javey. He was watching intently, the peel of his banana draped over his fingers.

"Do you want to know how it feels to have a cock inside you?" Phoenix asked him.

Javey gaped. "Yeah," he whispered.

A smile on his lips, Coast disappeared into my room, returning a minute or two later with a tube of lube. "Bend over the table beside her."

Javey swallowed hard, but pushed his jeans down his thighs and bent over beside me.

Coast opened the lube and squirted out a large dollop onto his finger. He tossed the tube aside and slipped his finger slowly into Javey's ass. "Bro, you're so tight." He worked him with his finger for a while before adding a second one. Then a third.

"Are you okay?" I asked Javey gently.

"Better than okay," he replied in the same tone. "This is…" He shook his head. He had no words for what this was. Something beyond good.

"Phoenix, he's ready for you," Coast said. He stepped aside to give Phoenix room, then moved in behind me.

I straightened up to watch Phoenix position himself outside Javey's rear entrance, then slide himself slowly, carefully inside.

Coast was already hard again after me sucking him off. He gripped my hips with firm fingers and shoved his cock deep inside me.

I leaned forward again, my nails gouging deeper marks in the top of the table.

"You were right, he is so tight," Phoenix said breathlessly. "They both feel so fucking good. Javey, I'm going to come inside you, okay?"

"Yeah," Javey said with a grunt. "Do it."

Phoenix couldn't hold back any longer, he pushed into Javey with a couple of long strokes, before grunting and groaning as he came.

He pushed Coast over the edge into a second orgasm, grinding and thrusting hard into my body. That in turn made me come, half a heartbeat behind both of them. The kitchen was filled with the sound of bliss and the smell of sex and cum.

I was still coming when Coast slipped out of me and was quickly replaced with Javey.

In the space of less than half an hour, I'd been fucked by three different guys. How was this my life? Whatever, I wasn't going to question it, I was going to enjoy every moment of it.

I rolled back against Javey, pushing him harder and harder. His breathing was harsh and ragged, aroused as hell. He'd been fucked and was now fucking me. He probably wasn't sure how this was his life either.

"Come inside her," Coast said. "Fill her with a third pussy full of cum. She can take all of it. All of our cum."

I came again, at the same time Javey came inside me. I cried out his name as he cried out mine. He slammed into me several times, drawing out both of our orgasms until finally they faded and we slumped together, breathing heavily.

"You are all everything," Phoenix said softly. "All of you."

I was too breathless to agree apart from giving a nod or two. I was going to need another shower and I'd be late for work, but it was completely worth it. With every second and every single drop.

CHAPTER 32

Wren leaned forward, blue eyes all but bulging out of her face. "You think Aidan set you up? Why? Wait, do you think Elenna was in on it?" She sat back and shook her head. "No, she couldn't be. Could she? I suppose she could. I don't want to think that about her though."

I turned my wine glass around in my fingers and let her continue with her monologue.

Everything she said had gone through my mind multiple times already. Especially since the guys left for their away games in Canberra and Sydney.

They hadn't wanted to leave, but I'd insisted. They couldn't put their jobs on hold indefinitely, not for me. Not even for each other. They were under contract. Not to mention the fact their determination to win wouldn't let them walk away unless they were injured or tied down to my bed.

Yeah, I was tempted, but in the end I'd had to let

them go, assuring them Wren and I could take care of each other in their absence. It was only a couple of nights anyway. We'd probably gossip a lot, drink and cry over romcoms.

A standard weekend before I started seeing any of the guys.

"If she was, she didn't mean anything by it," I said. "It would have been Aidan who orchestrated this. I know he doesn't like me, but to involve the guys?"

I exhaled and shook my head. "This might be all about me. Maybe they, I don't know, got caught up in it because they're with me."

That made sense, I supposed. Aidan would do almost anything for the team, but he'd throw them all under a bus if it meant keeping Elenna safe. He wouldn't think twice or even blink. There was nothing in this world he wouldn't surrender for her.

"It might not be about you at all," Wren argued. "Someone told Kylie to say that and it might not have mattered who she said it to. Either way, she would have stirred up shit."

"Right." I couldn't argue with that logic. "I have the strangest feeling I'm going to go into work on Monday morning and she won't be there. Her desk will be empty and no one will remember anyone named Kylie having ever worked there. They'll put me in the back of a white van and ship me off to... Wherever they ship people off to when they're losing their minds."

"If that happens, then I blame aliens," Wren said.

I arched an eyebrow at her. "Aliens?"

She shrugged one shoulder and smiled. "Yeah, aliens. Things like that only happen in science-fiction. Some alien goes through and wipes everyone's memories."

"Except mine." I propped my feet on the coffee table.

"Because you're the protagonist. You're the one who's supposed to figure out that it's aliens. Before they ship you off in that white van. Or spaceship."

I choked back a laugh. "If that's the case, I'm not going to work on Monday. It might be better to stay here and wait to be abducted."

I believed in the existence of aliens, but not their involvement in this particular situation. Although, it would explain so many things.

"Good thing I'm here with you then," she said. "We can get abducted together. Maybe by a pair of hot alien brothers who have massive cocks and two tongues each. Or better yet, two cocks and a huge tongue." She grinned.

"I didn't think there was such a thing as reading too much, but I'm starting to wonder about that," I teased. "Especially if you're thinking of running off with some big purple alien."

"Who said he's purple?" Her eyes shone. "He might be blue."

"You might be out of your mind." How had we gone from talking about Aidan to talking about blue aliens? I knew which topic of conversation I preferred, but one was slightly more realistic than the other. Which was unfortunate, because two cocks and a big tongue sounded pretty good to me.

"I might be, but in the best way," she said. "It took your mind off things for a while, didn't it?"

I sighed. It had, but now it all came rushing back. "Do you think we should speak to her? I don't want to talk about Elenna behind her back." Even if she was doing the same to us. I didn't believe she was, not really, but this whole situation was twisting my brain inside out. Okay, more so than usual.

"Let's call her and invite her to lunch tomorrow," Wren suggested. "We can talk about everything over a nice meal."

"That's a good idea." I nodded.

"I have those once in a while," she said. "Don't tell anyone, they'll start to expect things of me."

"We already expect things of you," I said. "Because we know how amazing you are."

She sat back and rested her elbow on the arm of the couch. "Are you sure you're not the alien?" A slow smile crept onto her face.

She ducked to the side, but I managed to lean over and sock her on the arm.

"I'm not an alien and you are amazing," I said. "One of these days, you're going to see it too. You should already though. I've never seen anyone make jewellery as pretty as yours. You have a natural talent for design.

If I even tried, it would look like... I don't know. Terrible."

"Only because you'd try to make a pendant shaped like a dick and balls," she said.

I laughed. "I wouldn't even know where to begin to do something like that." I hesitated for a moment. "Are you projecting, by any chance? You're really the one who wants to make a pendant like that?"

"Don't knock it, they'd sell like crazy," she said. "I'd do it, but my father would lose his mind if he saw them. He can be such an old fuddy-duddy sometimes."

"The keywords here being 'if he saw them,'" I said. Not to enable her or anything.

"You said it yourself, they'd sell like crazy. You could make a ton of money from them and set up your own business. You could call it—" I held up a hand in front of me. "Wren's Junk." I frowned. "No, that makes it sound like it's rubbish."

I lowered my hand and went on thinking for a few moments.

"I know, Dangly Dicks." I bit back a giggle.

She didn't bother to hold back her laugh. "Beautiful Balls. But then, if I did those, I'd have to do pussies as well."

"The Gilded Genital." I pressed my fingertips to my lips and chuckled.

She tipped her head back and laughed. "That sounds like a gentleman's club."

I snorted. "Scratch that then. Seriously though, you

should think about it. It wouldn't hurt to make a bit of extra money, right? I'd buy one. I'd happily wear a cock right beside my heart."

She laughed even harder. "When you put it that way, I might have to. I could make ones with little piercings in them. Maybe engraved ones with things like, 'You're only allowed to touch mine,' on it."

"I'll take three," I said. What could be better than three dangly dicks next to my heart when the guys weren't around? They could each have a pussy charm to wear to their games.

"You can be my first guinea pig… I mean client," she said with a grin.

"You better make them extra-large then," I said. As if the guys didn't have big enough egos as it was.

"Three extra-large cocks coming up," she said lightly. "Pun totally intended."

I raised my glass and she clinked hers against it. "I can't wait. I'm sure they'll be gorgeous." They were dicks after all.

"You know what else would be fun?" she said thoughtfully after taking a couple of sips of wine. "Pendants of a hand with the middle finger sticking up." She demonstrated by flipping me off.

"I'd like one of those for every time I have to talk to Aidan." I looked at her speculatively. "Let me guess, you want one for every time you have to talk to Bray?"

She groaned. "You know me too well. But then, he'd

have a giant rubber hand made, for when he has to talk to me. He's such a prick."

"I'm sorry," I laughed. "A giant rubber hand like that would be pretty funny. I have a feeling all of the guys would want one of those."

"Please don't tell him that." She shook her head. "He'd do it. Especially if he knew I thought it was a bad idea. He likes nothing better than to get under my skin."

"Are you sure it's your skin he wants to get under?" I teased.

She stuck out her tongue and made a face. "Probably not, but I'm telling you, it's not going to happen." She exhaled out her nose. "Right now, I'm having enough trouble with Tiger. I don't need any with Bray. Or even Lex."

"Lex?" I looked at her in surprise. "I didn't realise you were seeing him."

I saw them talking to each other in Hazards, but at the time, it just seemed friendly.

Admittedly, my attention was on my guys, rather than on who she was chatting to as we played pool. I made a mental note to pay more attention. I wouldn't be much of a friend if I was clueless.

"We've been texting a lot," she admitted. "Just friendly stuff mostly. GIFs and funny memes. But lately they're getting more and more intense."

"Intense how?" I asked. "Is he sending you dick pics?" I didn't know the coach well, but he didn't seem like the sort of guy to send unsolicited *anything*, much less pictures of his cock.

She shook her head vehemently. "Nothing like that. He's told me stuff about his childhood and I've told him stuff about mine. Then we share a couple of penguin GIFs and laughing face emojis and... That's about it. I have a feeling he's going to ask me out at some point."

"Where does Tiger fit into all of this?" I asked.

Her love life sounded even more complicated than mine. The situation was difficult at times, but we were starting to figure out where we stood with each other. We still had a long way to go, but I was certain we all wanted to try. That was at least half the battle, wasn't it?

"I have no idea," she said, her voice slightly higher than usual. "We've met for drinks a couple of times and sometimes he seems really into me and sometimes he's really distant. I have no idea what he's thinking or feeling. Usually I'm good at figuring people out, but in his case I'm absolutely hopeless. I think he wants more than to get into my pants, because he hasn't even tried to yet. I keep giving him hints and inviting him in for coffee, but he always makes excuses and takes off. He's so hot and cold I don't know if I'm coming or going."

"It sounds like you'd be coming more often with Lex," I said. "Pun intended this time too."

"Why do men have to be so complicated?" she asked.

"Because vibrators can't talk?" I suggested.

She laughed. "Yet. Give them time."

"Let's put on a movie," I suggested. "Romcom or action? Or would you prefer some science-fiction? There must be something with hot aliens in it."

"I could do with an action movie right about now," she said.

I put my wine on the table in front of me and stood just as the lights went out, plunging us into darkness.

"Shit." I bumped into the coffee table. "Ouch."

My wineglass fell and hit the floor. Glass tinkled, wine splashed down my jeans and probably everywhere else too.

Fuck.

"Fuck. This is a great time for the power to go out." I felt around on the table for my phone.

"Don't turn it on," Wren said urgently. "The lights are still on across the street."

I peered out between the blinds.

She was right. The streetlights were still on too.

"Any chance you didn't pay your electricity bill?" she asked.

"No chance," I said. "It's set on automatic and sends a text message whenever it gets processed. The last one came three or four days ago." I tucked my phone into my pocket.

"Not a coincidence then." She stood slowly and grabbed my hand.

"Probably not," I agreed. "Stay close."

"That was the— What was that?" Her hand gripped mine so tight it hurt.

I didn't say a word or move a muscle.

Someone was at the back door.

The knob rattled, followed by a click. They weren't making any attempt to hide their presence. They could have broken the door down, but they didn't. They wanted us to sweat. They were playing with us.

I opened my mouth to suggest we try to sneak out the front door.

It also rattled.

Shit.

"Come on," I whispered.

I tugged Wren towards my bedroom, on the other side of the house. We trotted in as the back door squeaked open. Now would have been a really good time for Javey to be outside watching, but that was the point.

They'd waited until the guys were away to make a move.

I pulled Wren over to the window and gritted my teeth as I undid the latch. It probably wasn't audible outside the room, but it sounded loud as fuck to me.

I slid the window open as far as it would go and placed my palm on the fly screen. I pushed it up and grabbed on tight, trying to keep it from dropping onto the ground outside the window. I managed to hold onto it and lower it down silently.

"You first," I whispered. I stepped back and shoved her towards the now open window.

She didn't argue or hesitate. She swung one leg over the sill and held on with her hands. She transferred her weight to her other foot and swung her other leg over.

"Get out of here." I gripped the side of the window. If they came while I was climbing out, they'd catch us both.

"Not without you," she whispered back. "Come on."

I swung my leg over just as a blaze of light moved into my bedroom doorway.

That was followed by the cocking of a gun.

"Stop right there," a cold, male voice said.

I didn't look outside. I hoped like hell Wren ducked down in time to avoid being seen.

"Hey," I said lightly. It didn't hurt to try to be friendly when someone had a gun pointed at you. Whatever it took to appear harmless.

"Step back inside," he ordered.

I did as he said. I stood with my hands raised to either side so he could see I wasn't armed. I was pissed off at someone coming into my home like this, but I wasn't dead yet, so that was a bonus.

"Out this way," he barked. He turned his phone towards the doorway, the light indicating the front of the house.

Keeping my arms raised, I stepped towards and

then around him carefully. There was a difference between wanting someone alive and leaving them unharmed. I was all too aware of that fact.

"Out the front door," he said.

A couple of other figures dressed entirely in black, stood just outside. And one in jeans and an emerald green hoodie. Wren.

Fuck. I thought… hoped she got away.

Under other circumstances, I might have made a smartass comment, saying if they wanted me outside, they could have waited until I climbed the rest of the way out. I had a feeling something like that would go down like a balloon with a brick inside it.

No, it would be best to keep my mouth shut. The less pissed off the people carrying guns were, the more likely I was to make it out of here alive.

"This way," another one of them ordered.

If this was a romance novel, they'd put us in the back of a car, possibly a limousine, drive us to the airport and put us on a private jet to go to Sydney to see the guys.

Since this was real life, they shoved us into the back of a black van, one of the gunmen watching over us. They slammed the door and climbed into the front.

"Well, this sucks," Wren said. She sat down against the side of the van and tucked her knees in against herself.

"You should have run when I told you to," I said.

She shook her head. "It wouldn't have made any difference. They were waiting."

I settled back and rubbed my fingertips over my temples. I shouldn't have asked her to come over to my house. She should be safely in her townhouse.

I turned to the gunman. He pulled the mask off his face and sat with his eyes narrowed, gun trained on us.

He looked younger than me, but with that air that this wasn't his first time doing things like this. I didn't recognise him. He was nothing more than a hired gun. He probably didn't know anything, but I decided to try anyway.

"What is this about?" I asked.

"Quiet," he snapped.

"In other words, you don't know." I leaned my head back and closed my eyes. "That makes three of us. I hope they're paying you well for this."

What was I saying? Of course they were. Men like this didn't abduct women for shits and giggles. Not in my experience anyway. And not if they didn't want a whole bunch of angry hockey players coming down on them like a bunch of brick filled balloons.

The guys were going to be ticked when they found out, to say the least. Blood was going to be spilt.

I considered my options and the chance of us overpowering one guy and getting out of the van. The first part would probably get one of us killed. The second part would be more difficult for whoever was still alive.

I ruled out trying, for now.

What would the guys do? I considered, then decided they'd do exactly this. Bide their time and wait. Right now, that was our best chance of walking away from this in one piece. I doubted this was about Wren or me. We were a means to an end. Bait.

That didn't mean they wouldn't kill us, but they probably wouldn't kill us *yet*. Not until we'd fulfilled our purpose.

We sat in silence for twenty or thirty minutes before the van pulled to a stop.

The front doors opened and slammed shut before the other two of our abductors walked around and opened the back of the van.

They'd both taken off their masks as well, revealing faces only slightly older than the guy that travelled in the back with us. Like him, I didn't recognise either of them. They worked for whoever paid them the most, that was all. It was unlikely they cared whether we lived or died, unless our deaths meant they didn't get paid. Then they'd work really hard to make sure we didn't die.

What do you know, we had something in common.

"Out." Gun still trained on us, the guy inside the van indicated for us to climb out before him.

I followed Wren out and found myself outside the front of an old motel. Judging by the darkness of the reception area and sign on the street, it was closed, possibly abandoned.

"This way." One of them jerked his head towards an old door. The worn number twenty-six on the front was barely visible.

"Otis, you first." He nodded towards the youngest of them.

Otis nodded. He turned the door knob, pushed the door inward and stepped inside.

"Roach, stay behind me," the same guy said. He must be their leader.

Roach nodded and waved to his gun for us to hurry up and follow Otis.

I glanced at Wren, but stepped inside.

What choice did we have? Alive didn't necessarily mean with functioning legs. Or hands for that matter. Since I was attached to both, I stepped over the threshold and moved to stand against a grubby wall near the window.

Wren hurried to stand beside me.

"You gonna call them, Gus?" Roach asked, keeping his voice low but loud enough for me to hear.

"Yeah, keep an eye on these two. If they try anything, aim for their feet." Gus grinned at us as if he'd said something hilarious, then stepped back outside and closed the door behind him.

I exchanged glances with Wren, knowing she was thinking the same thing I was. He probably had a tiny cock. Guys like him liked to overcompensate in all sorts of ways.

We both bit back smiles; we were also attached to our feet.

"You might as well sit," Roach said, nodding towards the only bed in the room. The covers didn't look like they'd been changed since nineteen eighty-five.

"I think I'll sit over here." I lowered myself to the carpet which was just as disgusting. I had a feeling Roach wasn't the only cockroach in the building. The place should have been torn down, or blown up, years ago.

"Me too." Wren lowered herself down beside me. "This place is delightful."

"It's no five-star resort, that's for sure," I muttered back.

"No stars sounds more accurate," she agreed. "This place should come with a health warning."

"It probably does." Hired guns didn't always follow health warnings or do what was best for people they abducted from their own homes. I had a sneaking suspicion it wasn't high on their list of priorities.

"This was not how I expected the night to end." She sighed and sagged against the wall.

"Really?" I looked at her with one eyebrow raised. "This is a pretty standard Saturday night for me. A few drinks, a random abduction. Ending up in a shit hole around about dawn."

Wasn't this every girl's dream date? Yeah, maybe in one of those romance novels, but not in real life. The reality was that this sucked shit.

"Later on, you and I are going to have a talk about better ways to have fun," she told me. "Because if this is your idea of a good time, you clearly need some educating." She smiled.

"I'll be more than happy to have that conversation with you," I said. Just about anything would be better than this. I'd rather have a long, drawn out conversation with Aidan. No, really, I'd much prefer that to this.

I fell quiet, listening to Gus speaking outside. He wasn't trying to keep his voice down and the paper thin walls meant I could hear almost every word.

"Yeah, we've got her and a friend of hers," he said. "I figured, two for the price of one. If one doesn't do the trick, the other will." He was quiet for a moment, listening to whoever was on the other end. "I don't know, some redhead. If you don't need her, me and the guys can— Okay, okay. We'll leave them whole, for now. I'll hear from you in a couple of days then. Yep. Later."

CHAPTER 34

COAST

The second game in Sydney was a tough one. We won, but only by one goal.

As usual, Aidan was wound up tighter than a flea's asshole afterward. We got the standard, 'yes you won, but if you played better, you could have won by a handful more goals.'

We gave away a couple of easy opportunities we shouldn't have, but I spent half the game being bounced off the fucking boards and being on the defensive and not the offensive.

We were on the back foot right up until the third period. That was when I drove the puck to Tiger, managing to slide it between two of the opposition players. He drove it all the way back behind the goal and slid it back to me. Before they knew what hit them, I passed it to Javey, who passed it back to me, and I slammed it into the goal, missing the goalie's glove by half a hair.

It's shots like that, tight games, that I lived for. A walkover is too fucking boring. And frustrating if it doesn't go our way.

I was exhausted but all I wanted to do was get back to Sinclair. I messaged her a bunch of times, but she'd only responded in GIFs and the occasional emoji.

I figured she was too busy to reply properly. Unless she was still pissed at me for knowing what Aidan was doing and not telling her sooner. I'd make it up to her. There was no way I was going to let her be mad at me for long.

She was mine, she'd forgive me.

I followed the other guys off the plane, across the tarmac and slumped down in a seat on the bus. That would drive us back to the arena in time for the team meeting before we went home. Or in this case, Sinclair's place.

I'd have to figure out a way to get my place ready faster for her to move in there. Or find somewhere for all four of us. This situation was getting more and more permanent by the day.

"Hey." Phoenix flopped down in the seat beside me. "If you keep thinking that hard, you're gonna end up uglier than you already are." He grinned.

I flipped him off. "If that was the case, you'd be smokin' hot." Which he was, but I was still trying to get my head around any potential relationship between me and Sinclair, much less me and him. Knowing she was mine was easy.

Thinking of him that way wasn't as simple. We'd been friends for so long I couldn't just flip that switch. Could I?

"Unlike you, I can be smoking hot and a deep thinker at the same time." He sat back and laced his fingers behind his head. "It takes a special kind of talent."

I snorted. "If you say so."

"You're special all right." Tiger turned around in the seat in front of us and scowled at Phoenix. "A special kind of dumbass."

"Fuck off," Phoenix said. "You can talk about being a dumbass."

"Yeah I can, because I know one when I see one," Tiger sneered.

I sat forward. "What exactly is your problem, Pennington? You need to get laid? You should try, it might lighten you the fuck up."

"You offering?" Phoenix asked.

I sat back against the seat with a thud and crossed my arms. "Not him." He was a talented hockey player, but he had a bigger stick up his ass then Aidan.

Phoenix gave me a look like he wished I'd make that offer to him, but then looked away.

I caught movement in the corner of my eye and looked up to see Elenna making her way through the bus. She sat down next to Tiger and asked him something.

I sat up straight. "What did you say?" I asked.

Tiger glanced back like he was going to say it's none of my business.

Elenna put a hand on his shoulder and said, "I was asking if he's heard from Wren. Have you heard from her or Sinclair?"

I frowned. "Yeah, but she hasn't been chatty."

"Not with me either," Phoenix said. "I figured…"

"Wren has only responded once or twice," Tiger admitted grudgingly.

We all looked across the aisle to Javey, who clearly caught the end of the conversation.

"Only a little and she has no reason to be pissed at me." He wasn't bragging, just stating a fact as he saw it.

"There is that whole stalking thing," I said. "But if both of them have gone quiet, what does that mean?"

Elenna shook her head. "I'm worried." She looked up at her guys, who'd all followed her down the bus and stood beside her now.

Aidan closed his eyes for a moment and looked pained. When he opened them again, he nodded. "I'll tell the driver there's a change of plans."

"Well, this just got interesting," Finley said as though that was a good thing.

Orion contradicted him with a glare, but Finley didn't bat an eyelid.

"I've had enough of fucking interesting," Tiger

growled. He made no move to stop Aidan as he made his way to the front of the bus and spoke to the driver.

"We all have," I said. I hated to agree with Tiger, but he was right in this case.

Chances were, there was nothing to worry about. Sinclair and Wren probably got drunk and passed out on the couch in front of the movie.

For two days.

That was how long had passed since Sinclair's last real reply. I should have figured out sooner that something was wrong.

If anything happened to her, and I hadn't flown back to do something…

Fuck, I shouldn't have gone in the first place. To hell with my contract. She was more important to me than hockey.

More important to Phoenix and Javey too. They both looked like they were ready to rip off arms and shove them down throats. I was right there with them.

All I could do was hold my breath and wait while the bus drove through the streets of Dusk Bay, towards Sinclair's house.

"It's empty," I growled. I wanted to kick someone or something. I could do nothing but curl my hands into fists and hold them at my sides.

One window was wide open, the screen popped out.

The front door was closed, but the back stood open. There were no signs of a struggle, no blood. The splashes of red on the coffee table were wine.

The TV was on, the screen indicating the end of some movie. Fast and Furious sixty-nine, or something.

Unless it had something to do with the Kraken, then it wasn't my kind of thing. I preferred action movies, or ones about sport.

Although, if Sinclair asked me to watch it with her, I would. But I'd spend the time watching her watch the movie. Yeah, maybe Javey was onto something. Watching her was an underrated pastime.

"There's no specific indication of who took them," Aidan said. "No ransom note. We can make a few assumptions though."

"Fuck assumptions," Tiger snapped. "I'm ready to rip some fucking heads off."

"Get in line," I told him. "I want to start with some balls and work my way up." I could start with Sawyer and Nicholas and go from there.

"Ripping off heads and balls won't help them," Aidan said. "There's no trophies for guessing what they want." He looked directly at me.

"Done," I said with a shrug. "Ring them up and ask them where they want me." The only thing that mattered now was getting Sinclair away from them.

"It won't only be you they want," Aidan said.

"No," Elenna told him. "I'm not doing this again.

You're not handing yourself or anyone else over to them."

"We still don't know if Sawyer is working with Nicholas and Celine," Finley pointed out.

"This has Sawyer written all over it," Phoenix said. "Nicholas and Celine would have approached us directly. Sawyer prefers more underhanded methods. He thinks it gives him an upper hand that being civilised doesn't. He's as much of an asshole as his mother was."

I nodded. "Phoenix is right. Nicholas likes to think he's some kind of gentleman businessman, or some shit. Sawyer is the one who is as subtle as a pile of cow crap on a rock."

"Then we know what to do," Javey said.

All eyes turned to Aidan.

We could have gone off and done whatever we wanted to, but he was good at coordinating and leading the rest of us. If I tried, Tiger would question me and vice versa. Both of us would listen to Aidan and do what he told us to.

After a solid minute, Aidan nodded. "Fine. We're going to need weapons and a plan. We can't just jump on the ice and hope like hell to win." He turned to Elenna. "You're going home. Finley, go with her. I'm not taking her into this." His tone gave no room for argument.

She looked like she might try anyway, but when

Finley took her hand, she kissed Aidan, then Orion before letting him lead her away.

I managed to catch Aidan's eye and jerked my head to the side. "A word."

He nodded and followed me a few steps away.

"What about Tank and BJ?" I kept my voice low. Having them here was bad enough if we couldn't turn our backs on them. Taking them into the lions' den might be a bad idea.

He looked irritated on top of conflicted. "We have to act quickly. Chances are they know we've arrived back in Dusk Bay. They probably have someone watching this place. They already know we're coming, we just have to keep an eye on both of them and get to them before they try anything with us."

I nodded. "They'll be toast if they do." I'd make sure of that. Both of them would regret being born if they pulled anything.

He clapped me on the shoulder. "Yes they will. Come on, let's go and deal with some assholes." He actually seemed to be looking forward to this. Apparently it wasn't just Finley with a masochistic streak. Or me, to be honest.

If this didn't involve Sinclair in any way, I'd enjoy every moment of it. Killing people was almost as much fun as playing hockey. But slightly less violent. Depending on the circumstances.

I followed him back to the bus and flopped back into

my seat. Phoenix was right beside me, Javey and Tiger in front.

"We'll find her," Phoenix said. "Both of them," he added when Tiger glared at him.

"We fucking better." It was Bray who sat in the seat on the other side of the aisle. "My stepsister is a major pain in the ass, but my mother and stepfather will never let me live it down if anything happens to her." He looked like the last thing he wanted to do was help Wren, but apparently his fear of his family's disapproval was stronger than his dislike of her.

Whatever. I didn't give a shit what motivated any of the guys. As long as they did what they were told and we got my woman free.

If any prick lay a hand on her, I was going to kill them the most, but also the slowest. I might ask Ice to help me make it even more painful. They'd regret the day their great-grandparents were born.

CHAPTER 35

JAVEY

None of us gave a shit whether we agreed on anything in the past or not. Coast and Phoenix were as pissed off as I was, determined to get Sinclair back.

We all fumed quietly on the way to the warehouse, where we secured weapons before getting back onto the bus.

Aidan looked like he might suggest some people sit out, but he didn't and no one would have accepted anyway.

I appointed myself to keep an eye on Tank and BJ, both of who seemed just as excited as the rest of them. *Them*, not me. Excitement wasn't uppermost in my mind.

Cold fury, vengeance and focus, along with a sliver of fear that Sinclair was already dead.

I didn't let that sliver in too far. I couldn't afford to.

That would mess with my focus and replace it with despair.

If she was gone…

I gripped the gun in my hand a little tighter. Shoved away the thought and let the words Aidan was speaking filter into my brain.

"They may be expecting us," he said as he paced up and down the aisle of the bus. "I'm banking on them not realising we'll be so quick. Whatever their endgame, they won't get past us."

"Fuck no they won't," Coast agreed.

"Just let them try," Tiger grunted.

"They won't even *get* to try," Phoenix said.

"They should be kissing their asses goodbye as we speak," Bray called out.

Aidan nodded. "Yes, they should. We'll be stopping a block away and walking from there. We need to be subtle."

Yeah, a bus with 'Dusk Bay Demons' written down the side would be anything but subtle.

Personally, I would have kept us on here and driven straight through the front of the building. If there wasn't a chance we'd kill Sinclair too, I'd suggest it.

Not that Aidan would agree to it. Using the bus for this was one thing, damaging Demons property was another.

The bus drew to a stop by the side of the road. Aidan gestured for us to follow him off.

Gravel crunched under my shoes until I moved over

to the grass. I stood in the shadows near a tree and waited, watched as the bus pulled away.

"You good?" Phoenix asked gruffly as he came to stand near me.

"I will be," I said. "Once we take out these assholes, everything will be peachy."

"Who uses words like peachy?" Coast teased, but his tone and expression were tense.

I shrugged. "Usually not me." I didn't want to admit the pressure was getting to me. "You got a problem with that?"

He grinned. "Nah, brah. No problem at all." He patted my shoulder. He made to step back, but then gave me a quick bro hug, then gave one to Phoenix.

The one they shared lasted a little longer than might have strictly been necessary. It was about time Coast realised there was something between them.

"Okay." Aidan held a gun loosely in his hand.

Orion stood with him, his usual unreadable expression on his face.

"You know what to do. Stay close and don't do anything stupid." Aidan's gaze slid to Coast, before taking in the rest of us. He even lingered on me for a moment or two before moving on.

We moved as quietly and carefully as over twenty guys could. I stayed close to Phoenix, but kept part of my attention on Aidan and the rest on Tank and BJ. If they were going to pull something, it would happen soon. Not yet. Not while they were outnumbered. But soon.

We moved down the quiet road.

It was dark, apart from a flicker of lights up ahead. Every so often, I glanced back over my shoulder.

The further we went, the higher we climbed, revealing the lights of Dusk Bay spread out behind us. I would have preferred to share the view with Sinclair and have a picnic.

I made a note to do that once we got her back. Maybe the other two guys could join us. I'd figured the details out later.

We approached a large house set back from the road. Not one of the cliffside mansions, but big enough.

It was surrounded by a tall fence, but the gate was currently ajar. A glance at Aidan confirmed that was his doing. He had someone on the inside. Someone with enough guts to leave the gate open, but who still wanted to keep their presence a secret and was nowhere to be seen.

Or they snuck out through the gate and were long gone.

Either way, we slipped through the gate and back into the shadows, moving as quickly as we could. If anyone glanced out a window, they wouldn't miss seeing a bunch of us filing through.

None of us would rule out the possibility they were lying in wait and this was a trap.

"Here's where Reuben sending us help would have actually helped," Orion whispered to Aidan.

Aidan glanced at him and grunted in response. Apparently that was a sore point for them.

I can't say I was too surprised Reuben *hadn't* sent help. If this went badly, he and Caleb could say they knew absolutely nothing about it. If it went well, they'd happily claim credit.

Sometimes I wondered why any of us were loyal to either of them. Then I remembered they'd probably have us killed if we weren't. Threats of death were usually effective motivation.

"We've got this," Coast whispered. "We don't need help."

His confidence buoyed my nerves. That and Phoenix gripping my hand and giving it a quick squeeze before he let it go. Getting to know the goalie was one of the biggest surprises in all of this. Like me, there was a lot more to him than he let on.

"Just as well, because we ain't getting any," Tiger said. "Let's do this."

In spite of the cold, sweat trickled down my forehead. Pure nerves. When the adrenaline kicked in, those would dissipate. For now, I had to shut them away and stop them from getting the better of me.

'I love you too.'

Sinclair's words echoed around and around in my head. And the way she smiled. The way she smelled.

The way she sounded when she came. The taste of her lips.

I needed to feel her body under my hands. On my tongue. I wanted her curled around me. I needed her more than I needed to breathe.

If I died here tonight, it would be worth it as long as she was safe. But I'd do whatever I could to make sure that didn't happen. I wasn't going to miss out on the rest of our lives together. I wanted to spend at least the next seventy or eighty years reminding her how special she was. She was my forever.

"We're going around the back," Aidan whispered.

Any other time, someone would have made a smartass comment in response. Tonight, we simply followed, keeping to the shadows as we moved around the large house. We stepped away from the lights and into the deepening darkness.

Our feet barely made a sound on the neatly mowed grass. Little more than the occasional swish, apart from the crack of a twig here or there. The shuffle of leaves. Animals running from us and hiding.

Yeah, I'd run and hide from us too.

"Anyone else have a bad feeling about this?" Phoenix whispered.

"Nope," Coast whispered back. "I don't have time for bad feelings. Let's get this done."

Phoenix muttered something unintelligible under his breath, but didn't slow.

"We've got you," I said as close to his ear as I could without stopping. "We'll get her out of there together."

I sensed his surprise and nod of agreement. "Yeah, we will. Then we're going to have a nice long talk and get drunk."

"Sounds like a plan." I inched closer to the forms I knew to be Tank and BJ.

Tension seemed to ooze off them more than it was of the rest of us. Either they were up to something, or they realised they were being closely watched.

Whatever it was, they knew there was risk to them. That might make them desperate and desperate people make mistakes.

That realisation put me even further on edge. Mistakes and guns usually didn't end well.

If it wasn't for the need to be quiet, I'd consider dispensing with them right now to make sure a mistake didn't happen in my direction. Or in the direction of Phoenix and Coast. Especially not in the direction of Sinclair or Wren.

I had to remind myself it wasn't just my woman whose life was at stake here. Wren was important to Sinclair, which made her important to me. They were both the priority.

"We've got you too," Phoenix whispered.

"Yeah, we do," Coast agreed. "Whatever happens, we're brothers now."

Later, his words would sink in better, but right now they floated on the surface of my mind, making me feel a part of something in a way I hadn't in a long time. Like somehow I was even more of a Demon than I was before. Less of an outsider and more...

Connected. An insider rather than an outsider watching from the stands. Later I'd tell him how gratifying it was to hear that, but it might make his ego even bigger. If there was room for growth. Knowing him, he'd find a way.

"Quiet," Aidan hissed.

We were close enough to the house that they might hear our whispers. Even over the sound inside. Some kind of sporting event on a big screen. It didn't sound like hockey. Probably some kind of football. My guess would be rugby union. Something involving tackling, judging by the commentary.

A couple of voices inside the house jeered. Apparently they didn't like the umpire's ruling, or the commentator's commentary. Standard couch jockey stuff by the sound of it. We were all guilty of it from time to time.

I tried to remember if the Dusk Bay Smashers were playing tonight, but I couldn't. Keeping up with our roster of games was hard enough, without keeping up with theirs. I tried to catch a game whenever I could.

Before I played hockey, I played rugby. Now I preferred to watch, but I knew a few of the guys on the team. I saw them around places like Hazards often enough, as surrounded by jersey chasers as we were.

We reached a smaller back door. The kind that led

into a laundry, rather than the wide one that led to the pool area. That was a bit further on.

I glanced over, but it was covered by a heavy curtain. Only slivers of light escaped here and there. I bet it was a lot warmer inside than it was out here.

I barely finished that thought, when a couple of drops of something landed on my face. I thought it was raining until I saw a sprinkling of white drifting past and melting on the ground.

Just what we needed, snow. From the look of it, it wasn't going to be heavy, but it was going to make us colder. Was Sinclair warm? She better be. If they weren't keeping her comfortable, they'd have her three guys to answer to.

I'd happily keep *them* warm by setting them on fire. It wasn't something I'd ever done before, but, you know what they say, there's a first time for everything. Especially when it came to my woman. Nothing was off the table or off-limits. Nothing.

Aidan pulled something out of his pocket and inserted it into the lock. Of course the head coach of a professional ice hockey team knew how to pick a lock. Our coach anyway. The rest were probably normal. Maybe.

The lock clicked and he pushed the door inward.

One by one, we followed him inside.

CHAPTER 36

"How long has it been?" I whispered.

Wren glanced at her watch. "Too long."

"That's very unspecific, but at the same time accurate," I said with a sigh.

My ass was sore from sitting on the thin carpet. There was nothing under that but a concrete slab, cold and hard, like the expressions of the men who guarded us.

They sat side by side on the bed, guns still pointed at us. I waited for a moment when they looked bored or distracted, but it didn't come. However much they were paid, it was enough to keep their attention. Luckily for them, they kept their hands to themselves.

So far.

"Any chance of a cup of coffee?" I asked Roach.

He twitched. Apparently he'd like a dose of caffeine too.

"Quiet," Otis snapped. "You'll get coffee and food when we're told to give you coffee and food."

Their leader, Gus, stepped out a few hours ago, giving them orders to stay put and not move until they heard from him. Whether or not he meant it literally, they were taking it that way.

They must both be as hungry as I was. Not that I gave a fuck about them, just me and Wren. Although, it might be to our advantage to pretend for a while.

"I don't suppose there's food in the minibar?" I nodded towards it. "I'd share a chocolate bar with you if there was one." I carefully avoided mentioning packets of nuts. Giving them ideas might be a bad idea right now. The last thing I wanted in my mouth was either of their nuts.

"If there's food in there, it's probably been there for a decade," Wren pointed out.

"I'm hungry enough that I almost don't care," I replied. "What's the worst that could happen? Death by chocolate?"

"I was thinking more along the lines of vomiting and diarrhoea," she said. "This isn't exactly the place for it."

"Quiet," Otis snapped again. "I won't say it a third time."

I've always thought that was a strange expression. If he wasn't going to say it again, then there was no risk in us talking our heads off, was there? We already knew they wouldn't kill us unless Gus told them to. While he wasn't here, we could chat about anything and everything. Whether or not we talked wouldn't matter if he gave the order to dispense with us.

In spite of that, it might be better not to antagonise Otis or Roach, just in case.

I leaned my head against the wall and closed my eyes. All I wanted right now was to be in my own bed curled up in clean comfort, surrounded by my three guys.

My three guys. That was surreal. I'd joked about it when Elenna got together with hers, but never seriously thought it would happen to me. Not at all and especially not with three guys who were so different. So complicated. I wouldn't change any of them for anything. They kept life interesting, fun and sexy as hell. I was a lucky girl. When this was over, I was going to tell them that as many times as it took for them to believe me.

I wished they were here. No, I wished I was wherever they were right now. They'd hate every moment of this. One of them would have tried something by now. Something that might have gotten them killed.

Where were they right now anyway? Did they have any idea we'd been taken? They would have returned to Dusk Bay by now. They had a late afternoon meeting before they'd head home.

Coast and Phoenix might have gone to Phoenix's apartment, but Javey... He could have gone to his place or straight to mine. Was he sitting outside, watching the door our abductors closed behind them, not realising no one was there?

No, he wouldn't have sat there and waited. He would have walked up to the window and looked inside at the very least. When he saw no one there, he would have tried another and another until he found my open bedroom window. Then he would have known I was gone.

What would he do next? He'd probably let himself into the house and look around, trying to figure out what happened.

Would he at some point call the other guys and tell them? If not them, then maybe Aidan. The head coach would have told the other guys, wouldn't he? I decided he would. He might discuss it with Elenna and she'd insist.

The idea of that conversation made my breath catch in my throat. What would Elenna think when she knew we were gone? She'd be frantic, the same as I would if it happened to her. She'd want to find us. I hoped like hell she didn't do anything silly that would put herself at risk.

What was I thinking? Even if she was inclined to, Aidan, Finley and Orion wouldn't let her. Not unless she snuck off by herself without them knowing.

I could imagine her doing something like that. For a moment, I pictured her bursting through the door with a flamethrower on her shoulder, ready to free us. She'd be dressed from head to toe in army fatigues, that black stuff smeared on her face like they did in movies.

She'd probably have a cool line like, "Burn in hell motherfuckers." Then she'd turn the flamethrower on them and incinerate them on the spot.

Why a flamethrower, I didn't know. Burning the world down for me was more my guys' thing than hers.

Yeah, at times my imagination was as active as hers. I should try writing some of this down some day. I doubted anyone would read it. Although, a flamethrower would be cool and effective. As long as Wren and I managed to stay out of the flame.

No one burst through the door. No flamethrowers appeared. No one in army fatigues. Not even someone with a security guard badge.

Nothing until the door opened quietly a couple of minutes later. It startled me out of a light doze.

My eyes snapped open. I jerked my head around to see Gus step inside. The sight of him was like a bucket of cold water straight on my head.

Not who I was hoping for. Not even close.

At this point, I'd be ecstatic if Aidan walked through the door. Anyone but Gus. Or anyone else who worked for the Fiorellis or Mancinis.

He glanced in our direction before closing the door behind him. He didn't immediately order them to kill us, nor did he do it himself. That was a good start. Wasn't it?

I decided it was. If only because I had to have something to cling onto. While we were alive, there was hope we'd make it out of this yet.

Gus was carrying a large paper bag in his arms. He set it down on the table and unrolled the top. He pulled out a burger wrapped in wax paper and tossed it to me. He threw another to Wren before keeping a third for himself and handing the bag to Roach.

I unwrapped the burger and took a bite, but only after Gus did the same with his.

It was silly. If they wanted to kill us, they didn't need to bother with poison. Admittedly, poison would be quieter than a bullet, but slower.

Regardless, I was too hungry to resist.

"No coffee?" I asked once I swallowed my first couple of mouthfuls.

"I just had one." Gus looked smug. He fished out another burger from the bag and started to open it.

How many more were in there? Right now, I could eat sixteen of them. Okay, maybe two. They weren't the biggest burgers in the world. Or the best. Of course they weren't, they weren't from Hazards. Theirs were twice as big and three times better. And didn't have beetroot on them unless you asked.

I caught the look of annoyance on Otis's face. Evidently I wasn't the only one Gus pissed off by not bringing us coffee. Good, let them be pissed off at each other. If it helped us in some way, then I could handle missing a few cups.

"Can I go and get one—" Otis started.

"No going anywhere," Gus told him. "Be glad I brought enough food for you too." He looked meaningfully towards Otis's gun, which had dropped slightly while he ate with the burger in his other hand.

Otis brought the gun back up. He didn't stop eating. He must have been starving. He was almost twice my size. A guy like him needed a lot more food than I did.

Use it on Gus, I silently suggested. *Asshole didn't bring you coffee, or tea. Surely he deserves a bullet.* Okay, maybe that was a little extreme, but firstly, we were talking about caffeine, and secondly, if they turned on each other, it wouldn't break my heart.

It seemed that Otis didn't agree, because he didn't shoot Gus. That sucked, but he didn't shoot me either, so I finished my burger and licked my fingers clean.

I admit the hamburger was more or less edible, but it would have tasted a whole lot better if I was anywhere but here.

"I suppose you're all wondering if there's any news," Gus said slowly. "The Demons won their game last night. Only just. I hear they played like shit. Of course they did, they're a team of losers."

If he thought he'd get a reaction from me, he thought wrong. I wasn't going to be drawn on the guys' playing. We all knew they were doing better this season than they had in the last few. If he wanted to provoke me, he was going to have to try harder than that.

"They arrived back in Dusk Bay a couple of hours ago. They went from the airport to the arena and then went off to their homes." He glanced tauntingly at me and Wren. "It seems like they didn't even notice they were missing anything."

He leaned forward towards us. "Or maybe they don't give a shit."

I looked back with no expression on my face. I knew better than to think the guys didn't care about me. And, in spite of her tumultuous relationship with both of them, I knew Tiger and Bray cared what happened to Wren.

"Either way, it seems you're in our company for a while longer. I hope you're comfortable down there on the floor, because you're not going anywhere anytime soon."

He leaned back.

"Were you the bully?" I asked.

He frowned at me.

"Were you the bully?" I asked again. "Or were you the one who got bullied? In school, I mean. It's one or the other. Guys like you turn out fucked up because of it."

His face turned red.

Shit. I should have kept my mouth shut.

He stepped around the bed, crouched down beside me and backhanded me across the face.

He hit so hard I was slammed back against Wren's shoulder. My cheek stung like a bitch.

"If I were you, I'd shut the fuck up," he growled. "There's a lot more where that came from and I don't mind dispensing it. There's nothing I hate more than mouthy women. Unless their mouth is around my cock."

For a few moments, I feared he'd unzip his jeans and try to make me suck him off.

Instead, he glared at me until he stood and stalked away.

"Are you okay?" Wren whispered.

All I could do was nod and press my hand to my face. I believed him when he said he'd hit me again. They needed us alive, but that wouldn't spare us from being beaten if they felt like it.

Silence fell for at least an hour after that, finally broken by the sound of Gus's phone ringing.

He pulled it out of his pocket and pressed it to his ear. "Yes, boss." While he listened, he turned to look at me and Wren.

His expression filled me with dread.

CHAPTER 37

PHOENIX

I could almost feel Javey trembling beside me. Okay, maybe that was me.

Not with fear, no way. I was shaking with rage. Carefully controlled rage, but still.

This was the opportunity I'd been waiting a long time for. My family had its share of enemies, but we deserved better than we currently had.

The DiMarcos should hold as much power as the Brantleys, not the Fiorellis. Their days were done. We'd spent enough time in the shadows. It was past time to walk out and claim what was ours.

This was a big step toward that. My brother Ric would be grateful for what we did here tonight. He fucking better be.

Although, no one was fooled that he held the power. His girlfriend Daisy Lasalle was the one people increasingly turned to. They called her Daze. She was as dangerous as they came and just as gorgeous. Not compared to Sinclair. Before I met her I would have happily wet my cock in Daze. Even if it meant pissing off my brother.

Okay, especially if it meant that. I was done standing in his shadow too. I'd show them all I was more than Ric's little brother. More than a goalie.

Tonight, I'd make my mark.

I gripped my gun carefully, keeping it in front of me as my gaze swept back and forth.

Javey and I were a few steps behind Aidan and Orion, but I wouldn't let my guard down in case they missed something. One tiny detail and we might all be fucked.

Aidan stopped suddenly, his hand raised.

I narrowly avoided walking into the back of him.

Coast stumbled into me, grabbing my arm with his spare hand to keep us both from falling.

Fuck, his touch sent a rocket of heat through me. One I struggled to contain.

He'd kept me at arm's length for so long, I shoved the feeling away out of habit. It was harder this time than it ever was before. Hard like my cock was getting.

Down boy, I told him.

Now was not the time for an erection. Not until Sinclair was safe and we'd finished what we came here to do. Then, we'd make time to clear the air, once and for all.

Figure out where all four of us stood. I knew what I

felt for Sinclair. I loved the woman the moment I first lay eyes on her. Like I did with everyone else, I used my gruff exterior to keep her away.

Between Coast bringing me along for the ride, and her natural magnetism, I was quickly done for. I was loving every minute of it. Even this part. She'd know how hard I'd fight for her. I'd risk everything. I'd die for her, if I had to.

Aidan gestured for half of us to go to the left and the other half to follow him. Several of the guys slipped down a side corridor. The rest of us followed Aidan into a huge living area.

Two people sat on a huge sectional, curled up around each other in front of a fire and a massive television screen.

To my disappointment neither of them was Sawyer. One was his younger sister Kaya. The other was a guy I didn't recognise. Both of them were focused on the rugby game on the TV.

According to the score, the Dusk Bay Smashers were leading by ten points. Good for them.

Aidan stepped up behind Kaya and cocked his gun.

She froze.

The guy with her turned around, jumped up and leapt away. "What the fucking hell?" he shouted.

"Where's Sawyer?" Aidan asked coldly.

"He's probably upstairs," Kaya replied, her tone surprisingly calm.

"Where's Sinclair?" Coast snarled.

"I don't know any Sinclair." To her credit, Kaya hadn't flinched or moved a hair. She sat perfectly still, hands to either side of her, palms pressed down on the black leather.

"I don't know any Sinclair either," the guy stammered. "I swear."

"Henry doesn't know anything," Kaya said. "Whatever my brother is up to, he hasn't said anything to either of us."

"That's right." Henry looked close to panicking. Luckily the floor was tiled, because any moment now, he was going to piss himself. "I don't know anything. I just came over to watch the game with my girlfriend." He held out his hands to either side. His eyes were wide.

"You better find a way to get Sawyer down here," Orion said. "Without shouting."

Kaya nodded. With hands also raised where we could see them, she leaned forward to pick up her phone. She reached behind her to offer it to Aidan.

"The code is one two three seven. Sawyer is in my contacts. He won't know it's not me messaging him."

Aidan took the phone and tapped on the screen. He put in the code and grunted when it actually opened.

There must not be much love lost between Sawyer and his sister, because she seemed only too happy to throw him to the wolves. Presumably she realised cooperating gave her a slight chance of making it out of this alive.

"Everyone step back," Aidan ordered. He pushed the phone into his pocket and stepped back himself. "Sit down, Henry. Relax. Our beef is not with you."

Henry swallowed, and for a moment I thought he might make a run for the door.

Instead, he sat beside Kaya, but he made no move to give her any comfort. Some boyfriend he was. He was more worried about his ass than hers.

After a minute or two, footsteps started coming down the stairs that led to the living area.

"Kaya? What's so important that you couldn't—"

"Sawyer, it's a trap!" Henry shouted. He leapt up and ran. He made it three or four steps towards the door before Coast put a bullet in the back of his head.

Kaya flinched, but otherwise didn't move. Smart girl. She might make it out of this in one piece yet.

Sawyer reached the bottom of the stairs and stared at us. He had his gun in his hand. He must have suspected something funny was up.

To be honest, if I was as big an asshole as him, I'd be armed all the time too. Someone would always be wanting to kill me.

"Nice of you to join us," Coast said. "Why don't you come and sit down with your sister?" He aimed the gun at her head.

In the corner of my eye, I saw Tank and BJ stiffen. Yeah, it figured. Of course they wouldn't want her threatened if they were working with her brother. Unless…

I looked at them both full on. They weren't angry, they were scared. For her. That made sense. Their loyalty wasn't with Sawyer, it was with Kaya.

"If Sawyer does as he's told, she doesn't need to get hurt," I said, my voice low and even.

Coast and Javey looked at me in surprise, but quickly realised who I was looking at and why.

"We don't want anything to do with him," Tank said. "Please, don't hurt her. She's not a part of any of this."

"But you are?" Javey narrowed his eyes at them.

"No, we're not," BJ said quickly. "She wanted us to keep an eye out for anything he did so we could make sure it didn't come back on her." He gave her a look that both said what he felt for her and that he'd do his best to protect her.

"So Henry was—" I looked at them questioningly.

"A decoy," Kaya said softly. "So my brother didn't suspect I was working behind his back."

"Fucking bitch," Sawyer snarled. "Are you working with Nicholas and Celine?"

She looked over at him, unflinching. "No. I'm working for myself. I want nothing to do with them or you."

"Aren't you just putting the fun back into dysfunctional?" Coast said cheerfully.

"None of this is getting Sinclair back," Javey said. He pointed his gun right at Sawyer. "Where is she?"

"Why should I tell you?" Sawyer hedged. He gave Javey a look like he was something he scraped off the bottom of his patent leather shoes. Or expensive as fuck Nikes.

"Because if you let her and her friend go, we might let you live," Aidan said. "We don't care about you either. Until this, you were a blip on our radar. You can go back to being exactly that. Or you can be as dead as Henry there. Your call."

Sawyer glanced down at the dead man and swallowed. The fact he even hesitated suggested to me he wasn't very bright.

No, there was more to it than that. His gaze flicked towards the door to the other side of the room.

I aimed my gun right at his face. "Expecting someone? Because if you are, I'd tell them to fuck off before I put a hole right between your eyes."

"If you do that, you'll never find her or her friend," he said. "If they don't hear from me, they'll kill both of them. Don't think you can fool them with a text message. They need to hear my voice."

"Then get on the fucking phone and tell them to let her go," Coast said. He smiled, but it was a dangerous, vicious look. He wouldn't hesitate to kill everyone in this room if he had to. Even me.

Aidan slipped Kaya's phone out of his pocket and handed it to Sawyer. "I suggest you be quick. The guys have had a long day and they're tired. When they get this tired, they get…" He considered his words. "Trigger-happy? Impatient? Violent?"

"All of the above," Coast said without taking his eyes off Sawyer.

Sawyer glanced at the door again before tapping on the screen of the phone and putting it to his ear. Apparently she trusted him with the pass code too. With this phone anyway. A girl like her would have a phone she used in public and a private one for personal use, like calling BJ and Tank.

"Gus, this is Sawyer. How are our pretty little packages?" He looked right at Coast when he spoke. He had some balls to taunt a man who had a gun aimed at his face. If he had a death wish, he only had to provoke us a little more. I half hoped he would. That would serve the prick right.

"Good to hear they're doing well," Sawyer replied to the person on the other end. "We have a change in plans."

For a heartbeat, I thought he was about to tell this Gus guy to kill them. He'd be dead before he finished speaking the words.

Instead, he said, "I want you to let them go." He listened for a moment. "You heard right. We don't need them anymore, let them go."

Why the fuck did he look triumphant? Even if this was a trap, he was still the one staring down the barrel of several guns.

Sawyer ended the call and handed the phone back to Aidan. "They're at the old Seahawk Motel near the beach on Collins Street."

"Coast." Aidan nodded to him.

"I'm on my way." Coast tucked the gun into his jeans.

"I'm coming with you," Tiger said. He had that expression on his face like it wasn't worth arguing with him. Nothing was keeping him from getting to Wren.

Aidan nodded and ordered a couple of the other guys to go with them, including Bray. "The rest of us will stay here until we know they're free and alive."

There was something in his eyes that put me on edge. I wanted to go with Coast, but I wasn't one of the ones he sent. Neither was Javey. Aidan never did anything without good reason. He better have a fucking good one for keeping me from Sinclair.

Coast glanced at me and gave me a nod. I gave him one back.

I thought that was it, he'd step out the door and go to her. I'd stay here and wait, and hope like hell she really was okay. At the last moment, he stepped towards me, kissed my mouth and then turned and left.

That was so unexpected I was tempted to run after him, but I had to stay firm. When all of this was over, we'd sort it out.

I exchanged glances with Javey who smiled. His expression was tense. He wanted to go with Coast as well.

"So what's—" I started to say.

The entire room was shaken as the front door was blown apart.

CHAPTER 38

"It looks like you ladies are free to go," Gus said regretfully. He tossed his phone up in the air and caught it a couple of times before shoving it back in his pocket.

I glanced at Wren, not quite believing what he said. Her eyes were wide, but she pressed her palms to the wall behind her and pushed herself to her feet.

I followed a moment later.

"Just like that?" Otis asked. "We let them walk out of here?"

"Just like that," Gus agreed. "That was the plan all along. The boss knew exactly what they'd do and they did it. They walked right into his trap. Those dickheads are nothing if not predictable."

I tried hard not to bristle and snap at him for calling any of my guys a dickhead. But he was still armed and he could easily claim he let us go and had no idea why we mysteriously disappeared.

I gripped Wren's hand and placed my other on the door knob. I held my breath and waited for one of them to stop us as I opened the door and stepped out into the cold darkness.

A light snow fell. Here and there, piles began to form. Keeping close together to share warmth, we headed out to the parking lot.

The ground was icy. We'd have to go carefully, it was slippery and treacherous.

"What now?" she whispered.

"We keep walking," I said quickly. "Get out of here as quickly as possible."

I didn't dare to look back in case we were being followed. Or worse. If they were about to shoot us in the back, I didn't want to see.

Listening for the shot out of pure instinct was bad enough. I wasn't just shivering from the cold.

We made it to Collins Street without dying or falling on our asses. Only then did I dare to look over my shoulder.

The door to the motel room was closed, but the lights of the van flared on when the engine started.

"Remember that movie where the guy in the car chased down that—" Wren started.

"Yeah, I remember." In spite of the ice under my shoes, I started to trot, keeping as close to the side of the motel as possible. My heart was racing, ready to leap right out of my chest and take off down the road at a sprint.

The engine revved.

"Shit." Wren sounded panicked.

The headlights grew bigger as the van roared up behind us.

Wren's panic was contagious. It crept up my spine and right into my brain, where it quickly spread. My thoughts became muddled, semi-coherent.

Calm down, I told myself.

The van drew closer.

"We're almost to the end of the building, we just need to—" I flinched hard as the van drew up beside us.

Laughter came from inside.

Gus.

The engine revved again before the van roared past us and sped off into the night.

"Holy fucking hell," Wren said breathlessly. "I thought…"

"Me too." I tugged her hand and headed around the corner. "We need to find somewhere warm." Preferably somewhere with coffee. Lots and lots of coffee. And a comfortable, dry bed that didn't smell like mould and urine.

"We need to tell the guys where we are," she said.

"We need to get somewhere safe first," I said.

I should have insisted Gus give us back our phones before we left. How fucking stupid was I to forget something like that? Oh, right, I was in a hurry to get out before he changed his mind.

"Shit," she said. "He was talking about them. They walked right into… Something."

I stopped mid-step. "Fuck. You're right." I felt the blood drain out of my face. Without our phones, we couldn't even warn them. We couldn't do anything. I couldn't remember ever feeling so helpless in my life.

I kept on walking. "We need to find somewhere warm with a phone," I concluded.

We might already be too late, but I couldn't let myself think like that. I wasn't giving up until I saw my guys alive and well with my own two eyes.

Until then, I'd cling to that thought. None of them were that easy to kill. Whatever they'd walked into, they'd walk out of it. They had to.

"Right." Wren nodded. "They'll be fine. They have to be."

"They will be," I said.

We walked down a street full of empty buildings, some with lights on, illuminating furniture or used cars. Others were abandoned and in various states of disrepair.

This was a far cry from the mansions of Dusk Bay, or even the city or suburbs. This was the industrial side of the city. The place where people came during the week to do business.

On the weekends it was a ghost town. The perfect place for people to keep abducted women. Before it was abandoned too, one of the buildings here was used for human trafficking. I didn't know which one and I didn't want to. That was a side of this life that I didn't want to think too much about. A side that guys like Orion were trying to stop from happening anymore.

"You don't realise how much you rely on your phone until you don't have one with you," Wren remarked. "For example, I have no idea which way to go."

"Me either, but we keep going straight ahead," I said.

We passed another block. The ocean was on our left. The beach was dusted with a light covering of snow. It would all melt in the morning, but it looked beautiful right now. Cold as fuck, but pretty.

"I'd love a hot chocolate right now," she said. "Good thing we're not travelling on an empty stomach."

"Yeah." The burger sat heavy in my belly, but it was better than nothing.

Every so often, I looked up and down the road, watching for cars. Hoping like hell not to see the van return.

If the laughter from Gus was any indication, he'd enjoy toying with us like that. For all I knew, they weren't letting us go, they were just fucking with us. Seeing what would happen when they opened the door to the cage and let us fly. The idea they might be waiting for us, to take us back into that motel room, allowed a sliver of despair into my heart.

It started as a tiny pinprick and quickly grew from there.

I shoved it away violently. I couldn't let thoughts like that win. I couldn't even let them into my brain. The only reason they were there was because I was tired. I hadn't slept in a couple of days, not really. I hadn't had more than a light doze here and there.

That much time spent with guns on us, sitting uncomfortably on the floor…

No wonder I was starting to unravel. No one could go through that and come out completely unscathed. I was going to need therapy.

"You okay?" Wren asked softly.

I hadn't realised I'd stopped until now. I glanced down at my feet, then over at her.

"No," I admitted. "I'm not okay. I'm starting to understand why Elenna has nightmares. I've killed people and it hasn't gotten to me the way being locked up in there did."

She put her arms around me and gave me a squeeze. "It's perfectly understandable. I feel the same way. It's one thing to defend yourself and people you care about, and another to sit and wait and wonder what the hell is going to happen to us. They could have killed us at any moment. Or worse. And there was nothing we could do about it. If we'd tried to attack them, we'd be dead right now. Sometimes the smart thing isn't always the easiest thing, but it can be the most stressful and terrifying thing. I wished neither of us went through that, but at least we had each other."

I squeezed her back and rested my head on her shoulder for a few moments. "I still think you should have run when you could."

"And miss hanging out with you in a dirty hotel room, eating terrible hamburgers?" she joked. "Not a chance."

"Next time, let's find a different way to bond," I suggested. "Skydiving or bungee jumping might be safer."

"I'll watch while you do both of those," she said. "I like my feet firmly on the ground."

"We should get going," I said. "It would suck to get out of there only to freeze to death." I'd love my Oodie right about now. That would keep me toasty warm while we found a place to shelter, and a phone to borrow.

"Yeah, let's not have that happen," she agreed. She started to hum *Winter Wonderland* while we walked.

I didn't have the heart to remind her that it was a Christmas song and we were in Australia. The sound cheered me up. It might be just what we needed to get through this next while.

We walked for at least ten minutes before seeing another set of headlights. They pulled into the street with the motel before I could make out what kind of vehicle it was.

It was probably a complete coincidence, but the thought it might be the van made panic rise again.

Why would they go there when they knew we weren't there? I had no answer for that, I just walked a little faster, almost dragging Wren along behind me.

"We have to be nearly *somewhere* by now," she said.

"Of course we are." I suspected that wasn't anywhere near the actual truth. We were still a long way from anywhere that was occupied, warm and had a phone. Unless we broke into one of the buildings and used theirs.

I was toying with that idea when headlights pulled out of the same street and headed towards us. They flickered and danced, bouncing off the increasing snow.

"Shit," I said under my breath. I started frantically looking for somewhere to hide. If that was the van coming back for us…

"There's a gap between those buildings," I started to say. If we moved quickly enough, we could slip in between them and potentially find a place to hide until they were gone. If we didn't freeze to death first. It was better than being—

"Wait." Wren's urgent tone made me wrench my head around and look at her. She was staring right into their headlights.

"What?" I looked too. My lips dropped apart. "Is that?"

"The Demons' bus," she finished for me. The closer it

got, the easier it was to make out the words, and the team logo on the side.

I'd never been so happy to see a bus in my entire life.

It pulled to a stop beside us, skidding slightly on the icy road. The door slid open and I almost burst into tears.

Coast ignored the steps and leapt out down to the street. He gathered me up in his arms and pulled me to him.

I leaned into him and sobbed silently. He rubbed his hand up and down my back and said soothing words in my ear that barely registered. All I knew was the feel of him and his voice. And the absolute relief that he was alive and so was I. He squeezed me harder like he couldn't quite believe this was happening either.

I was vaguely aware of Tiger doing the same to Wren.

"Thank fuck you're okay," Coast said. "I was ready to kill a bitch."

Kill? Oh shit. Where was Phoenix and Javey? They couldn't be… No, Coast would have said something if they were dead. Wouldn't he?

I pulled back. "It was a trap. They wanted all of you to walk into it, that was why they took us."

Coast smiled. "Of course it was."

CHAPTER 39

The bus came to a stop about fifty metres from Sawyer's home.

We stepped off the bus into virtual silence. The snow stopped falling, but the air was freezing as hell. Someone had fished out an oversized coat for Wren and one for me.

I was still itching for a coffee, but that wasn't important in the scheme of things. Especially not after Coast tried to call Aidan, but got no response. He'd tried Phoenix and Javey as well, with the same result.

By the time we were halfway here, he wasn't smiling anymore. He was stressed as I'd ever seen him and clearly conflicted.

If he'd stayed to help the other guys, they might all have come to find Wren and me.

But if he hadn't, we might have wandered the streets

of Dusk Bay, and fuck knows what might have happened.

I was conflicted for the same reason. If anything happened to them because he'd come to look for me... We would have found someone sooner or later. We could have been sitting in a warm room drinking coffee right now.

All of this regret was getting me nowhere. We were here. What we did now was the only thing we had any control over.

"Get back on the bus," Coast said to me. "It's warm in there and you'll be safe."

"I agree with the first part of that sentence, but not necessarily the second part," I said. "I'll be safe with you, and I can be helpful. You need someone else to have your back."

I already had a gun from the spares the guys secured before coming here the first time.

"Who knows what might happen if we're left alone in there." I jerked my head back toward the bus.

"Sinclair," he started. He closed his eyes and shook his head. "You know what, you're right. If I try to leave you in there, you're only going to follow me."

"Exactly," I said. "Wren should stay on the bus with Tiger and Bray."

"Fuck that," Tiger growled. "I'm going to kill the motherfucker who ordered that asshole to take Wren."

"Same," Bray said simply. "Unless Wren *wants* to hide out on the bus." He gave her a look like he knew exactly how to push her buttons and didn't mind doing it.

She flipped him off. "I've never hidden anywhere in my life. You must be confusing me for yourself."

He snorted derisively. "Typical Wren, you're still out of your fucking mind."

"Don't make me shoot you in the ass," she said darkly. "Let's get this done. If we wait too long, the reality might sink in and Bray will piss his pants."

"You fucking wish," he said. He stomped behind her as she started off towards the house.

Coast shook his head but trotted to catch up with them.

I followed along behind, with Tiger and the other guys sent to find us.

"Did they… Do anything to her?" he asked like he was ready to rip off arms and legs with his bare hands.

"They only deprived us of coffee," I said, as if that wasn't bad enough. "They didn't touch either of us." Except the slap. I suspected if they'd done anything worse, he would have begun tearing off arms and legs and gone from there.

"Good. I would have snapped them in half and made them suck their own cock," he said.

I managed to smile. "I actually would have liked to see that. Maybe that's something you can do when you catch up to them."

"Count on it," he said gruffly. "Assholes like that are

nothing but cowards. If they want to come after a guy, they should. Leave our fucking women alone."

"You really care about her, don't you?" I asked, my voice low.

He glanced over at me. "Don't tell anyone. They wouldn't believe you anyway. Everyone knows Tiger Pennington doesn't have a heart. It's a family thing. We come from a long line of coldhearted motherfuckers."

"I'm sure you're not that bad," I said.

He grunted. "Yes, I am. Everyone acknowledges that my older brother is an asshole, and he's the golden child of the family. Beau fucking Pennington. King of the fucking keyboard. Musical genius. Arrogant prick extraordinaire. Compared to me, he's a sweetheart."

I knew about Penn, the keyboard player for the band Wolf Venom. From what I've heard, Tiger's description of him was relatively accurate. He was as obnoxious as he was talented.

I'd always thought it was better not to believe everything I heard though, even if it was coming from his younger brother.

"You're Tiger fucking Pennington," I told him. "First line winger for the Dusk Bay fucking Demons. You have your own talent. You're good at what you do. Better than good, you're incredible."

He murmured something that could have been agreement. Clearly this was a touchy subject for him.

I had the distinct impression his parents had doted on his older brother because of his musical talent and his brother had rebelled because he was stifled. After that, they might have undervalued, or downplayed, their younger son and his abilities. It wasn't fair, but it happened.

"Besides which, a little birdie told me she likes you as much as you like her." I glanced in Wren's direction.

She hadn't so much told me as indicated by the way she talked about him. She'd clung to the idea that he would come and find her while we were in that motel room. We'd both stuck to whatever kept us from losing our minds. Giving up would have been the worst thing we could do. Both of us were too stubborn for that.

I'd never admit how close I came though. How slivers of despair crept into the corners of my mind, trying to trick me into surrendering to it. How, for a while there, I started to think we'd never walk out that door again. They'd find our bodies, another stain on the already grimy carpet.

I blinked the thoughts away. We were out of there now. Nothing and no one could make us go back there.

Tiger glanced over at me, his expression unreadable. "We should be quiet now."

The moment he finished speaking, shouting sounded from inside the house. That was followed by a gunshot, then another.

I winced and ducked down when the others did.

"No one panic," Coast said. "Chances are, that's our people dealing with the problem before we get there."

"Better leave a bitch alive for me," Tiger grumbled.

It was Bray who patted his shoulder. "I'm sure they'll bear you in mind and spare one."

"Otherwise, they can resurrect one for you to kill," Wren said.

Tiger nodded. "They fucking better."

When the house fell silent again, Coast gestured us forward. "Looks like they left the front door open for us."

In fact, there *was* no front door. Where it should have been was a gaping hole where it was blasted open.

What was it with this family and blowing up doors? First the arena, now here.

Coast led the way up the front steps and inside, still keeping low and ready.

There was something about seeing him like that made my pulse race. This might not be the best time or place to ruin my panties, but it was what it was.

A man who knew how to handle both a gun, and a situation like this, was irresistible to me and my pussy. That I was in love with him was an added bonus.

I was right beside him while we moved slowly through the house.

"This isn't the time, but I love you," I whispered.

He glanced back at me and grinned. "I love you too. When this is over, I'm going to wreck the hell out of your pussy."

I smiled back. "I'm going to let you."

He turned back as we stepped toward the kitchen and living area. Several bodies lay on the floor. A guy I didn't recognise lay in the doorway, a bullet hole in the back of his head.

A muffled shout and another gunshot came from a dark hallway off to the right.

Stepping slowly and carefully, we headed in that direction.

The hallway led to another living area, this one illuminated by a single lamp. It wasn't much, but enough that my eyes had to take a few moments to adjust.

Three cream coloured couches were arranged in a horseshoe shape. Beside each sat simple but elegant tables. Painting and framed photographs hung from the walls, but no television. This was the kind of room where people gathered to talk and not be distracted by a screen.

Apparently Sawyer was more civilised than I gave him credit for.

Coast raised a hand to stop us from stepping out of the darkness of the corridor. From here, we could see without being seen.

Several figures crouched behind a couch that was side-on to the doorway.

I let out a soft, silent breath.

Aidan. Javey, Phoenix and a few of the other guys were beside him.

Alive, thank all the fucks. And apparently completely unaware of our presence.

Sawyer and a handful of his minions were crouched behind another. Also blissfully unaware of us.

From here, I couldn't make out who was behind the third couch. The seat faced us, the back hiding all but the occasional movement. The top of a head, the muzzle of a gun.

"Well, shit," Tiger whisper-drawled.

I wasn't sure what he was specifically referring to, until I saw a young woman's body lying to the side of the room.

Celine Fiorelli. So much for not taking the direct approach. This wasn't just a trap for our guys. Apparently it was for Sawyer as well.

Nicholas and Celine must have thought they could get rid of all of us at once. Instead, they'd taken her out. I couldn't say I was sad about it.

Nicholas must have been in contact with Gus and the other assholes. When he knew the guys were here, he struck.

Was that who was behind the third couch? I had a feeling it wasn't. He sent Celine and others to do his dirty work for him.

We'd have to deal with him later.

"Hey, motherfucker." Without warning, Tiger stepped out into the open and shot Sawyer in the head. He took out a couple of Sawyer's minions before ducking down beside Aidan, out of sight of the other four.

"You're outnumbered," Aidan said. "Your boss is dead. Throw your guns down and get the fuck out of here. Last chance."

Apparently when Sawyer was gone, so was the loyalty. All four of them threw their guns over the top of the couch and onto the floor. They rose with their hands to either side of their faces.

They all braced themselves, ready to die, but Aidan jerked his head towards the doorway. "Out," he barked.

With only a tiny measure of hesitation, all four turned and ran.

"Your boss is still alive," Aidan told the last group hiding behind that last, third couch. "I don't think we can leave you alive. Unless—"

"Unless what?" A voice asked from behind the cream leather.

"Unless you take a message back to Nicholas that I'm going to kill his ass," Tiger said. "That's a threat, a promise and a guarantee."

Aidan nodded to him, apparently satisfied with the content of the message. "Throw your guns down first."

The longest pause fell before the guns were thrown over the couch to join the others on the floor.

"And the other two," Aidan said.

Another pause before the last two joined the rest. He must have counted the clatters and knew exactly how many people we were facing.

I barely registered Nicholas' minions leaving, I was caught up in an embrace with Javey, Phoenix and Coast.

"I knew you'd be all right," Phoenix said. "You're too much of a badass to let assholes like that kill you."

That was a stretch but I appreciated the sentiment. "Same with you three," I said.

I could hardly believe they were okay, alive and in one piece.

Of course they were, the Dusk Bay Demons weren't defeated that easily. Not anymore.

This might not be the time, but before we went any further, there was something I desperately needed to say.

"Phoenix." I turned to him and took his hands in mine. "I haven't had a chance to tell you. I love you."

He looked a little awkward, unaccustomed to being sentimental and talking about emotions. He cleared his throat and squared his shoulders. He didn't have to say anything back, but I could tell he wanted to. This was as important to him as it was to me.

Yeah, we could have picked a more romantic time and location. Sometimes the words need to be said when they need to be said. That was better than never saying them at all.

"I love you too." He kissed my mouth before Coast shoved him aside to do the same. He in turn was shoved by Javey so he could kiss me too.

"Can we get out of here?" I said finally. I needed a hot shower and a hot coffee and to clean the smell of blood and dirt out of my nose and mind. And I needed sleep and a lot of orgasms. Not necessarily in that order.

"Of course we can." Coast took my hand.

We stepped toward the doorway but froze.

BJ, Tank and a woman I recognised as Kaya Mancini stood in the faint light from that single lamp.

Shit—

Kaya nodded at me, but her gaze slid to Aidan. "We don't want any trouble."

"Don't cause any," he said simply. "Stay out of our way, and we'll stay out of yours."

"Coach," BJ ventured warily.

Aidan sighed and tucked his gun away. "I expect you on the ice for the morning skate. Don't fuck up."

I registered relief on the faces of both players before my guys tugged me away.

CHAPTER 40

"I'm going to burn every bit of that." I stepped out of my clothes and kicked it all aside.

"I'll bring the match," Coast said. "Hey, here's an idea, why don't we burn *all* of your clothes? Naked looks good on you." He looked me up and down and grinned.

I shook my head at him and stepped into the shower. I turned the water on nice and hot and stepped under the flow. Steam flooded the room in moments, fogging the mirror and shower glass.

"After all you've been through, we can't let you do that by yourself." He was out of his clothes in a flash and stepping in with me.

He gestured for me to turn around, and squirted a handful of body wash onto his palm. He rubbed it all around my back and down to my ass, massaging and lathering as he went.

I leaned back, letting the water pour down my face, washing away the last couple of days.

"Mmm, that feels so good." I closed my eyes and let my cares wash down the drain.

For now at least, I could put them aside and forget about them. Wren and I were safe and all of the guys were alive. I wasn't going to spare a moment to think about who died. I'd dwell on all of that later.

"You feel so good." He pumped more body wash onto his hands and lavished extra attention on my ass cheeks.

The shower door opened and closed. I cracked an eye open to see Phoenix and Javey step in with us.

Javey reached for the shampoo and started to wash my hair, while Phoenix began to clean Coast's back.

"Turn around." Javey tilted my head back so the shampoo could wash away. Satisfied it was rinsed enough, he massaged in a handful of conditioner.

Coast went to work washing the front of me, taking special care with my breasts and pussy. "Can't go neglecting these."

I let Javey rinse the conditioner out of my hair and returned the favour, washing his hair and body while Coast and Phoenix washed each other.

"I was so worried about all of you." I took extra time to wash his cock and the curls at the base of his stomach. My touch made him nice and hard.

"We were worried about you," Javey said. "If those

assholes..." His face was pink from a combination of anger and heat from the water and steam.

"They didn't," I said quickly. I stroked my hand up and down his length, until he was moving his hips, thrusting slowly. "We wouldn't have let them anyway. We're badasses, remember?"

"We're still going to hunt them down and kill them," Coast said. "No one fucks with our woman and gets away with it."

"No one but us." Phoenix was washing Coast's cock as carefully as I was working on Javey's.

"Exactly," Javey said with an irritated grunt. "Just us."

It wasn't that long ago that he wouldn't have included the other two guys in that equation.

All of us had come a long way, there was no doubt about that. So many times I thought we'd never get this close. I'd almost given up on this as some kind of pipe dream.

Now, I wanted to laugh and cry at the place we'd reached. And laugh a little more at the idea that the guys would have *let* me give up. Once they'd decided I was theirs, there was no going back for any of us.

Javey slipped his hands down to my ass, grabbed me firmly and pressed my back against the shower wall. He lifted me until my legs were around his and pulled me onto his cock.

He let his aggressive side take hold, slamming into

me over and over. Our wet skin slid against each other slick and slapping with each violent thrust.

"I didn't think I'd be able to do this again," he admitted. "All I wanted to do was bury myself inside you just like this."

"All I wanted was to have you fill me," I panted. I shook water out of my eyes and looked down to where Phoenix was on his knees, his mouth around Coast's cock, sucking as frantically as Javey and I were fucking.

Coast caught my eyes and smiled. He ran his hands over my breasts, down to where Javey's cock pounded into me, and over my clit. He deliberately let his fingers graze Javey each time he pounded into me.

Javey's eyes widened. "Fuck, that's…"

Coast worked us both with his fingers while slowly thrusting in and out of Phoenix's mouth.

I moaned. "Yes it is." There wasn't way he could finish that sentence that I wouldn't have completely agreed with. Hot, incredible, amazing… There were too many perfect words to list them all.

I let my body do the talking instead.

"I'm so close…" I bucked against Coast's hand in time with Javey's strokes.

"Come for us," Coast said. "Come on beautiful girl. I want to see you come around Javey's cock." His own tone was breathless. He must be close too.

I shattered into a million pieces, screaming in ecstasy as I clung to Javey to keep from sliding down the wall.

I slid instead, into a place of perfect bliss. Somewhere between universes. Maybe before the first universe was born. Whatever it was, it was incredible and I didn't want it to end.

Javey coming with a harsh cry, made me come again when I was halfway down from the first.

This was longer, stronger and more intense. My vision went black. All I knew was how I felt in that moment. Absolute pleasure and the connection between me and two of my guys. The awareness that Javey was spilling himself deep inside my body. Coast's fingers rubbing my clit until it was too sensitive to take any more.

I came back down, panting, hot water rushing over our bodies.

Javey set me down carefully, his own breathing still ragged.

Coast slid his cock out of Phoenix's mouth and turned off the water. "We're all going to be prunes if we don't move this out of here."

Surrounded by my three guys, I stepped out of the shower. We all grabbed towels and helped to dry each other off. All of them took turns with my hair.

It was Phoenix who grabbed a brush and started carefully working out the knots until the bristles could pass all the way through without stopping.

He slapped me lightly on the ass a couple of times before tossing the brush back onto my dresser. Taking my hand, he led me over to the bed. A faint smile on his lips, he lay me back and climbed over me, his weight resting on his knees between my legs and his hands to either side of my shoulders.

"How are you so fucking gorgeous?" he asked.

Before I could answer, he leaned in and kissed my mouth.

I raised my knees so his cock was positioned outside my pussy, and gave him a nudge to slide inside.

Coast stood back and watched us both for a minute or two before he reached into the drawer for the lube. "Care to do the honours?" he asked Javey. He handed the tube to the winger and sat beside us.

Javey swallowed audibly before squirting lube onto his fingers and sitting on the other side of us, beside Phoenix's ass. He waited until Phoenix nodded before spreading lube around his rear hole and slipping a finger inside.

Phoenix's eyes half closed. "That feels…strange, but I like it. Don't stop."

Javey slipped his finger in deeper, thrusting in and out slowly, stretching Phoenix, making him ready. After a few minutes of that, he slipped in another finger, then a third.

"He looks ready to me," Coast said, his voice husky. When Javey slid his fingers out, he moved around behind Phoenix and waited for him to bend forward over me.

I watched both guys as Coast pushed his cock carefully into Phoenix's ass. He moved oh so slowly, stopping every couple of moments to let Phoenix adjust.

"Holy shit," Phoenix breathed. "I…" He quivered, his body trembling against mine.

"You okay?" Coast asked.

"More than okay." Phoenix moved carefully, thrusting into me again.

Coast set the pace, driving into Phoenix and pushing him into me so deep he touched everywhere inside me.

"So fucking tight. I'm going to come." Coast's eyes were crossed. "You're so fucking… Ahh." He thrust a couple more times before he stilled, eyes wide, spilling his cum into Phoenix's ass.

"Come with me," Phoenix whispered. He sounded like he was barely holding on to control.

"I…" I came again at the same time he did, our cries mingling together like a chorus. I felt him fill me as my muscles clenched tight around him, gripping him and drawing out every drop of orgasm from us both.

When I finally came down from this final orgasm I was completely boneless. Exhausted, spent and thoroughly satisfied.

Panting, we all flopped down onto the mattress together, a tangle of arms and legs and hearts.

EPILOGUE

SINCLAIR

The guys all stood watch while the electrician finished installing the last of the security alarms and packed up to leave.

Each of them had their own way of pretending they weren't following them around and watching every move. It was adorable, but no one was fooled.

Coast would pass them by on the way to nowhere in particular and stop for a chat every now and again.

Phoenix must have run around the outside of the house a hundred times, exercising while supervising.

Javey, apparently tired of sticking into the shadows, openly watched them his with arms crossed, eyes narrowed.

I had a feeling they finished more quickly and packed up faster because of it.

Either way, our new home was as secure as a place could be. Iron gates, cameras everywhere, alarm systems that would wail and send a signal to a security team.

There was almost nowhere in our huge house that I could go that I couldn't be seen on one camera or another.

Instead of sitting in his car, or standing under a tree, Javey could sit in the control room and watch me.

Coast and Phoenix teased him for doing it, but he shrugged them off and went on watching when I wasn't spending time with him and the others. Fortunately, the security system was finished, so that could happen more often.

"I still don't like leaving you and playing away," Coast said.

The Demons had made it all the way to the playoffs, but lost by a goal. They'd gone away disappointed, but more determined to win the cup this season.

"You have access to every camera in the house, on your phone," I reminded him. "The only place I can go that you can't see me is the toilet." Was it a little excessive and obsessive? Yeah, but I got to keep an eye on them as well.

When I was at work and they were at home, I could check to make sure they were alive and safe. Some day, I might learn to relax again. According to my therapist, the hyper vigilance was normal.

Besides, when they were in the gym they built into our new house, I liked to watch them get all hot and sweaty.

"Yes, but you have to leave home to go to work," Phoenix pointed out.

"Which all of you can track with the car's GPS and the tracker in my earring," I said. "I can't sneeze without you all knowing about it."

Literally. After the first couple of cameras were installed, I sneezed and got a message from Phoenix to say 'bless you.'

Sometimes it felt like I'd gone from having one stalker to three, but I wouldn't have it any other way. I felt safe and loved with them around.

Even when they weren't, nothing and no one, except a violent act of nature, was going to get me in here. Since the house was built to withstand fires, floods and everything but a nuclear device, there was nowhere safer for me to be.

"We worry because we love you," Coast said. He pulled me to him and kissed my nose.

"I love you all too," I said. The next thing I knew, they were all surrounding me, arms around me and each other.

"I love all of you," Phoenix said.

"Back at you," Coast said.

"What he said," Javey agreed. Neither of them were big on talking about their feelings, especially the ones towards each other. But everyone knew.

They were such *men.* I wouldn't have them any other way.

. . .

Phoenix here, if you loved our story, as much as we did, leave a review tell your friends and all that shit.

Wren's story is up next in Power Play

You probably noticed, I have a bit of a kink. Probably more than one, but the whole thing about fucking Sinclair while she was asleep, that's in the bonus scene, which you can get here.

ABOUT THE AUTHOR

Maggie Alabaster writes reverse harem romance.

She lives in NSW, Australia with one spouse, two daughters, one dog, and countless birds.

Jo Bradley writes contemporary romance.

Sign up for Maggie's newsletter! Sign Up!

Join Maggie's reader group! Join here!

Follow Maggie on Bookbub! Click here to follow me!

Check out Maggie's website- www. maggiealabaster.com

Sign up for Jo's newsletter

ALSO BY MAGGIE ALABASTER

Dusk Bay Demons

Puck Drop

Breakaway

Power Play

Brutal Academy

Book 1 Heartless

Book 2 Cruel

Book 3 Vengeful

Court of Blood and Binding

Book 1 Song of Scent and Magic

Book 2 Crown of Mist and Heat

Book 3 Sword of Balm and Shadow

Book 4 Whisper of Frost and Flame

Dark Masque

Book 1 Bait

Book 2 Prey

Book 3 Trap

Saving Abbie

Book 1 Pitch

Book 2 Pound

Book 3 Session

Book 4 Muse

Book 5 Rhythm

Book 6 Encore

Novella Venomous

Saving Abbie books 1-4

Saving Abbie books 4-6 + Venomous

Ruthless Claws

Book 1 Ivory

Book 2 Crimson

Book 3 Elodie

Harmony's Magic

Book 1 Summoned by Fire

Book 2 Summoned by Fate

Book 3 Summoned by Desire

Shifter's Vault

Book 1 Discarded

Book 2 Deceived

Book 3 Disgraced

My Alien Mates

Book 1 Star Warriors

Book 2 Star Defenders

Book 3 Star Protectors

Academy of Modern Magic

Book 1 Digital Magic

Book 2 Virtual Magic

Book 3 Logical Magic

Complete Collection

Summer's Harem

Book 1: Shimmer

Book 2: Glimmer

Book 3: Flicker

Complete collection

Short reads

Taken by the Snowmen

Jingle All the Way

Also by Maggie Alabaster and Erin Yoshikawa

Caught by the Tide

Book 1–Pursued by Shadows

Book 2 Pursued by Darkness

Book 3 Pursued by Monsters

ALSO BY JO BRADLEY

Dusk Bay Sharks

Prequel Novella Sidelined

Spike

Punt

Intercept

Snap